TWO KINDS OF BLOOD

JANE RYAN

POOLBEG

CRIMSON

Published 2020 Poolbeg Press Ltd
123 Grange Hill, Baldoyle,
Dublin 13, Ireland
Email: poolbeg@poolbeg.com

A catalogue record for this book is available from the British Library.

ISBN 978178199-356-9

www.poolbeg.com

ABOUT THE AUTHOR

Jane Ryan studied with Chartered Accountants Ireland and works in the technology industry. Her short stories and articles are published online and in print and she was shortlisted for the Hennessy Literary Award. Her first novel *47 Seconds* was published in 2019 and shortlisted for the inaugural John McGahern Book Prize.

Her work has received praise from Jo Spain, Jane Casey, Eoin Colfer and Patricia Gibney.

Jane lives in Dublin with her husband and two sons, you'll find her at @ryanerwriter on Twitter and Instagram.

Two Kinds of Blood is her second novel.

PRAISE FOR JANE RYAN

'A gripping thriller' *Sunday Independent*

'Ideal for fans of *Line of Duty*' *Evening Echo*

'After devouring *47 Seconds* in one sitting, it is safe to say that fiction needs to make room for another master of crime fiction. Gritty, emotional, and utterly enthralling from start to finish, this book left nothing to chance and completely blew me away and desperate for the sequel!' *Booksofallkinds*

'Really enjoyable read. It totally drew me in and I could not put it down. Characters are beautifully drawn and subtly revealed over the course of the book. Plot is intriguing and cleverly constructed. There are shocks and surprises to keep you on edge. Highly recommend as a thoroughly engrossing page turner' Catherine MacDonald, *Goodreads*

'Highly recommend' *Compelling Crime Drama*

'Suspenseful crime drama with interesting and multi-layered characters. Thoroughly enjoyed the many twists and turns and the likeable, if prickly, protagonist Bridge. Look forward to learning more about Bridge and her nemesis, Flannery, in the sequel(s)!' Fiona, *Goodreads*

'Excellent. Couldn't put it down' John O'Connell, *Goodreads*

'Fantastic book, loved it! Great for fans of Harlan Coban & Jo Nesbo, reminded me of *Line of Duty*. Can't wait for the next book!' Padraig Murphy, *Goodreads*

ACKNOWLEDGEMENTS

As ever, heartfelt thanks to my family the McNamaras and the Ryans for their endless support and interest in my work. To my friends, book club girls, the Eyelash fans, the Willow and Rock girls who ever have my back.

Thanks to my writerly friends and the Irish crime-writing fraternity for making me feel so welcome. To the booksellers and book-bloggers, I've found my tribe. To my publisher Poolbeg – Kieran, Paula, Gaye, David, Caroline and Lee. I could not wish for a better team.

To my boys, Ron, Adam and Conor.

I'm writing this after the most extraordinary St Patrick's Day I've experienced in my lifetime. Covid-19 is changing everything. It's the fear of the unknown and while grief and loss will touch many of us, I know there will be joy in our lives again. If you feel lonely, please know you are not alone. We are in this together.

-Jane

Dedication: For Ron, Adam and Conor

PART 1

*Whoever fights monsters should see to it that in the
process they do not become monsters.*
Nietzsche

Chapter 1

2019

A siren scream.

Detectives sprang back from me as though I were a biological hazard. Shock and fear on their faces. Liam O'Shea's bald head was corrugated with concern.

'My mother.'

My mouth couldn't keep up with my brain. I ran from the briefing, Liam O'Shea at full pelt to keep up with me as I made for the car park.

'*He has my mother, Liam! Seán Flannery has my mother!*'

I was deranged.

'I'm driving, Bridget,' said Liam. He pulled open the driver's door of the nearest car and jumped in.

My fingernail caught as I pulled open the passenger door. A section ripped off the nailbed and started to bleed. I put it to my mouth and sucked, the pain in tune with my thoughts as I scrambled in.

'Where are we going?' Liam reversed and headed for the rear entrance.

'Oaken Nursing Home on Colliers Avenue in Ranelagh.'

The words were sand in my mouth.

'Show me what he sent,' he said.

The barricades inched down.

'*Hurry!*' I was screaming.

'Show me what he sent, Bridget! They can't get the barricades down any faster.'

I opened the WhatsApp and clicked on the message. My hands shook, my fingers thick with fear and fumbling. I hit play, and Seán Flannery's reedy voice, talking to my mother in sing-song, filled the space.

'*Liz-zee? Look at me, Liz-zee. Where's Bridge? You remember me, don't ya, Lizzie?*'

My mother's small face, smiling to cover her confusion. Her eyes searching his face and her mouth full of unspoken fear.

Then nothing.

'Liam, faster!' I rocked in my seat. 'How did he know where she was?'

'Calm down, Bridge.' He hit the talk button on his TETRA radio. 'Urgent assistance requested at Oaken Nursing Home, Colliers Avenue, Ranelagh. Any units nearby?'

A backscatter of voices and static. 'FH 188 in vicinity.'

'Traffic corps out of Donnybrook.' I stated the obvious, an attempt to shape a formless situation.

'What are we looking for?' came from the radio.

'Mrs Elizabeth Harney, possible elder abuse, patient has dementia. Please stay with her until we get there,' said Liam.

'Understood.'

He threw on the sirens and drove at speed. Up the narrow street of Morehampton Road forcing other motorists onto the path, taking the hairpin bend at an angle

4

and reaching Colliers Lane. The nursing home was set back off the road.

I was out of the car and running. The sight of a patrol car gave a second's ease of piled-on fear, emotions too jumbled together to differentiate. I punched in the door code of the nursing home and ran down the ammonia-smelling corridor to Mum's room.

'*Mum!*' It was more of a sob than a name. 'You're OK.'

She looked small and frightened in her bed and her mouth made shapes for words refusing to come out. Her eyes were how she messaged and she didn't know me. One of her nurses held her hand, two uniforms I hadn't acknowledged stationed at her door.

'She's fine, Bridge,' said the nurse, an Englishwoman who had welcomed Mum on her first day into the nursing home. 'Everything's OK. You need to breathe.'

She stood and took my arm, massaging the white inside skin in small circles. I wanted to lay my head on her shoulder and weep, but some impulses I won't give into. Instead I squeezed her hand, accepted a tissue and blew my nose. I kissed my mother on her head, forcing the trembling in my body to quiet.

Outside, I barked to the uniforms: 'Stay where you are until you're relieved.' A frightened dog snapping, my hand flared up to my face. 'Sorry, lads, I should have started with thank you.'

Liam watched from the mouth of an empty resident's room. I turned on my heel and headed for the manager's office, down a long corridor in an offshoot to the main building.

'Bridge! Slow down!' It was Liam.

The director of the facility was called Helen. She paled

when she saw me and turned, stumbling down the corridor towards her office.

But I'm fast.

'Bridget!' Liam caught me. Hauled me up from behind, thick arms banded around my chest.

My lanky legs flailed in the nothing, blonde ponytail whacking him in the face.

'Jesus, keep her away from me,' said Helen, a runty-looking woman.

Liam ignored her.

'I'm going to let you go now, Bridge. Deep breaths. We're going to talk about this like adults. OK?'

'All right,' I said, furious, and he put me down. 'Liam, it's my mum. Do you have any idea how vulnerable . . .' My voice failed.

'I know, Bridge,' said Liam.

'Excuse me?' said Helen. 'I will not allow threatening behaviour of any kind –'

'I'll stop you right there,' said Liam. He stared her down, which wasn't difficult given the height discrepancy. 'You had a known criminal in this nursing home today. A dangerous individual.'

I showed her the video on my phone.

'In Mrs Harney's bedroom,' said Liam.

'Do you know what he's capable of?' My body shook with leftover anger. '*Do you?* He held a man down and stabbed him in the rectum.'

'Bridge! Enough!' said Liam.

The colour drained from Helen's face and she leaned against a wall.

'I'm sorry – he was here looking at the premises this morning. Told me his mother had dementia and they

6

couldn't keep her at home, said she'd wandered off last week. We brought him to the Darcy Wing, the recreation room, and Elizabeth was there . . .' Her voice trailed off.

My knuckles pressed through the thin skin of my hand, but I'd found some self-control amidst the panic.

'She's safe at least.' I showed Helen a recent photograph of Flannery.

'That's him, Miss – sorry, Garda Harney. I'm so sorry. I'd no idea who he was.'

'I'm going to need all the details you have on him – phone number he used, address he gave. Any information you have. When did he arrange the appointment?'

Helen opened her office door and went to a cabinet behind her desk, pulling out a folder.

'He contacted us last Thursday, 10th of October, and booked for today, Tuesday 15th. He said it was the only day he could do, and it had to be early.'

She handed me the folder. The name, phone number and details Flannery used were false – no doubt a burner phone long ditched.

'Seán Flannery told you he was Martin Cahill?'

'Who?' said Helen.

Her eyebrows were raised punctuation marks on her forehead, but my tone of voice gave her some warning and she worried the navy button on her suit jacket.

'The General, psychotic thug from the eighties. He nailed an associate to a pool table and put a bomb under the state pathologist's car. Man still walks with a limp.'

Helen blanched.

Chapter 2

Detective Superintendent Niall O'Connor was in full flow when we sidled into the back of the squad room. A block of a man, he'd done something with his hair – instead of his usual cue-ball head, he was growing out his thinning hair and sporting a crinkly comb-over. It didn't suit him, and I put it down to wife number three's advice.

'My thanks to Detective Chief Superintendent Graham Muldoon for taking the time to brief us on this evening's operation. Everything you hear is confidential – top priority,' he said, for the pleasure of hearing himself speak. He clicked a memory stick into the server linked to the overhead. He was in danger of spontaneous combustion at the thought of being involved in an operation with DCS Muldoon, An Garda Síochána's best boy.

Graham Muldoon headed up the CAB – the Criminal Assets Bureau. That was the first unit in An Garda Síochána, or any law enforcement organisation, to have worked across government departments and followed organised crime's cash – confiscating cars, homes and anything else acquired from ill-gotten gains. Not a man to sit still, as though born without the ability, DCS Muldoon was thin and angular with a bristling grey crewcut which showcased surprisingly delicate ears. Books had been written about the man from the Midlands, using high-blown hyperbole to describe his methodology. DCS Muldoon thought it was all 'cack' and said as much, but the international Maritime Analysis and Operation Centre (Narcotics), based in Lisbon, rang him not the Garda Commissioner when they had news the Venezuelan cartels were packing their 'marching powder' into shipments and heading for open waters.

'Thank you for your attention,' said DCS Muldoon. He cleared his throat. A gunshot in the silence. 'We have received intel from MAOC. A shipment of drugs is coming into Dublin port this evening.'

Groans from the room and a shadow of amusement crossed DCS Muldoon's face. He raised a hand for silence.

'The cargo vessel containing the primary shipment docked in Guinea-Bissau from Puerto Cabello. We believe the shipment in Bissau was unloaded and repacked into several containers, possibly as foodstuffs, but MAOC's intel is sketchy. Police on the ground lost sight of the shipment. However, it's possible the cargo went overland to Morocco. We found two ships with manifests for Dublin and Southampton with similar bills of lading. MAOC are tracking both.' He paused and ran his eyes over his audience.

A new detective garda mouthed at me. 'What's MAOC?'

'Maritime Analysis Operation Centre (Narcotics),' I murmured, 'but everyone says MAOC. M–A–O–C dash N doesn't roll off the tongue.'

That got a smile and she bobbed her head in thanks.

'We'll be searching for a straw in a heap of dung, as each secondary cargo vessel has over eight thousand twenty-foot containers,' DCS Muldoon continued. 'But I mean to check all of them.'

The silence had an overstretched elastic quality and I cast my eye over the assembled detectives. My colleagues were doing the same, making calculations on available people versus size of search. Everyone was coming up short.

I saw Niall O'Connor staring at me and inched behind Liam O'Shea's bull's back out of his line of sight. O'Connor and I had a history of clashing.

'Will we get more manpower, Chief Super?' Liam asked Muldoon.

'You can pull in from Kevin Street and Store Street. We can take about thirty in total. My office already has those calls out.'

Some shoulders fell back down at the small reprieve.

'We'll need every detective with drug-squad experience to lead individual search parties. This is not an exclusive CAB initiative. These shipments are large, and we believe they are here for the Halloween and Christmas rush. Our intel states it's from the *Fuentes cartel*.' He said the last words with emphasis.

DS O'Connor scuttled to switch on the projector. It made an angry-wasp noise and a florid display of cartoon Simpson faces popped up.

'Some of you may know this, but a recap for those who've just joined,' O'Connor said. 'The Fuentes cartel has changed its shipping instructions. They were using geometric shapes to denote locations and the gangs they ship to. We now understand they're using cartoon characters. For instance, Homer's face means bound for Ireland – include Marge in that combination and it's headed for Seán Flannery's crew. Moe the bartender means bound for UK with Bart denoting the Ahmeti mob working out of South London, etc. You can see on the slide's legend that we've deciphered what we can – however, this is a new system so we don't have all the characters and combinations worked out. We believe they're still using emojis for weight but keep your eyes open for any new symbols. Questions?'

I had plenty. O'Connor gave me a vice-grip of a look that closed off my throat. The air was rank with testosterone and the salty anticipation of the fight to come.

'Will we be looking for trafficked individuals?' a male voice asked behind me.

He meant women. Dublin was fast becoming a tourist sex-destination with pop-up brothels in the Airbnb unregulated space. The irony of complaints from Irish pimps who couldn't get clients to wait on corners for local girls. If the intel was solid regarding Flannery's drug shipment, there'd be no girls shipped.

I'd been banished from the DOCB – Drugs and Organised Crime Bureau – to the Sexual Assault Unit, ostensibly because of a breakdown after my partner Kay was murdered. Few people knew the correct reason. And while none of the DOCB detectives turned the other way when I approached, they didn't strain themselves trying to make eye contact. Apart from Liam who, out of loyalty for Kay's regard towards me, was ever on my side. None of the others wanted me near the squad room. I was a reminder of a cocked-up case and dead detective all in one and many believed my disgrace might be contagious.

I pictured the fierce Queen's University Belfast team I

had debated against in a pro-republican motion at 'The Hist' when I was at Trinity. My voice now needed the baked-in depth of conviction I'd had that day.

My body inched its way out from behind Liam's back.

'Flannery doesn't go in for human traffic – it's not his thing,' I said. 'He makes the dealers stamp his stuff with a five-point star, or he won't supply them. It's called "red star" and users ask for it by name.'

'He's a right little marketeer, isn't he?' said a voice at the edge of the briefing.

Laugher from the lads, but I wouldn't be derailed.

'Whatever's coming in will move fast. Flannery deals at least forty-per-cent pure so his cutting time is less than other gangs and he keeps his operations tight. He'll use a rip-on/rip-off system.'

'For our civilian colleagues from CAB, please elaborate, Detective Harney,' said DCS Muldoon. He gave me the level stare of someone who'd read my file, including the many psychological evaluations.

'Rip-on/rip-off involves loading in the port of departure and recovering in the port of arrival,' I said. 'Fuentes had someone in Caracas when the cargo was loaded – this is the 'rip-on'. Trusted operatives of Fuentes travelled to Bisson Guinea, a new port for drug traffickers, but it's lawless and easy to use. From there, the shipment went overland to Morocco, using the old cannabis routes, too many for any organisation to police. Once in Casablanca it's more difficult to find willing officials in the current climate, but Fuentes fixers will manage.'

An educated guess was coming up, but I couldn't look tentative in front of the dull burn of Niall O'Connor's eyes.

'Flannery's people will check the cargo here and peel off

in Casa, making their way back to Dublin, separate from the shipment. Flannery will have two or three people in Dublin Port. Could be security, crane operators or dockers and someone senior more difficult to pinpoint. Flannery's people will be given access to the loading area prior to any checks and "rip-off" the shipment.'

I knotted my hands together to stop them flying around.

One of the Revenue Commissioners officials who worked in CAB looked at me with a-less-than-polite raised eyebrow. 'You sound like part of his gang,' he said.

Before I could answer, one of my old colleagues from the DOCB butted in.

'Flannery's a bit of a hobby for our Bridge.'

The room rumbled with laughter and I was grateful for 'our Bridge'.

'Anyone could tell you all that about Flannery!' said O'Connor. He was all but baring his teeth.

A couple of my colleagues at the front shuffled back.

Someone said, 'That's good intel on Flannery.'

O'Connor eyeballed his audience, searching for the source in the room of lowered heads.

Emboldened by a nod from DCS Muldoon and wanting to take the heat off whoever had stuck up for me, I continued.

'The Fuentes cartel will put in guns as a sweetener. Flannery favours the Glock 19. He doesn't like the usual Walmart tat.'

It was a gamble to bait O'Connor and I'd no way of knowing what to expect in a shipment – if the Fuentes didn't have Flannery's brand it could be a bunch of Kochlers and some pre-loved AK47s, something Flannery would never touch – but if the end shipment was destined for him then the Glocks were a possible identifier.

'Flannery isn't the only one to favour the Glock 19,' said O'Connor. 'You're again looking to put value on your own theories.'

DCS Muldoon took a half-step away from O'Connor.

I gave O'Connor a flash of teeth and he looked as confused as a K-9 on the scent of a score the prevailing wind whipped away.

'We'll move out in tactical formation,' said DCS Muldoon. 'Two Drugs and Organised Crime Bureau detectives with every Armed Response Unit. Criminal Asset Bureau personnel travelling in unmarked Garda cars with armed detective protection.'

I stood to one side as the briefing broke up. Teams formed, with detectives checking guns on hip-holsters, no impossible pulling out from under jackets or sweaty armpits. Everyone looked tense, an urgency pushing away rational thought. A sour rashness to the atmosphere, demanding momentum for the sake of action. I took a chewy sweet from a greaseproof wrapper and popped it in my mouth, releasing its peppermint oil. The sucking sensation helped me concentrate.

'Stay out of O'Connor's line of sight,' said Liam, a lemon slice of amusement in his tone but hazel eyes intent. 'You'll travel with the CAB personnel. You're back in it now, Harney, however you've managed it.'

I tugged at his elbow. 'This doesn't strike you as odd?' I magicked another sweet out of my pocket and handed it to Liam. 'Let me check something first, will you? I would've said more at the briefing but –'

'Yeah, I got that, Bridge, but I suggest you put a lid on it and make sure you're available to the CAB people. Or do

14

you want to stay in Sexual Assault for the next ten years?'

I pulled him into a side office – the automatic sensors there weren't working despite the dusk peering in at us.

'You think I haven't learned anything from last year? Running around when Flannery cracked the whip, thinking I was in charge because I got his girlfriend to be my tout and chasing down dead ends while he fed me information. What do I have to show for that time other than Kay's death if I haven't learned to question neatly packaged information? I'm going to ring my tout.'

Liam's eyebrows drew right down, a black hieroglyphic. He stood staring, stroking his dark goatee, as I punched the keypad on my phone.

My call was answered on the fifth ring.

'Thought it might be you,' said a voice cracked from cigarette smoke.

'Why's that?'

'Youse all tearing around getting ready to do the big man at the Port?'

'Don't be cryptic. It doesn't suit you. Where's the shipment?'

'It's in and gone. Flannery plays a mean game. Yizzer looking under the wrong shell, and it'll tie youse up for at least ten hours. Stuff will be in the Farm and cut before yis have repacked all them containers.' The voice gave a throaty laugh. 'Love to see you lot fucked around.'

The phone went dead.

'So?' said Liam.

I shook my head. 'Tout says the shipment has already been ripped off.'

He banged the veneered desk, water tumblers and a finger-stained jug jingling in protest.

'You believe this source, Bridge?'

15

'Yes, it's real. We've got to get out in front of this or it'll be a mess. Muldoon will close down the Port and the media will get wind of it. If they haven't been tipped off already. Viral videos of us looking like tosspots.'

'What can we do? Do you know where he's taken it?'

'He's taken it to a place they refer to as the Farm. It's in Kilkenny. Tout told me about it a couple of months ago, but nothing when I went there to see other than an old man telling me to get off his property with a legally held shotgun.'

'Nice.' Liam was overheating in the small office and ran a finger around the inside of his shirt collar.

'We need to stop them.' I pointed at the pack filing out, jostling and blocking one another. 'Who do we say it to? O'Connor or Muldoon?'

Liam looked at the ceiling as if counting the Styrofoam tiles. 'I'll say it to Muldoon. O'Connor won't listen. You stay in here and watch from the sidelines. Don't get involved, no matter what.'

He threaded his way through the exiting gardaí and tapped DCS Muldoon on his navy-suited arm. DCS Muldoon, not a short man, had to look up at Liam.

Muldoon's face gave no indication of his thoughts. DS O'Connor was a revolving radar circling them, trying to catch every word. I wanted to run and warn Liam. O'Connor shouldered his way into the conversation, his mouth chewing words. Muldoon was unreadable, and Liam climbed in on himself as O'Connor's eyes searched the room. I pulled back behind the door.

The round-face clock on the wall squinted down at me and gave an uneven *tock*. I waited.

Liam looked around the plyboard door into the darkness, his pupils pinpricks.

16

'Where are you? I can't see a flipping thing,' he said.

'Here,' I said.

'Well, O'Connor has offered the opinion that you're certifiable, but the Chief Super is willing to let the two of us go to Kilkenny.'

'He's going to go through with closing the Port and checking all those containers?' My voice was spiky.

'Listen, Bridge, you're bloody lucky. If it was up to O'Connor you'd be on a pushbike giving out litter fines.'

'We can't go down to the Farm with no back-up. Can we get uniforms from Kilkenny?'

Liam's pupils had widened to accommodate the darkness and he looked alien. 'Now you're talking. I can pull in a few favours.'

We walked out of the meeting room and all but collided with DCS Muldoon. He looked down his knife of a nose at me.

'Garda Harney.'

'DCS Muldoon.' I felt a line of blonde hairs under my ponytail lifting. 'Thank you for your support –'

'Don't thank me yet. You've made some large claims at the briefing. I hope for your sake you can back it up.'

Chapter 3

The dark evening cold snatched at me through my clothes as I made for the station car park. A squally wind caught us, grit lodged in my hair and found the corners of my eyes.

Electricity charged around me, crackling on my skin, giving my movements a jerky quality, an over-eagerness for action to blunt the anxiety pooling inside me.

'Who's driving to Kilkenny?' I asked.

'You going to make an issue about this?' said Liam. He looked at me with a vulture's eye, leaning in until I smiled. The top of the key ring clicked around his forefinger and thumb.

'If I say I'm a better driver you'll take the hump,' I said.

My phone trilled, a birdsong ringtone I couldn't change. The numbers on the screen spelled longing.

'Paul?'

Liam, not knowing his own strength, yanked the car door open and it groaned in protest.

'I wanted to see how you are? There's a lot of action in the Square today?' said Paul.

Despite extreme trepidation at the idea of chasing Flannery's drug shipment, Paul's voice pulled me up, out of myself.

'Yes, it's bedlam, won't see my bed this evening,' I said.

'Is that a good thing?'

'Are you flirting?' Hope is a four-lettered word.

'Nah, well, maybe. Stay safe, OK, Bridge?'

'Sure.'

It was enough. I got into the car beside Liam. His mood was as stultifying as the car air freshener was cloying.

'Can we ditch the tree?'

'Whatever you think best, Bridge.'

I reached up to the green pine-tree cut-out hanging off the rear-view mirror and snapped the elastic.

'What's with you?' I asked.

His face was shuttered and he splayed his fingers on the side of my headrest as he swung round to look out the rear window, reversing the car. Swinging it in a wide testosterone arc.

'Can we calm the *Starsky and Hutch* driving?'

He ignored my question.

'Why do you still have that stupid ringtone on your phone?'

'Kay put it on before she died. Just to annoy me.'

That quietened him.

'You OK?' he said after a spell and I nodded.

'Look, I know you never open up, but I've put myself on the line a bit here, speaking up for you in front of O'Connor and Muldoon.'

'I appreciate that, Liam,' I said, tensing as I awaited what was coming next.

'Fair enough, but are you ever going to tell me why you were transferred to the Sexual Assault unit and busted back down to Garda? When I'm talking to DS O'Connor I feel like everyone's in the know except me.'

'Joe never said?'

'No, Bridge, he didn't.'

I chewed on a tatty piece of the bandage covering the nail of my torn finger.

'It was the arm in the pig carcass in the docks. Turned out the arm belonged to Emer Davidson.' I didn't know how much I could dare to say.

'Her other arm was found in Birmingham, that much I know,' said Liam. 'It's what happened afterwards that I'm not clear on.'

'You'll remember the Burgesses, Anne and Mike? From Birmingham, with a second home in Dalkey?'

'Of course. Go on.'

'They had a son-in-law Declan Swan, married to their daughter Lydia. I liked him for the murder but it turned out he had an alibi. Emer Davidson was having an affair with Mike Burgess and Anne confessed to killing her. Moment of madness.' I sidled a glance at Liam. 'Seán Flannery was called in to dispose of Emer Davidson's body.'

'What! You never said anything about that! How in God's name did Mike Burgess know Seán Flannery?'

'They sailed together. Burgess had a yacht and Flannery crewed out of one of the Dún Laoghaire yacht clubs. He's being doing it for years.'

'Then why wasn't Flannery charged?' Liam's square face stretched in confusion.

'I lost the evidence needed to convict him.'

I was lying, but it was better than the truth. I had planted evidence to implicate Flannery, which wouldn't have survived a barrister's cross-examination, so then had to lose it, letting Flannery walk away. Our Joe Clarke and Chris Watkiss from the West Midlands Constabulary covered up for me. But I couldn't tell Liam. The words wouldn't get past my leaden tongue. My face burned.

'Happens to all of us.'

The gruff sympathy in Liam's voice acted like a can-opener and made me want to talk, but there was more than one neck stretched on the block of that story, so it wasn't mine to tell.

The silence condensed inside the car until the windows were fogged from our breathing. Liam turned on the fan to relieve the pressure.

'Let's have your grand plan – how are we going to catch Flannery?' he said.

I knotted my hands together. How to explain all the tentacles of Seán Flannery's grotty empire, the machinations of dealing with him, the twisted roots he dug into the soil of his community. Flannery was the definition of a man with a plan.

'First off, we'll need regional back-up,' I said.

Liam's head swung towards me.

'Why are you looking at me like that?' I asked.

He threw up a hand the size of a butcher's steak. 'I'm relieved, is all. I was afraid you were trying to go it alone. Right. Muldoon sent word to Kilkenny saying we'll be in contact, and I have a mucker down there. I'll call him when we get closer.'

'A mucker?'

'A friend.'

'If I said that, Liam, I'd never hear the end of it.'

'Tell me what you expect to happen and not the sterile version you'd give Muldoon.'

'I haven't got a plan, Liam. I'm going for an "emergent strategy" on this one.' I was rewarded with a smile. 'My tout is reliable.'

'What are you paying him?'

'The usual, so it's not about money. This person wants to get out from under Flannery's thumb. Someone desperate to keep their own family from going under. Prison. Escalating violence.'

Liam rubbed the cracked-leather steering wheel. 'It's gone up a notch all right. Since the cartels started shipping direct and sweetening everything with automatic weapons. It's a circus. Where are we headed?'

'M9 southbound. The Farm is in Kilmacow, about ten miles outside Kilkenny town.'

'Kilkenny is a city,' said Liam.

'Is it? It's not a county town?'

'No, you *Dublin jackeen*!' The air pressure in the car lifted as he snorted with laughter. 'I hope we find something, or Muldoon will be justified in handing us over to O'Connor and I can't take that man. Self-promoting article. He'd want to shave off those strings of hair. He looks like a clown.'

'Possibly his new wife asked him to let it grow.'

A sideways smile from Liam, then seriously, 'I've taken sergeant's exams.'

I sat up, the old seatbelt jammed and flung me back. 'You're going to leave the Square?'

The vehemence of my reaction surprised me.

'There's nothing so great about the Square, Bridge. That's you all over, thinking it's the epicentre.'

His comment niggled me, aggression coming first as I pushed away the unexamined panic.

'So you're going to go to a station in *To-mee-var-ah*?' I lengthened the rural vowels. 'Getting on your bike at lunchtime and looking at the lovely girls playing camogie?'

'Not everything in the countryside is an episode of *Father Ted*, Bridge – and you can be condescending when you want.'

'Well, there's a putdown! And if you don't mind me saying you're married to the DOCB and will go stir-crazy in some local station.'

'Maybe so, but I want a life outside the job, you know? Have a relationship.'

My eyes darted to the left as my brain accessed coils of memory. 'What about Mary? Marie?'

'Evie,' said Liam.

'I was close.'

'Miles off. Didn't go anywhere. It doesn't if you have to keep on breaking dates because of work. We spent more time on the phone than in person.'

'Sorry.' And I was. He'd liked Evie. I remember him being teased about dating a nurse and the hoots of laughter when he'd admitted they'd met in Coppers. 'We're a right pair! We should be out at forest bacchanals, not going home to a favourite hob-ring and meals for one.'

He chuckled. 'You?'

'Me?'

'What about yer man, Paul?'

'Oh! I'm not sure we're off the ground yet. He does like me, but I've no idea how to be in a relationship.'

I shut my mouth, mortified. The lulling motion of the car, the darkness outside and the comfort of knowing you couldn't do anything for two hours had made me loose-lipped – but Liam wasn't a gossip. The truth was, my spell in the Sexual Assault Unit hadn't kept me front and centre with any of my old colleagues and DS O'Connor had used his praetorian guard to isolate me.

Liam had the grace to keep his eyes on the road.

We were silent for a time and the road rolled on, the city blazing amber behind us. Stars spun in dotted patterns and circles, vast and unknowing. I was small and hidebound in my orbit. Not so Seán Flannery, who'd stepped out of his – if he'd ever been in one – long ago, unrestrained by societal rules. He knew we were dust, less, particles within the dust with no judgement or God behind the stars. Only more dust.

Liam scratched his domed head. 'I'm as bald as a kiwi.'

'That why you grew the goatee?'

He chuckled, but it had a layer of purple chagrin.

'Suits you,' I said and meant it.

He grinned. 'How're things with Matthew and the kids? Have you been down to Roosky?'

'I went over during the summer for a couple of days, but I haven't been down since.'

A feeling of loss. Kay had bequeathed me a dwelling inside each of her children's hearts and a linchpin loosened inside me when Matthew took his family halfway across the country.

'You know Matthew wasn't coping in Dublin, Bridge. He had to go home.'

'It's selfish of me to want the children close.'

'It's not, Bridge. You love them, but Matt needed his family. I don't have to remind you what a tomb that house was after Kay.'

The pain of her murder was a switchblade slicing and made me grip the door handle of the settee-on-wheels Liam had picked to travel in.

We followed two orbs of headlights, a destination in mind but the way not clear.

Chapter 4

Liam's phone pinged.

'What does it say?' He handed me his mobile.

I read the text. 'Nothing found at the Port. They're still tearing the place apart.'

'Your tout was right, and it's played out for you. You'll get kudos from Muldoon. Nice to have a favour there. He might give you your stripes back.'

'That's the plan.'

The side of Liam's mouth rose. 'Are we all dancing to your tune, Bridge?' His tone was playful. 'Where to now?'

'Head for the Mill House in Kilmacow, keep on the N7.' I flicked my fingers to increase the size of the map on the screen and looked up to orientate myself. In the surrounding dark I was a blue floating face. 'Says we're about twenty minutes out.'

'What's Flannery's going to do with the shipment? You think he'll be here?'

'Yes, I do, and what would *you* do with a tonne of cocaine?'

'Jesus! *How much?*'

'It's from the Fuentes cartel in Venezuela – direct to Flannery – Fuentes doesn't ship in kilos. Flannery has to break it up. We seized some of his five-point-star stuff at a party. He cuts it with Warfarin and Panacur.'

'The stuff for roundworm in cows?'

'How do you even know that? The Tech Bureau had to tell me what it was used for.'

'Grew up on a dairy farm, so why wouldn't I? But where did Flannery find out about it? He's lived in East Wall all his life.'

'Good question. It's his secret recipe – easier to snort, gets into the bloodstream quicker and less damage to human membranes and septum – he leaves it forty-percent pure and his dealers are obliged to keep it at the same level. Or face his retribution.'

Liam's face creased.

We were moving fast, the dark encapsulating us as the fields and hedgerows blurred by, the digital display shining red against its black background. 8.15pm.

'Time to call the back-up in Kilkenny,' said Liam. He handed me his cell.

Lost in thought at what Flannery might be doing, my eyes found the shape of Liam's thighs bulging against the material of his suit trousers compelling. Heat flashed up my neck to my face and I turned away.

'You OK?'

'Of course.' Embarrassment made me curt. 'Who am I ringing?'

'Cigire Charles Murray. He's out of Thomastown and mind your tone when you're talking to an inspector. They're no big deal in the Square, but they run things in the country. He's under Charlie M.'

I rang and Charlie M picked up on the second ring, recognising the number.

'*Conas a tá tú, Liam?*'

'I'm well, thank you, Cigire Murray – how are you?'

'Who's this?' Suspicious.

'Garda Bridget Harney. I'm here with Detective Garda Liam O'Shea. We –'

'Put me on speaker.' He didn't waste any niceties on me.

'I would if I could, Cig, but this is an old car and the Bluetooth isn't seeing Liam's fancy iPhone.'

I grinned at Liam who shifted around in his chair and motioned to me to punch the phone's audio button.

'You're on speak, Cig,' I said.

'Liam?'

'Howya, Charlie – we're looking for a bit of help.'

'I got an email from DCS Muldoon, saying you'd be needing back-up. What can I do for you?'

Liam and Cig Murray had the easy comfort of shared experiences in their voices.

'Yeah – we're following some information on a container, ripped off from Dublin Port and headed towards the Mill House in Kilmacow.'

'Lonely country, Liam, you won't see a light on for miles. Where are you now?'

'I'm not sure.'

We searched for the neon-blue signs the EU had part-funded, but their grand plan had missed this part of the country.

'Maps say we're in Knocktopher,' I said.

'Does your woman have marbles in her mouth?' said Charlie, laughing.

Liam mouthed an apology at me.

Undeterred by our silence, Cig Murray continued.

'You're about twenty minutes out from Kilmacow. Are these lads expecting us?'

'No,' said Liam, looking at me for confirmation.

I made a shim-sham movement with my hand.

'Well, maybe,' Liam said, 'but it's a big haul so they'll be tooled up and with workers to cut and package, some soldiers protecting. We believe their boss will be there too and he never travels light.'

'Not a small operation then?' said Cig Murray, his voice full of hyena excitement.

'What do you have available to us?' I said.

'Thanks to Muldoon's warning,' he said in a tone that signalled a clear rebuke to me for joining the conversation, 'I can give you eight armed detectives plus myself, but I'll ring into the city and get an armed response unit on the road. They'll be a good half hour behind us. Why the last-minute call, man?'

'Because we don't know how this will pan out,' said Liam.

'Not sure of your tout?' said Charlie.

'Coming up trumps for me now, though,' I said.

'*You're* running the tout?'

The surprise in his voice wasn't flattering, but I said nothing – he was ponying up eight armed officers.

'Meet me at Mullinavat, Liam. It's past Knocktopher. There's an Applegreen fuel station, only thing around for miles. I'll see you in twenty.'

He hung up.

'He's a good bloke. A bit old school,' said Liam, his jaw tight.

He said no more. There wasn't a whole lot to say when ten guns were getting together. We drove in silence and I spent my time planning positions and formations, a game of chess with live pieces, panic the size of a fire ant walking up my spine, biting each vertebra as it passed. Despite my bluster I was risk-averse, not wanting to chance lives against Flannery's capos.

'Remember, Bridge, Charlie is running this show.'

I nodded, too tense to make a fuss.

The petrol station appeared ahead, a blinding block of light in a farmer's field, a fuzzy neon nimbus making the darkness surrounding it bottomless.

Liam cut the lights in the car and slowed.

'Pull in here, Liam – stay well back and don't go into the forecourt.'

'Why? There's no one here, place is empty.'

It was a flicker, something deep in the loops of my brain.

'Stop the car. It's too quiet.'

'It's the middle of nowhere and well past eight o'clock,' said Liam.

'Even so,' I said.

It was picture-perfect and soundless.

Liam eased the car into the cover of a hedgerow and we got out, closing the doors with a soft click.

I magnified the serving hatch with my phone camera.

'Look at the clerk – he's by the hatch and barely breathing. The only things moving are his eyes. Does that strike you as late-shift behaviour?'

We stood in the quiet and I raised my head, a dog sniffing for lookouts. Nothing but cold country air.

I nudged Liam and pointed towards the truck-wash area. A juggernaut had its dark face pushed into the cone of light above the steam jets, an international shipping container on its rear axis. He took out his phone and snapped a picture, magnifying it with a flick of his fingers.

'No one inside, but it's a UK reg,' he said.

'Could be Flannery's. Tell the Cig to slow down and approach with caution.'

The whole garage was eerie as hell, more stranded spaceship than service station. A single operator and no other living thing in sight.

Liam texted to Cig Murray: **Set-up.**

'How did this truck get here before us?' said Liam. 'We never caught sight of it on the roads.'

'Tout never told me what time they left the Port – for all we know the truck's been here for hours.'

A ping in the ensuing silence made me jump.

Liam showed me the text on his phone: **Fan out.**

'Let's go.'

'OK,' said Liam.

Both of us were gun-range regulars, every month instead of the prescribed three times a year, and had our holsters unbuttoned, not our weapons drawn. The provocation of drawn guns was for television and escalated a situation. However, the Garda were not transparent in what constitutes reasonable use of force in these situations, never making Garda rules of engagement public. It's more act-first-ask-forgiveness-later and Cig Murray struck me as this type of individual.

He had eight detectives in an arc outside the halo of halogen light from the garage. Weapons drawn and gung-ho heads on them.

Of course, I was not above shooting Seán Flannery if it were him and me, with some modicum of fairness attached, but I wouldn't let anyone face a firing squad.

'There's no one in that cab, Liam. Signal your cig and get him to calm down. They've gone all OK Corral on us.'

I hadn't given Liam sufficient credit. He stared down

one or two of the detectives, all the while tapping his holstered weapon.

Tap. Tap. Tap.

Some of them got the message and put their guns back in.

Cig Murray was a cocked-and-locked cliché advancing forward. Apart from armed gardaí, no one else was on the forecourt.

One of the detectives walked over to the serving hatch as if he wanted the daily special. He rested his elbow on the silver drawer. The man behind the till shook his head until it was a blur and pointed to the truck.

The detective waved a hand at the rest of us. Said, 'Driver left half an hour ago. Told him not to move as they've a tap into his CCTV.'

'Christ!' said Liam. 'And he believed it!'

We converged and circled the truck. Human adrenaline had an odour and contrary to popular belief it wasn't fresh and fizzy, rather more burnt solder. Liam made a motion with his forefinger and thumb to indicate he was going to open the container. It had no seals. The shutter lock was open and dangled under the lock box. Liam and Cig Murray pulled the handles of the long vertical columns that kept the doors in place. They swung out and we scattered to each side – no one up to taking a bullet to the head.

Silence.

'*Gardaí!*' Our voices were an off-key choir.

Nothing.

We moved in pairs, one garda in front, hands free for his or her gun, the other garda at the back with a torch aloft.

The discs of bright light swept over cardboard boxes with *Aceite de Oliva Barcelona* stamped on the side. No faces caught in our beams.

'Clear,' said one of the detectives. 'No one here.'

Liam turned to me, nostrils flared. 'What's this? Food?'

I motioned for him to follow me and jumped up into the container, my blue gloves on in a moment. Four other detectives followed my lead onto the container platform. The horse-stable smell of cardboard was overpowering. I cut through the masking tape of the nearest box, pulling out a tortilla, solid, yellow and shrink-wrapped. I threw it at Liam. He caught it one-handed and dropped it, his face covered in surprise at the weight.

'I'm guessing we're going to find the tortillas are in fact cocaine and the olive-oil containers have floaters,' I said. 'Don't know how many of these little treasures there are in each box.'

Voices deeper into the container called out as other gardaí found similar packages.

'Automatic weapons here,' said a male voice.

The gun-oil solvent smell lay under the faecal pong of cardboard.

Liam made a small tear in one of the tortilla shrink-wraps with a short blade he carried and pressed down either side, letting white powder push up. It had a ground-aspirin texture.

'The yellow colour must've been painted inside the plastic,' said Liam. 'Clever, but the interior's cocaine.'

'Any identifying stickers?' I said.

'This,' said Liam, opening the inside flap of a box with a sun logo emblazoned on the side. 'And this?'

It was an FC Barcelona soccer decal.

'The sun is the Fuentes logo – it denotes their purity,' I said. 'The FC Barcelona decal might be Flannery's new shipping sticker. It was Homer and Marge, but Fuentes must have changed it. Much good it will do us – as soon as they see the seizure on the news, they'll change everything again.'

Nine pairs of eyes regarded me.

'Can't say she isn't worth the price of admission,' said Cig Murray.

No one laughed.

Then he was on his phone calling for the Tech Bureau, bagging up the packet in Liam's hand and telling his men to seal the area off. Puffed-up and shiny-faced with excitement, Cig Murray sensed his next promotion.

Liam didn't look so sure of himself and leaned in to me, so close his wet breath touched my ear. 'Why would Flannery abandon a haul this size? After all the effort of the rip-off? And in a fuel station where anyone could find it?'

'He didn't have any choice. Flannery knew we were following him so ditched the container. He wasn't going to lead us to the Farm.'

Liam's face cemented with the truth of my words.

'Flannery was tipped off,' I said. 'We have an informer in the DOCB.'

Chapter 5

We made our way out to Kilmacow farm in cold silence, Liam digesting my theory. I'd gone over old ground with him of when Flannery had been ahead of us in the past. Liam became more withdrawn with every incident I recounted until the stark quiet matched the landscape we found ourselves in.

We were following a couple of carloads of Kilkenny detectives with an armed response unit behind us. Reflected in the visor mirror was a huge jeep, phosphorus yellow with red stripes. All it needed was an ice-cream-van jingle to make us unmissable. We wouldn't be creeping up on Flannery.

'We're close,' I said.

'This tout of yours is gold. I've never had one that was so accurate. Or trustworthy.' His voice was bitter as a green orange.

'I'm being played, is that it? Or do you think I'm in on it? Is that what you're trying to say?'

The heat from his face was a thing in that small stuffy car.

'*No!*' He banged his hands on the steering wheel.

'What then?'

'You think someone in the DOCB is telling Flannery we're after him? Isn't it a more reasonable assumption that his man at the Port rang him and told him cops were crawling all over the shipments? It's not as dramatic but it fits.'

I didn't want to look sceptical or offhand so appeared to give his statement due consideration.

'Of course it's possible and much easier to swallow – no one wants to think there's an informer in the squad – but I believe Flannery knew the shipment was being tracked by MAOC. Remember, Flannery had that shipment ripped off before we got there. That kind of precision takes accurate information. And there's the timing of his visit to my mum – he was creating a diversion – knowing I'd lose the head. He had to book that appointment with the nursing home days ago, so he knew precisely where the shipment was and its trajectory.'

Liam was fighting the inevitable conclusion.

'Say you're right – how do you know this farm isn't a set-up and we're going to get a full-on war when we arrive, if we're not ambushed first?' He jabbed a thumb behind him. 'We're not travelling light or inconspicuous and if Flannery's the genius you claim he is, he'll be expecting us.'

I shifted around against the grooves of the car seat's corduroy material and wound down a creaking window. 'How old is this jalopy?' A bead of sweat rolled down my back and lodged in the lower curves of my body. It only added to the anxiety chewing at the wall of my stomach.

Liam ignored my question.

'He might be expecting us, but I'm hoping there's no one there,' I said. 'If he was tipped off and ditched the drugs, it stands to reason he'd clear the Farm out. That's the best-case scenario.'

35

'But he could've left a welcoming party, hopped up on cheap crack,' said Liam.

'Yes.' The word was lost in the speed of the car and the darkness outside. Drops streaked the windscreen – the rain was here.

'As long as Gavin Devereux's not there,' said Liam. 'He's a violent beast.'

I shuddered.

'Map says it's a mile up here.' I pointed towards a stalky hedgerow same as any other bush for miles around.

A crackle burst from Liam's radio and the car in front began to slow. '*Pull in up here.*' It was Cig Murray.

Liam parked the car and we got out, all Garda jackets and caps. A woman from the Armed Support Unit flicked a red ponytail through the eye at the back of her cap.

The rain had eased, leaving the smell of drenched briarwood everywhere.

'What's the plan?' Liam asked me.

A compacted dirt road led into the Farm.

We were standing in the thin light of the open car door.

'Approach with caution,' I said. 'We have to assume –'

'Have you been here before?' Cig Murray cut right across me. He was the type of man who asked questions if the answers made him top dog.

I shook my head.

'Charlie, no one knows Flannery like Bridge,' said Liam.

Cig Murray eyeballed Liam in front of all the armed detectives and waited.

'Eh . . . Cig,' said Liam.

Cig Murray, not high in my estimation, nose-dived.

'Right, you two, close the car door and let your eyes get

used to the dark. Don't want to explain to DCS Muldoon that one of you shot the other.'

Canned laughter in the background. We had been reduced to city idiots. It didn't bother me but I could see it rankled Liam.

'Right – I'm at the rear with my lads –' he pointed at two chinless detectives. 'Dubs in the middle where we can keep an eye on them. Armed Support Unit in front.'

The car light went out and the dark sucked at me. I blinked rapidly, willing my pupils to widen to catch whatever light was available. My surroundings moved into shades of black. The ASU had their night-vision goggles on.

The ASU were in a single-file formation, making themselves a more difficult target, and about to take the lead, which was the correct procedure with the rest of us well behind. Then Cig Murray changed his mind and walked to helm, not about to give up being bandleader.

He turned and held a hand up for attention.

'This is Kilmacow Farm,' he said. 'Used to belong to a family called Gillespie – last of them died couple of months ago and there's no family local, so I'd expect it to be empty.'

I was impressed with his local knowledge and would have said as much, but he wasn't for listening.

'This road's about quarter of a mile long – the homeplace is right at the back,' he said. 'Double time, lads!'

It was beyond ridiculous – no one jogged in this type of dark. We weren't reserve cadets on manoeuvres.

But I was damned if I'd slow anyone down.

'*Hand!*' I called out to the nearest ASU detective and she stepped in towards me.

I put my hand in the strap on her vest, made for this

purpose, and we broke into an easy trot. She was surefooted as a mountain goat and had night goggles.

Liam tagged my shoulder and kept step with us.

Cig Murray puffed, having set too fast a pace for himself. Others stumbled in the dark, either not knowing how or not wanting to attach themselves to an ASU officer.

'Nearly there, lads!' said Cig Murray.

He sounded giddy and it made me even more uneasy.

The Farm was squirreled away at the back of a wooded paddock as though the Gillespies had wanted to get as far back from their fellowman as possible. I could see its attraction for Flannery.

'Here,' said a voice. 'Use a torch – weak beam.'

My escort took off her night-vision goggles and flashed a torch at an old five-bar galvanised-steel gate leading to the house. When this house had been a real home, someone had painted the frame blue with every second bar white. Now a thick creeper with hairy veins had claimed a third of the gate and looked in no hurry to stop.

Cig Murray held up his hand in a needless fist – we were right behind him.

Liam's embarrassment hung in the air.

I said, 'We should check –'

'I have this, Garda Harney. *Visual scan complete. No danger. Proceed.*' He was so full of himself he couldn't see anything other than his hand waving us forward.

One of the ASU shouted at Cig Murray. 'Cig, it could be –'

An explosive bang threw everyone back.

'*Charlie!*' Liam yelled.

The gate was booby-trapped. The creeper was smouldering and the metallic smell of electrical charge blanketed the air. Murray was thrown by the blast and had landed on his back, an upended beetle. The smell of burnt flesh and he was shrieking.

An ASU garda ran to him.

'Murray's in shock, but it could have been worse,' said the garda. 'You lads take him back down the road and in to St Luke's – A&E will sort him out.'

Cig Murray had stopped screaming and someone shone a light at him. Tribal black burn-marks streaked his face. He blinked in slow motion, giving him a defenceless look, and I had a moment's pity for him. He'd expected some junked-up yob, intimidated by armed officers, spraying bullets and missing his target.

'This is a delaying tactic – we need to move – they might be still inside,' I said to Liam and the garda at the front of the ASU column.

The ASU crept forward towards the house. It was in total blackness. I stayed behind them in line with protocol.

It happened quickly and it was too dark for me to see how they knocked in the door.

Three more ASU officers swarmed in ahead of me. Grunts, exertion, then a call.

'*Clear!*'

Thundering feet came down the steep staircase.

'*Clear!*'

I ran inside the front door and flicked on the nearest switch. A naked bulb gave out a feeble glow. The house was double-fronted and shallow, main 'good' rooms at the front. Everything was swallowed in decay, the interior stuffed with rot. A bed in the front room was unmade with a rusting safety razor on the sideboard. It smelled of damp plaster and loneliness.

'Pity the poor so-and-so who was living here,' said Liam.

We moved towards the kitchen, the ASU still leading. The kitchen couldn't hold everyone. Of the two doors presented, one was internal so we took the sturdier door to the outside. Nothing but clotted gravel and a shed made of rusty sheet metal. No one was here. I twisted my neck to release the tension and pulled the night air in through my nose.

Liam was in the shed and stood in a slice of light from a naked bulb over an open chest freezer. One of the detectives around him was already on his radio calling it in and requesting the Technical Bureau.

'Bridge!' said Liam.

Experience told me there'd be another girl I'd failed in the freezer.

It was Lorraine Quigley. Saw the skinny elbows and remembered them sticking out of the short buttercup-yellow jumper that wore her. She was naked and packed away, an orchid bud starved of the light it needed to burst open, petals folded in on itself. Lorraine's hair was piled on the top of her head in her trademark barrette clip. Her face was unrecognisable.

'*Lorraine, what did he do to you?*' I whispered.

Her frozen face, or what Seán Flannery had left of it. I had seen too many brutalised body parts to cry. Instead I internalised it, a pocket for a tear.

'She was Flannery's girlfriend, wasn't she?' said Liam. 'You got her away from him and she was going to give evidence against him?' His hand hovered near my shoulder as though wanting to comfort me.

I leaned against him for support.

'I didn't get her far enough away. I was going to get her and her baby to safety, give them witness protection.

Christ, I had this idea she could stay in Birmingham, thought Flannery would never find her. It was possible – until she disappeared. Last time I heard from her she was making her way down to her cousin's caravan in Wexford. How did I let this happen?'

'Give yourself a break, Bridge – you got the baby away.'

I gave a stiff bob of my head. Baby Marie was with Lorraine's cousin.

'If this was Flannery, we might get DNA,' Liam said. 'She was beaten. Even if the assailant wore gloves there'll be sweat, blood, patterns, something. This took a lot of human contact.'

'Look at her – she's naked and I'd say doused in saline or something that will wash trace DNA off.'

I walked back to the house, the thoughts in my brain so much twisted cable running the same current. This was my fault. Different tune, same lyrics.

'*Garda Harney!*'

It was one of the ASU.

'*Over here!*'

He was shining an industrial torch on a looming box shape about as big as a family-sized bungalow jutting off the house. Had there been daylight we would have spotted it already, but the building belonged to the night, the outside painted coal-black.

The ASU guy came towards me. 'It doesn't seem to have an outside entrance.'

I ran back into the house – to the second door.

One of the other ASU officers was at the door checking for boobytraps. There were none apparent, no extra wires or suspicious connections, but everyone was on high alert after what happened to Cig Murray. The door jamb had been enlarged and one of the ASU tried the door handle. It wouldn't budge. He had a kit with him and made tiny anti-clockwise movements with a pliers deep inside the lock until the door snapped open.

It opened outwards and inside was a clean room of white plastic and chrome. Precise and square with machines for pill-pressing and dehumidifiers. Others, large as washing machines, were a mystery. At the centre of the room was a bagging machine and checkweigher, all pharmaceutical-grade even to my untrained eye.

'Get Liam O'Shea in here,' I said.

Liam's breath came in quick puffs from running. He turned wide-eyed to me.

'Have you ever seen a dealer's lab like this?' he said. 'It belongs in a hospital!'

'He's not a dealer, Liam. He's a corporation.'

'Can you imagine how much money he makes?'

'He'll need every penny to compensate the cartel for losing the shipment,' I said.

Liam faced me. 'You were right, Bridge – he was tipped off – but I don't think he had much time, otherwise he would have burned this place to the ground.'

He pulled me out of the doorway so he could enter. His foot rose with a heavy forward motion, but at the same time a black gloved hand gripped his ankle.

'*Trip wire!*' yelled the ASU who was squatting by the door.

We both looked down at the single strand of fisherman's wire across its base.

'There's a second inner door,' said the ASU. 'The door jamb was modified to make room for it – but look – it's wide open. They were hoping we'd just barge in. Both of you move back slowly. We'll need the bomb disposal unit.'

Liam and I went outside to the yard. The Tech Bureau were in situ but not moving out of their vans until the place was declared safe.

'Who has bombs and clean rooms? Who is this guy, Bridge? Paddy Escobar?'

I snorted back a laugh. 'Kind of.'

Chapter 6

The tartan blanket was stiff with black dirt, but filth never bothered Seán Flannery. It was one more type of disguise. He was sitting in the doorway of a 'to let' restaurant in Monkstown's crescent, a once-busy grocer's shop decades back. The cold October wind blew grit and the bitter tang of road tar into his face. The low winter sun had turned the roadworkers into a dayglo chain gang. Seán had watched their confused progression for two days, noting the local worthies were not pleased, holding their sharp noses a fraction higher as they walked by, too busy muttering about 'slipshod builders' and 'corrupt councillors' to drop a coin in Seán's tatty paper cup.

It suited him. The village was sleepy and quiet from the diverted traffic. A fear had gnawed at him since the abandoned Fuentes shipment and something like injustice at the stones on the DOCB for stealing his drugs and some Garda buffoon on television talking about teamwork and striking a blow at the heart of organised crime. It rankled. And they'd trashed the Farm. Gardaí had respect for nothing, tearing down a man's legacy. He rammed an ancient deerstalker hat further down his head, the fleece matted with grease from someone else's hair. He'd filched it from a charity shop as he walked through Blackrock. The invisible hobo. Insulated from the cold in an ancient parka, he watched the men working from his vantage point, lost in the beat of the steel rollers moving over the black-glitter glue of bitumen. The roadworkers folded in more gravel and rolled again, as though working toffee, the rhythm of their travails a meditation.

It took Seán away, his eyes half-shut and a layer of white flocculent sleep all but descending on him. He put his hand into his boxers. Right under the jock cup was a concealed pocket. He touched the teeth of his house key, their jagged edges soothing him.

Lorraine came to him. Not the shredded woman in the warehouse, too destroyed to recoil from the punches, but Lorraine as she lay frozen, the ice fogging and reshaping her into a serene Madonna. It was a peaceful scene until Seán remembered the baby girl he'd orphaned. She punctured his self-awareness, leaving it as pocked as the road surface. He should have killed the child – instead he left her to a motherless fate. Proof, if it was needed, that he was formed from original sin. It made sense of his cruelty and inability to feel remorse . . . but he had felt remorse about Lorraine's child. He struck his head, wanting to smack down the unassailable questions mid-air.

He shifted his thoughts away from that, to another girl walking around the backroom of his mind, so ripe at the age of nine. The soft downy skin on her arms and her dreams pulsing below the transparent skin of her eyelids. His desire was malevolent, dark as tar seeping into his pores, suffocating him.

He blamed original sin. The nuns in the Home said not

even Jesus could wash away his sin. Despite that, Jesus would try to love him. Without end. A millstone of forgiveness around his neck to wander through life with. Seán hadn't believed the nuns' fantastic stories of women turned to salt and oracle boys whose dreams came true – but original sin was different. St Augustine, who Seán knew about from his time in the boys' home named after him, declared that original sin was passed down through the generations when people had sexual intercourse and conceived a child. If the offspring was of an unwed mother, even baptism couldn't wash away the sin. Seán was doused in it.

A Nissan van screeched to a halt.

Seán's head whipped up while his legs thrashed out of the tangled rug. Four men from the road gang ran towards him. Another man tarring the road looked at the melee, the quick movements of the men drawing his eye. Seán's fingers scratched the pavement, struggling for purchase. The roadworker looked away from his terror. Those other men were unstoppable. Big, ugly conscripts with anabolic bodies. Fear bit into Seán and numbed his feet, turning them towards one another in his unlaced boots – he jerked his knees upwards to release his feet from them. A hand reached him. Grabbed the parka. Seán shrugged it off and ran. Past an empty pub in his bare feet, heading for the boiling tar of the new road surface. Four hands hiked him up before he reached it. His legs chopped the air, his left arm brought back to an unnatural angle and close to snapping.

'*Youuuu!*' Seán called out to the roadworker who had caught his eye, but the man shrugged and continued breastfeeding his shovel. This was not his fight.

'We have you now, Seán,' said one of the attackers. 'There's a good man and don't make a scene. Or I'll break your arm.'

'Do youse scum know who you're dealing with?'

'We do, Seán – but maybe you not – Big Man,' said another, the air of pack leader about him, despite his pinched features. He had a cheerful, chilling tone of voice and a Slavic accent. He mangled his English into horror-show bites and was soaked in Eau de Psycho. Here for the impersonal violence.

Seán swallowed his pain and terror. His chances of surviving would collapse with a broken arm. Two of the men hog-tied him with plastic cable-ties and slung him into the back of the white van with a single yellow stripe, head first. The deerstalker took most of the impact, but there was a crunch and a warm line along his eyebrow.

The abduction had taken less than two minutes. It happened so fast a bystander wouldn't have realised what they were looking at. The van looked commonplace yet official.

Fear and panic played on Seán so the van doors appeared to close in slow motion, peeling him back to the boy with his face pushed into ammonia-smelling black trousers.

Chapter 7

'Well, Miss?'

'Well!'

I beamed at Joe Clarke.

Joe was my sergeant when I'd first started in the Drugs and Organised Crime Bureau. He backed me to go to the UK when the Flannery arm-in-the-pig-carcass case gained national notoriety and the press were crawling around. He held me together when Kay died and lied to keep me out of prison after I'd falsified evidence. What had I given him in return? Made his name mud in the Bureau and a posting to a rural armpit. Yet, he still considered me one of his closest allies. I swallowed. I deserved no such regard from him, but I would be trampled underfoot for Joe if needed.

He was visiting me in my eyrie on the fifth floor of Harcourt Square. His uniform hung in pleated folds off a reduced body. His once dark hair was greying and needed a trim.

'It's good to see you, Joe.'

I was out from behind my desk and across into his bear hug, amazed my arms could reach behind his back.

'What has you here?' I asked. 'Visiting old friends or couldn't stay away?'

He gave a throaty chuckle. 'I got a start in the Criminal Assets Bureau. I go back a bit with Muldoon and the boredom in Wexford was lancing me. It's dead in the bed after summer, nothing but breaking and entering caravans or drunk patrol. You look surprised?' His face was lit with a broad smile and he slapped my shoulder. 'What has you up here? It's a bit grim.'

The Sexual Assault Unit was empty and lukewarm.

'Last time he was up, Liam said it was like a disused fridge no one had bothered to clean out,' I said.

'Well, he has a point. Is everyone out on the streets or chasing down the lads putting the girls on corners?'

'Hardly anyone on the streets now. Most online. We're looking at a particular scam targeting professionals using Instagram.'

'Any one we'd recognise?'

'Never seen them before. It's a Georgian gang based out of Longford. Starts off with a 'Hi, Handsome' comment on Instagram. When the mark accepts the follower request, their address book is copied – unknown to them. Sexting kicks off, the mark is encouraged to share a dick pic and, when he delivers, he's blackmailed with the threat of exposure to his work colleagues. It gets worse – some of the marks have allowed themselves be filmed.'

'Using trafficked girls?' said Joe.

'Of course – through Belfast, we think.'

His mouth formed a halo of fine lines. 'Why aren't you out there helping them? This is the kind of stuff you were born for.'

My foot tapped on the scratched parquet flooring.

'DS O'Connor has me hemmed in looking at tax returns of small-time hoods. All eighty thousand individuals and, when I do find something, I have to go cap in hand to the Revenue for more information.'

'They've no interest in helping us. Touchy about their employees being seconded on to CAB as well,' said Joe.

'Don't I know it. I was speaking to Miss Kelly – sounded no more than nineteen and called herself "Miss Kelly" when I asked for her name. But in fairness I got a batch of analysed work recently and it's good. Someone called "Amy" went to a lot of trouble to find patterns in the transactions.'

'Surprising,' said Joe. He was supporting himself by leaning against an old table.

The table was a study relic from the fifties, the veneer a chipped crackled crust from over-polishing.

Joe poked his head in the air, a quizzical expression on his face. 'Dettol?'

'Or something like it. The cleaner mops the hall with disinfectant, says the lino is rotten up here. Believe me, it's better than the original smell.'

The folds on Joe's uniform shook.

The tea lady and her trolley made an appearance.

'I'll do you two cups as a favour,' she said, nodding at Joe. 'I'm not supposed to, mind – cutbacks.'

She had quick movements, reminding me of a small bird, the way she moved delph around her samovar and produced cups of tea and custard creams out of thin air. She pushed the coarse clay mug I used towards me. The mahogany-coloured tea was sweet and the smell of freshly mowed lawn filled the dusty squad room.

'Thank you,' I said to her. 'Appreciate you coming up to me.'

'Much obliged,' said Joe.

She left, wreathed in smiles and a jangle of old wheels, her trolley having more in common with the temperamental supermarket variety.

'How's your wife?' I asked. 'Does she mind leaving Wexford?'

'She's grand, prefers Calahonda to Gorey. Over there now.' He put a hand up and rubbed a grey stubbled jaw. 'Put me on a diet these last months. I'm like one of those candles that's been shoved into a wine bottle.'

'Better for your heart, though.'

We drank our tea, enjoying each other's company.

I gestured at my surroundings. 'Any chance you'd ask Muldoon if I could be transferred to CAB?'

'After what you did?'

'You said you go back with Muldoon?'

'I do, but I'm not sure that'll cut it. He's a single-minded man. Nothing's as important as the job.'

'But you called him when you wanted to leave Wexford?'

'Called in the one favour I had. O'Connor made sure I'd no others.'

I flinched. 'Sorry, Joe.'

He waved a pasty hand at me. 'Water under the bridge. That arm-in-the-pig-carcass case made O'Connor. It should have been enough for him but he had to stamp on the both of us just because he could. I've heard he's never off the floor in the DOCB since his promotion. He should've let you out of limbo by now. Unless you've done something else?' His brows rose then fell to the bottom of his slab forehead.

'No!' My voice was high-pitched. 'I've kept my nose clean and done everything O'Connor told me to. Including monthly evaluations.'

'With Dr Paul Doherty? That'd be no hardship to you, from what I've heard.'

Joe gave an ill-timed wink and I flushed a hot pink.

'I'm kidding,' he said. A hand raised in supplication.

'I'll kill Liam O'Shea and his bog-baller's big mouth.'

Joe took a mouthful of tea and choked, laughter pouring out the side of his mouth.

This conversation was a cactus: thorny and going nowhere fast.

'So can you speak to Muldoon or not, Joe?'

'Course I can, but no amount of pull will get you into Muldoon's unit unless you're of use to him. You're an ex-barrister and your father's a retired judge, so I'd polish those connections and think on what you can bring to the table.'

'But I don't want to use my legal contacts and get stuck in some liaison-land between the Garda and the Director of Public Prosecutions.'

'Then I'd get pally with the tea lady – it's the only company you'll have up here.'

Chapter 8

Fifty-seven, fifty-eight, fifty-nine, thirty, one, two . . .

The van swerved. Seán rolled around, a lumpy turnip bashing into objects he couldn't see. The hat had fallen down over his eyes and the pain between his shoulder-blades was building to a fiery point. His fingers were lifeless. Blind and trussed up in the back of the van, he was a slaughterhouse delivery. The van accelerated and he shot into what felt like bags of calcified cement, mashing his ribs. Every so often he'd roll by turpentine rags, rearing his head away from the poisonous fumes.

Seán wanted to kill the men driving the van. All of them.

He tried kneeing the back door. It didn't budge.

The driver slowed and judging by the bumping and rolling it was a tributary road. Best he could tell, they'd been driving for over thirty minutes – he was counting and would do so until the van stopped. He had no idea if it was north or south but the Dublin Mountains were half an hour from Monkstown. People had met bloody ends there since before he was born.

He pictured the inside of the van and searched for the handle with his mouth but found nothing and snagged his lip on the musty-smelling door-fibre. Copper-tasting blobs bubbled on the pink membrane of his mouth. He licked them off and used the door as a prop to shove the hat off his head. As he'd suspected he was in a builder's van, with shelves and tools. His eyes lit on a scoring blade and wire cutters in a clear plastic drawer. The morons had stolen the van but hadn't bothered to clean it out.

He see-sawed towards the tools.

The van jolted to a stop.

The psycho opened the door. He grabbed Seán's upper body and hauled him out, the way you'd throw a leg of lamb onto a chopping board. The thin shirt Seán was wearing made a quick *rip-rip* noise and gave up trying. Damp air found his skin. He landed on his side with clumps of sharp rocks cutting into his legs. The daylight sliced into his eyes and he squinted at the surroundings. They were in some field behind thorny hedgerows choked with ivy.

The psycho had a knife, the kind that drew beads of sweat from Seán's body and shrank his privates. The man slashed it, right under Seán's nose.

'You and me, eh, Seán?'

'And the rest of them in the van? Putting on a show, are ye?'

The knife had loosened something in Seán – he was babbling.

'Ah, not so bright? I was the only one who got in. Rest of them got back on chain gang.'

Seán couldn't spare the brain power to process that statement. One obstacle at a time.

'You're going to hack me up with the tags on? What are you? A bitch?' he said.

The psycho's mongrel face contorted. He flung away his jacket and sliced towards Seán. A coldness moved down Seán's body and threatened to void his bowels. The psycho rolled him over on his stomach and he waited for the skewering burn of the knife to tear him from shoulder to buttocks. It's what he would have done. Instead, the psycho slashed the cable-ties.

'Let's go!' he said.

'Wait! Gis a chance!' Seán couldn't move his arms – from his armpits to the tips of his fingers was frozen.

A squally wind brought the psycho's meaty, excited smell towards Seán.

'Let me get some feeling back, give you a fair fight. Where you from – Azerbaijan?'

The psycho's face registered surprise.

'Georgia.' He hopped from foot to foot, not one foot behind the other, as Seán did, quartered in a fighter's stance.

'You near Tebilesee?' said Seán. He knew of a Georgian gang in Longford and they were from the capital. It was a shot in the dark.

'Tbilisi? How you know about –'

Seán chopped the psycho's feet from under him but his reflexes were fast and he drove the blade towards Seán. Seán zig-zagged, fearful his bare chest was too easy a target, and lunged for the pyscho's discarded jacket. In a fluid movement he trapped the psycho's knife-hand with the jacket. He put his bare foot in the crook of the psycho's elbow and mounted him up to his neck. Seán hooked the man's jaw and used it as a fulcrum, throwing his own body off the man's shoulders.

Momentum carried him down to the other side.

Snap!

The psycho's bewildered face made him look child-like.

Seán had entered his fourth decade and had few real skills, but he could kill a man. He should have disarmed the psycho, questioned him, found out who he worked for or how he had tracked him down, but at a certain point something took over and it had become a ballet or a swinging trapeze, one action begging the next.

Chapter 9

'Bridge?'

It was Paul. The sound of his voice hoisting me up with excitement. I tried to keep it light, the tone of a casual acquaintance but, by the expression on his face, I'd failed. My feet had taken me off the cement backstairs of Harcourt Square and onto the third floor Human Resources' foyer, replete with green Connemara marble tiles. Where I had no legitimate business.

'Hey, Paul.'

He put a hand out to me, a jerky movement stopping short of my body. We stood beside the brushed metal of the lift doors and our meeting had all the clumsiness of an engineered encounter.

'What are you doing out and about on this cold Tuesday afternoon?' I said.

I shut my mouth, dismayed at the hope in my voice, and shifted my weight from foot to foot. He looked formal in his pressed trousers and retro tweed sports coat. I drank in the dark-brown eyes, the moulded cheekbones, the dangerous charm and the undertow of clean male skin. His salt-and-pepper manscaped beard gave him a squared-off, devilish look. Because he needed more appeal.

'I'm not out and about, I work on this floor and it's six pm, hardly the afternoon,' he said.

No smile raised the outer corners of his mouth. He stretched himself to his full height, up and away from me. I wanted him to bend down, to soften his voice, to quell my jangling nerves as I picked up some unknowable signal he sent out in those sour-sounding words.

'Sorry. Are you usually on walkabout? Fancy a coffee?' I grinned to take the green desperation out of my voice. Nobody found needy attractive.

'Do you want to step in here?' Paul gestured to the door, his hand empty inches away from my back as he shepherded me through the dark-maple double doors into Human Resources. He moved me the way a seasoned waiter would navigate a flambéing plate for a tricky customer.

Ashleigh the receptionist sat at her desk, past her working day. She purred a greeting at Paul and curled her lip at me, her blunt face lathered in make-up. I knew she had the hots for Paul and wanted to pee on his shoe. It made an already awkward situation into cringing comedy.

'Can I help with anything, Paul?' she said and contrived to look down her squat nose at me from a sitting position.

He didn't answer, instead directed me toward a meeting room with a non-committal smile. The continued effort of trying to look laid-back was making my mind numb.

We walked by a standard stationery cupboard and I touched the painted door, trying to conjure the time we'd made love in a similar cupboard on the fifth floor.

He avoided my gaze.

'What's wrong, Paul?'

The door was solid wood with a vertical glass inset – it

closed with metallic cylinders clicking into place. He kept his back to the glass, blocking any outside view, and faced me in the heavy, unventilated air.

'Your behaviour isn't appropriate. If the professional interest I have shown has made you think there's anything more than collegiate interest, my apologies. It does happen where a patient or client develops unreciprocated emotions for a psychologist, while working together. After all, we see clients at their most vulnerable, even if the client is unaware of their own mental state.'

His expression never changed as his formal words tattooed themselves into my skin.

'*What?*' I said.

He put a pianist's hand to his face and rubbed the creppy skin under his eye. A grain of yellow sleep floated down onto the table. He didn't notice. I wanted to reach over and absorb it with my fingertips. Taste it. Taste him.

'What's going on? Why –'

His detached expression cut me off.

'This,' he wagged a forefinger back and forth between us, 'was a mistake. I blame myself. I took too much interest in your rehabilitation.'

'What are you talking about? I want it to be the way we were. Hanging out and chatting, going for coffee and an occasional date –'

'Please, Bridget. If anyone found out we had a friendship it would derail both of us, and you-know-who's always watching.'

His unwillingness to name DS O'Connor irritated me.

'People have mentioned I've shown you professional favouritism,' he said, 'which I haven't – but those types of accusations hang around forever. We shouldn't be fraternising.

I never get involved with someone I'm working with, much less someone I evaluated for return-to-duty protocols. I'm sorry, Bridge.'

He opened the door, gave a strained smile and was gone.

I stumbled into the corner, a blind spot for anyone passing the narrow glass panel in the door and screamed into my palm, clamping it over my mouth. The pad of my thumb hooked into the soft muscle of my jaw. Pain to cover pain.

I'm not sure how long I stayed there, until a glimpse of a Super's navy-and-brass-button uniform passing took me out of my stupor. I pushed myself off the cold brick wall and took a mouthful of dusty water from a tray laid for a meeting days ago. The room pressed in at me on all sides. My blood, given unexpected impetus, roared in my ears and I sneezed. A shocking mucus-filled sound in the silent room and my sinuses blocked. My body's reaction to Paul's rejection was to flood me with adrenaline and snot.

Cold nipped at my nose in the carpark as I made for my mother's ancient motor. I sat in the car, sanded raw from meeting Paul. The underground carpark was an inky black with a few ruptured ceiling lights trying to pry the dark open. The rear-view mirror caught my pale face.

'Cop yourself on, Bridget Harney. All this over a lad?'

Chapter 10

His body was heavy. Seán rolled the psycho over and checked his pockets for the van keys, tearing the inside of his finger on cheap coat-hanger wire the other man had fashioned a key ring from, with a Dinamo Tbilisi badge he must have brought from home. Red pops beaded between Seán's fingers. He stared at his own blood but knew better than to suck at his finger. The cold made blood coagulate quicker and he used an icy pebble to help the small wounds clot.

Never one to miss an opportunity, he eyed the dead man's body and stripped him down to his underwear. He had an overworked physique with a matching steroid rash on his back and was sunbed-tanned, in the way all those cheap Euro mobsters were, but his clothes were clean and new.

The serrated knife caught the sun on the ground and glinted – as if Seán would have left it behind. He rolled the man's uncooperative body into a shallow ravine, watching his designer underwear revolve until the body was face down in a gulley stream. The shirt and pants were baggy, but chance had given Seán perfect-fitting boots. They were good for kicking forestry-service-cut logs on top of their previous owner. It was temporary – he'd send some lads up to take the body. He'd left trace evidence of course, but if there was no body to be found the gardaí wouldn't be examining this site.

For now other things rushed at Seán. Such a blatant attempt on his life scoured his insides. He turned the van engine over, it fired first time and he drove out of the field onto a road with a green-and-white sign for Ballyedmonduff Road. He drove through Sandyford and kept to the coastline, ever drawn by a thread to the sea. A scoop of winter sunshine lay melting on the Poolbeg Chimneys, making their silver-coin lights flicker. A respite from the anxiety sucking at him.

Seán made for the Gardens, determined not to draw anyone's attention. His rising panic forced his foot harder on the pedal and into the rubber-lined base, the tyre-spin setting small stones flying. He wound down the window, breaths of chlorine-tasting city air filling his lungs. The familiar air calmed him and, with his body pushed back in the driving seat, he stayed the impulse to speed. He traced back, moment by moment, what had happened during the abduction. The men were strangers. Seán wasn't sure if they were even a crew. He knew of few gangs with the clout to infiltrate a company, place their men resurfacing a road and have them walk back to the job, business as usual.

The clock on the van's dashboard showed 2.30pm. Seán drove into the cul-de-sac of St Martin's Gardens. Built on land from reclaimed mud flats, the Victorians deemed it too salty and left it to the working class. For Seán it was home and everything that implied. The people knew one another, their lines unbroken from the first stevedores-turned-privateers. Rumour had it they ate their young, a bogeyman tale for naughty children in their middle-class beds.

Sheila Devereux was standing in the middle of the cul-de-sac. She looked at him in a way that made every hair on Seán's body rise in a spike.

He shunted the van to a stop. The coal tar and salt smell of Dublin Port greeted him as he got out.

'Seán?' said Sheila Devereux.

Her face was unreadable and Seán didn't have time to work out what she was up to. He swung his head around. Nothing. No children, no gossiping shrews slugging designer coffees, no lads prowling, nothing but the lone yapping from a caged dog. Dread, rising inside him, put a hot hand around his neck and squeezed.

The wrongness of the situation set Seán's teeth painfully on edge. He looked around for Gavin but couldn't see his car on the road or in the bubble at the end of the cul-de-sac.

'Where's Gavin?' he asked.

'Gone somewhere,' said Sheila. Her eyes were narrow slits in a watchtower.

Every nerve exposed, Seán ran for the cover of his front door. His hand caught on a sharp ridge of his house key as he pulled it out of his jocks, and opened the cut on his finger.

Inside his home nothing but quiet. The house was freezing. His breath puffed in a cold cloud at the empty rooms. His back door was open. Where were his dogs?

Where was everyone?

His hands were shaking as he put his house key on the van key ring. It was slippery with his blood but occupied him while his mind writhed around his brain, searching for answers. Nothing came other than a poisonous fear, crawling up inside him.

He had to leave.

He tapped the internal wall between his hall and living room. The thick satisfying sound of a space filled with cash insulation. He was about to kick a hole in it when a leg took his feet from under him. Seán fell, putting a hand out to an ornamental table, an idea forming in his mind to throw it at his attacker.

They were too quick. One held Seán down while the other injected the base of his neck. Two laughing black faces with teeth as white as chalk.

One spoke to the other. 'Remember to take the tracker off the van. Then call the road crew and get them to burn it out.'

The second one looked at Seán with eyes full of laughter. 'We're going to take you on a little holiday, Seán.'

Chapter 11

'Walk with me?' said DCS Muldoon.

Not so much of a question.

We were on Harcourt Street and this meeting didn't have the smack of chance. I turned for a panoramic view, in time to see his driver and car moving off into the traffic. My eyes found the lane with tram-tracks sliced and over-sliced into the tar, a Frankenstein surgery stitching the street together, a monster spanning a bridge from old technology to new.

'Joe spoke to me,' said DCS Muldoon. 'He thinks you'd be a good resource for the Criminal Assets Bureau.'

Muldoon took military strides, long and sharp. I fell in with his pace.

'It's something I would be very interested in, DCS Muldoon. And I'm grateful for the support on the Flannery drug seizure.'

He waved away my thanks.

'Why would you want to leave the Sexual Assault Unit? Joe told me you were exceptional when you worked serious sexual assault prior to your time in the DOCB.'

'I don't want to leave, but the work I'm doing in the

SAU is sifting through piles of data, trying to find evidence of tax avoidance for pimps and brothel-owners. It's not that satisfying.'

Too much the diva, but how to explain to DCS Muldoon that Flannery's seizure would change the criminal stage in Dublin and this was the chance I'd waited for? With all the friction and uncertainty the seizure brought, Flannery and his cohorts would fall off their pedestals.

'What do you think we do in CAB, if not sift through mountains of data? It's a core skill for my group.'

'I am aware of that, DCS Muldoon, and I believe I've given a significant amount of analysis – albeit about small-time criminals – to Revenue and DS O'Connor. Actionable data. But in CAB I'd have a chance to work it myself and have access to other resources. The pressure we could exert on Seán Flannery! With the support of a superintendent or above, we can deem that property is the proceeds of crime and confiscate it –'

'Before you get too carried away, Bridge, one of the key duties you would be performing, should your application to transfer to CAB meet with success –'

DCS Muldoon could be an officious bugger when he wanted.

'– is adviser to the superintendents on the Policing Authority.'

My face must have fallen off my head and he guffawed behind a spidery hand.

'Well, it's your ex-brethren they're up against. Police reform, risk management, mid-year performance reports, analysis of the recent commissions of investigations and all in full legalese. Do I need to go on?'

With three sitting judges and a prestige of dusty civil

servants the Supers assigned to the Policing Authority were called 'tributes' by their colleagues.

'If I hear another "ten-point plan" or "lessons learned at An Cosán" it will be too soon,' he said. 'You see what we're up against? The meetings are biannual and I won't need you to be present – just to prepare whatever Super is going in.' He shook himself, a great dog throwing excess water off his coat. 'Still interested, Bridge?'

'Yes, DCS Muldoon.'

Anything to get into a fair fight with Flannery.

'Might I ask, DCS Muldoon, if I must finish the monthly evaluations? DS O'Connor is insisting I do them.'

'How many do you have left?'

'They're at the end of the month, so I still have October's to do, then November and December.'

DCS Muldoon gave a small smile. 'You may consider them finished.'

No more spilling my guts in Paul's office.

'Thank you, DCS Muldoon.'

'You're welcome, Detective Garda Harney.'

Back in the game.

Chapter 12

A withheld number rang my phone.

'Bridge?'

I recognised his voice straight away. 'It's not a good time, Chris.'

'No, it's not a good time for me neither, little 'un,' said Detective Chris Watkiss. 'But, if we don't get this sorted, we'll be in a sight less of a good time than we are now. The West Midlands Constabulary and the Garda Síochána got commendations over our joint case. If I were you, I'd listen.'

I was on the fourth floor in a pokey communal office where administration had moved anyone waiting for a seating allocation or, in my case, until the main Criminal Assets Bureau office-space was reconfigured to accommodate new personnel.

A woman wearing a burqa moved and I jumped, having mistaken her for a solid object. An impulse to crack a joke about the fascist Norwegians who mistook six empty bus seats for women wearing burqas hit me. I wasn't sure if I could make it funny or at my own expense, so I said, in an overly loud voice, 'Can I help you?'

The woman gave a slow headshake in the negative, the kind you'd give someone with impaired faculties.

'Who's that?' said Chris.

I exited the office.

'I've just made a total fucking eejit of myself in front of a woman in a burqa.'

'No need for all the effing and jeffing!'

I tried to choke back a laugh. His north of England burr was soft as peat-smoked whiskey.

'Sorry,' I said.

'You don't see a woman in a burqa every day in Dublin. Sure it weren't a niqab?'

'Looked like a burqa to me, but it could have been a fancy niqab. I'm not sure I'd know the difference.'

'There's some'at coming in about headgear in the new year here. My two are furious.'

'Why? They're Hindus – they don't wear any headgear, do they?' I said.

'No, but they're protesting everything at the minute – you'd want to see them on climate change! Their mother isn't allowed use cling film or paper towels anymore. And they've me walking down to get a fish supper instead of taking the car.'

I pictured Chris's twins – strong, smiling girls. 'They still playing Union for their school?'

'Aye, made the team for the county schools cup.' He was in danger of spontaneous combustion.

'Well, wish them luck from me and send over a couple of photos of their next match. But you didn't call me to talk about sport. What's with the new number?'

'I'm on the wife's phone. Brace yourself. Anne Burgess's conviction might be unsafe.'

Shock put my hand out to a wall. It had ended a metre before and I stumbled through a half-open door. My reflection in the glass panels of the office door, making giant sidesteps to stay upright, was pure bumbling chorus girl.

'You all right?'

'No!' I found an obliging piece of knotted carpet on which to park and slid to the floor. 'How's Anne Burgess's conviction unsafe?'

Chris said something, but panic bound me, endless gossamer threads of unintended consequences tightening around my neck. An exquisite noose.

'Bridge? Bridge?'

'I'm here.'

'We might've missed something about the Burgesses. Declan Swan's in the wind – do you remember his alibi? Said he was with a female reporter. She's now saying Swan left the morning Emer Davidson was killed and came back later that night. Puts him in the timeframe for Emer's murder. I would imagine this journalist's memory cleared up right around the time she realised Swan wasn't coming back for her. I spoke to Anne Burgess, told her Swan was in the frame but she's sticking to her confession.'

I knew this case in runic detail, could lay the stickmen facts and watch as they became more than the sum of their parts, but perhaps we'd started with the wrong question.

'Spoke to the accountant out in Burgess Data Centre. Small man with big feet, looked a bit like a penguin, remember him?'

'Vaguely,' I said. Information quick as closing credits flashed past my eyes.

'Well, I've stayed in contact with him. He called me, said money's missing.'

'What!'

'He reckons Swan helped hisself on the way out. Burgess Data Centre is getting an audit courtesy of Her Majesty's Inland Revenue.'

'Did this financial controller tip them off, Chris?'

'Wouldn't think so. It's standard procedure for Inland Revenue to look into criminals with a profile like the Burgesses. Andy – that's his name – is a decent bloke and always had his suspicions. The Burgesses and Swans were a fast set.'

Chris sounded schoolmarmish.

'There's money missing from asset replacement accounts for one, deposit accounts that business had, nigh on two million pound,' he said.

'That's disappearance money.'

'It's a tidy sum, but Inland Revenue will find how it was done. I can promise you that.'

'Are there any other entities associated with BDC?' My mind reeled through possible places for a business to stash money.

'What, like OCGs? That's Organised Crime Gangs.'

'Jesus, Chris! I know what OCG means! No police force apart from the UK uses it in conversation. The rest of us say 'gangs'. And here's another thing, OCG comes from a European directive, the irony being the UK are leaving Europe.'

'Do you want your OCG back then?' said Chris.

I stepped off my soapbox. 'Sorry.'

'There's a logistics company, Slowell Holdings Ltd, that Burgess Data Centre use for everything, but it's legitimate,' he said. 'Andy says they use 'em for deliveries, invoicing, cash collection. Owt to do with the business.'

71

'We may need to look at what they've filed in the last few years, get a feel for them.' A desk drawer yielded a spiral pad and I scribbled notes in my loopy writing. 'We'll need to dig around in Companies House – it's all online now.'

'Oh God no! You know I'm not a filing-and-figures man.'

'We need to check for bitcoin too.'

'Why? That's pretend internet money,' said Chris.

He pronounced it *mun-neh* which made me smile.

'No, it's a proper crypto-currency and attractive to bad boys on the dark web, where you can wash bitcoin then pop it, neat as a pin, into a bank account and take out crisp notes.'

'It's that easy?'

'Yes, Chris. I mean you have to have connections with dark wallets, but if Swan was embezzling on that scale, he'll have connections. And Mike Burgess knew about this too.'

'Aye.' Chris sounded glum.

'What's up? This not good for you?'

'Well, yes and no. Mike Burgess isn't doing so well in Winson Green. Got a bad beating week before last and was in the infirmary for four days. I went and told Anne Burgess he were in a bad way and the bint just looked at me and smiled.'

'That's cold.'

'She's a strange one. I'll keep working on her. If we've missed something about Declan Swan due to a false alibi, Maitland will accept that. We'll have to sweeten the pill though, by having the real story about Burgess Data Centre.' He let out a gassy sigh. 'While we're on it, deep sea diver brought up bits of a body caught in wet fibre in the Irish sea.'

'You've been busy,' I said.

'Fellahs working on behalf of some telco on the Solas cable – body was knotted up in it – they call it wet fibre –'

'Chris, is there a point to this?'

'What's left of the body was Kumran 'Shabba' Stephenson. He worked for Burgess. His butler.'

'The man we met in Burgess's house in Newton? How's he tied into all this?'

'I don't know as yet, but he were a native of Lozzell Grove, same as Emer Davidson and Declan Swan.'

'God, Chris, what a cluster!'

'To be fair, we weren't looking for it. Shabba and all the Burgess staff were on a night off when Emer Davidson was killed. Shabba were in a local Weatherspoon's with as many witnesses as you like.'

'You think Flannery was involved in his murder?'

'Same disposal as was used for Emer Davidson, so I'd say so. Shabba was weighted down with car batteries, but got caught in undersea cables, triggered an alarm in some network operation centre. If he hadn't, we'd never have found him. Head got caught in a loop of cable. Flap of skin on his forehead was preserved. Fish couldn't get at it.'

Oh that I'd exercised some restraint with the breakfast bread and marmalade . . .

'So you got DNA?'

'Not the assailant's. It were blunt force trauma. So I'd say Declan Swan took a rock to Shabba's head and got Flannery to dispose of the body.'

'You could be right. Anything to tie Flannery to it?'

'Nowt but a copper's gut feel. I've put into Interpol for a Red Notice on Declan Swan based on the recanted alibi and the missing money.'

'Not for Flannery?'

'Bridge, don't start – there's no evidence linking Flannery to this. But I'll say this, if we get Declan Swan there'll be no telling who he might implicate.'

It would have to do for now.

Chapter 13

Joe Clarke was waiting for me in the Criminal Assets Bureau, on the second floor of Harcourt Square. Despite being recently reconfigured to accommodate new staff, it was at full capacity, staff sardined into every available space. Desks either side of musty-looking partitions any decent charity shop would refuse, plastic swivel-chairs with blue padded backs and a jammed carousel with inmates elbow to elbow. With so many people packed into a tight space and a low Styrofoam-tiled ceiling, the level of noise on the second floor was something you built up resistance to. But now it was pin-drop quiet.

'Bridget, this is Miss Amina Basara.'

Joe tried to work out where to put his eyes which irritated me. She wasn't naked.

The woman in the burqa was quarantined in the middle of a trestle-like table, a free seat either side of her. She stood to meet me, a ghost rising. She must have been waiting for a seating allocation in the same administration office I was in. She proffered a small white hand.

'Bridget Harney,' I said.

'Yes.' She raised a gauze. Her eyes were a startling

turquoise and blazed with defiance. 'Amina Basara. I'm from the Revenue Commissioners. I believe we'll be on the same team, under Sergeant Clarke.'

She had the glottal accent of west Dublin. I'm not sure what I had expected, but it wasn't flat Clondalkin.

'Eh, you can call me Joe,' he said into the air above Amina's head, then looked at her civilian identification badge. 'We're over here.' He waved to three desks spooned into a corner. 'It's cosy.'

'Fancy a coffee?' I said to Amina. The bug-eyed silence from the rest of the office irked me.

'I don't drink coffee.'

Part of me was sorry. I was curious to know how she'd navigate the veil.

'I like a bit of bread and marmalade as a mid-morning snack. The canteen is good – hungry gardaí are not happy people. They make their own brown bread, need I say more?'

She shook her head and the layers of fabric swayed.

'They have a good mint tea?' I said, unwilling to give up once I'd started.

She didn't respond.

She followed me out into the corridor and a group of detectives walked by us, gawking.

'Close your mouths, lads, lot of flies about,' I said.

I eyeballed Tom Ryan, but it didn't stop him shouting *'Jaysus wept, lads! Scatter!'*

He was a narrowminded buffoon.

'Wha' are you looking at? Yellow streak of piss!' said Amina.

For a small woman she had a commanding voice.

Tom Ryan's hyphen brow rose. 'Potty-mouth,' he said.

Laughter burst out of me and Amina's shoulders shook.

'Big girl's blouse!' she said.

'They don't get out much,' I said.

It was a good opening and I had to start somewhere. My store of knowledge was about to be increased after a quick dive off the deep end.

'I don't know much about burqas so I'm going to ask questions? That OK?'

I was hunching in on myself, trying to make my six foot smaller and racking my brain for a frame of reference. I'd known some Muslim students in Trinity, but no one had worn a hijab never mind a burqa. We'd all been so self-consciously indolent, leaning against the handrail outside the Lecky drinking Diet Coke and smoking, talking with the swagger of the young about feminism and communism, while living off the allowances our parents gave us and allowing the boys to rate the girls. How would Facebook have sprung to life if we hadn't?

Amina was silent and I was damned if I was going to start a conversation with 'some of my best friends are Muslim'. I hoped there was more to me.

'You're direct for an Irish person. This is a niqab not a burqa. I wear it Gulf-style. The top is designed to fall right down to my eyelids and I wear an eye mesh too, common in Saudi Arabia but not many other places. A burqa is different – it covers everything in a single garment, including your eyes. So it can't be taken off in public. My dress is different – you can see my eyes when I lift this gauze. In fairness, most niqabs don't have eye-veils or gauzes.'

'So yours is a more extreme version?' It was a bad choice of words and I nearly gave myself whiplash backpedalling. 'Sorry, I meant a more traditional or –'

'It's fine,' said Amina. 'I do wear a more fundamental dress. Most Irish Muslims don't wear anything like this.'

After a moment or two she took off her badge and handed it to me.

'Thank you.' I peered through the plastic. The photographer's workmanship was poor, leaving Amina's features indistinct. 'Were you born in Ireland? You sound Irish.'

'No, I came in 1999 from Bosnia. I was five. My homeplace was Bjeljina.'

'Veg-ul-gina?'

She gave a gentle shake I took for laughter. 'Close enough.'

'Can't have been easy.'

'It wasn't a party. Your liberal press said children lined the route to our direct provision centre waving flags of welcome.'

'Did they?'

'Oh yes, but then they closed their doors when the television cameras went away and complained to their local county councillors about dirty refugees being dumped on them like landfill.' She looked at me, forcing her face up to an unnatural angle. 'Do you remember it?'

I was only fifteen at the time. 'A little. I remember politicians and the media being happy Ireland was taking refugees.'

Amina snorted. 'Congratulating yourselves! I was in direct provision for three years and our family was lucky.' She shrugged. 'I'm not going to go on about it, but Irish people believe they have a talent for welcome. Your national narrative is built on it, but underneath the plastic-paddy smiles you are slippery as salesmen and calculating as an ASBO teenager who wants to get out on a Friday night.'

I'd hate to see fury if this was Amina's attempt at light banter.

'Steady on! That's some amount of people to insult in one go. Give yourself a chance. You'll get around to everyone at some point.'

She gave a loud, barking laugh. A strange sound from someone so petite.

'Is a niqab comfortable?'

'Allah tells the children of Adam that he has bestowed upon us a garment to cover our shame.'

It was said with good humour, so I chanced a reply in the same tone. 'You don't strike me as someone who needs advice on what to wear. Your dress is as much a form of protest as modesty.'

'You think?' said Amina.

She sounded surprised.

'I'm the only member of my family who wears niqab. My sister doesn't wear anything, and my mother wears a hijab, a headscarf.'

She pulled me towards the ladies' toilet. Once inside she checked the blue wooden cubicles, banging each door right into its adjoining wall. When she had established all were empty, she unclipped the veil of her niqab. She had swirling depths to her eyes out of the shadow of her veil, porcelain skin and her nose was raised at the tip, as though it had caught on something in her mother's birth canal. She offered me her hand again.

'Amina Basara, Bosniak.'

'Bridget Harney, ex-barrister at law and all-round South Dublin girl.'

'Posh and privileged? With private-school education?' said Amina. A hit of twinkle to ease the stark facts as she dropped my hand.

'Guilty as 'chorged'.' I gave her my best South Dublin vowel-switching, nasally accent.

'You're hurting my ears. When I first arrived, I was baffled by all these distinctions. Even now, having been in this country nearly two decades, I'll never understand why Dubliners believe the world revolves around them – and their viewpoint that people from Cork feel entitled, that Galwegians think they're spiritual and bohemian, while everyone else is a culchie.'

'You're not a culchie, you're from Clondalkin – that's a category all on its own.'

She clapped her hands and snorted out a laugh, a steam-train puff in the cold air.

'Here's to protests in our own time.' She paused. 'I should tell you I asked to be stationed with you.'

My eyes widened.

'Human Resources in Revenue are so politically correct now they spend most of their time rewording their own newsletters. I could have asked for a detail on the Detective Chief Superintendent's staff and I'd have got it, but I sent you information and it was acted on. We got somewhere, no?'

There was a timidity about the way she phrased her question, at odds with the cloaked provocation of her dress.

'That was you? I thought it was someone called Amy.'

'A–M–I – you can only put three digits in for your name on that system. But you liked my work?'

'Yes, I did. Thank you.'

I set my stall out. 'I'm not going to pretend I understand your choice to wear the niqab, don't understand some of my own choices, but it's your decision. And that decision shouldn't preclude you from working with dignity in a tolerant environment. Everyone's entitled to that.'

'I agree.' She gave a playful smile, then became serious. 'You asked about my niqab . . . can I ask you about your dead partner? What was she like?'

I didn't mind the question but couldn't put Kay into a few short sentences, so settled for details.

'We were friends from the first day of basic training in Templemore. She softened something in me and I hardened something in her.'

Amina saw through my words. 'She was a big part of your life.'

'Yes.'

'Why did you become a garda? I'm not saying you aren't a natural fit in here, but they,' she indicated to the squad rooms outside, 'talk about you. The barrister who plays at being detective.'

I sucked on her words for a good ten seconds. Silence didn't flap Amina.

'Have you ever been in the Criminal Courts of Justice?' I said then. 'Watch them swooping out of the bar council before court begins its afternoon session, a clique of crows coming from a single doorway on the fifth floor. Circling down on some of the most poor, deprived, and sometimes depraved members of society.' I made a clicking noise with my tongue. 'It was too removed from any kind of truth and I wanted something else – possibly as badly – the freedom to choose, not to follow my father into the bar, but to be a garda. To make my own decisions no matter who I offended. I struggle with the "you can be as different as you want, as long as it's our kind of different" thinking that prevails. It's just another form of control.'

Amina nodded. 'Me too, hence my elaborate niqab.'
'Bet that's fun to put on in the morning.'
Amina threw her head back and laughed.

Chapter 14

The coastal Dublin Area Rapid Transit to Booterstown was laden with tired bodies, rank breath from hungry stomachs and peppered with alcoholic exhalations from lunchtime drinkers. I made my way through the sticky mass and out of the station. The marsh was full, a rare sight, and its briny tang mixed with the soft rain falling. I didn't have a coat so broke into a trot up Booterstown Avenue, making a left at the top onto my road. My flat-soled shoes slapped off the shiny pavement in a tap-dance rhythm. I reached our house and keyed in the gate code, walking into the grounds of my family home. So much room for two people.

Nata was at the door in a fur coat and a full face of make-up.

'Mr Justice Harney, he eaten,' she said.

Nata gave my father his full title, as though she were senior counsel making a motion.

'Off on a date?' I said. 'You're all glammed up.'

'*Agh*, coat is fake, hope date not,' she said. 'You should try a new man? Be good for you. You spend too much time at job, no enough meeting men.'

Nata gave me a wink and squeezed my arm, a banded

platinum ring on her middle finger. I hoped it was from her new boyfriend. She saw me looking and threw her eyes skyward.

'Is fake too, TK Maxx. Maybe one day real thing. Left nice stew for you.'

'Thanks, Nata.'

Her presence warmed our house and I was so grateful for her scraps of mothering. I thanked the economic crisis in Moldova that had sent Nata to Ireland. Then felt guilty for such selfishness as she bustled off.

My father was in the kitchen. His routine hadn't changed much with the event of my mother being taken into residential care. He visited her every day in the nursing home and was home for his walk in the nearby park with Ted, my retired assistance dog, too soft for the K9 unit. Dinner was at 5pm – any later and my father believed his digestive system would be under pressure.

'Judge,' I greeted my father but stayed standing warming my backside against the Aga eating a hot bowl of paprika stew laden with chunks of chorizo, white beans and black pudding, Nata's cassoulet.

'Sit down, Bridget. You'll get stomach-ache eating standing up. And you're wolfing your food.'

Ours was a complex relationship.

My father gestured to the eating area in our kitchen, an alcove with ample room for a holiday of caravans. Cosy it was not. I walked over with a slouch, the moody teenager my father's voice had reduced me to, and he followed me in.

'How was Mum today?'

'Good.' He gave a precise nod. His economy of movements always fascinated me. 'I believe she's settling in. Elizabeth has a current penchant for jigsaws which is good according to the nursing staff. Help her keep whatever mental functions she has and perhaps slow down the degenerative nature of the disease. I bought some on my walk this morning, from the craft shop in the shopping centre.' He looked at a stack of boxes. 'We might start off with the easier ones and progress.'

'Good idea, Judge. I'll go down tomorrow.'

'You can't go down on a daily basis, Bridget. The weekend is fine. You're a good daughter, your mother knows that.'

But she didn't. Most of what she knew was lost in the toxic matter clogging the branches of her brain, green worms at the centre of the tree. She had described her head as gunk-filled years ago, when we could laugh together, when we had no dread of dementia and the pain it would leave at our door.

Ted snuffled in and licked my shoe, then my hand as I popped a sweet silver of pork-skin into his mouth.

'Dog has the run of the place,' said my father. 'To your basket, sir!'

Ted slunk away, injured but reeking of adoration, and sat in one of the many baskets my father had dotted around the house, to facilitate them being in the same room at all times.

Dad's ears were becoming fleshier over time, peach begonias stuck either side of his head, but his face was still as large as ever, no harrowing with age for him. He was still a tall man but had a stiffness of gait suggesting a problematic hip. Not bad for someone who was seventy-five. There were times when he was more vigorous than me.

He cleared his throat as though something unpleasant had lodged there. 'Richie Corrigan wants to visit your mother. In the nursing home.'

I stopped mid-bite, the food tasting of ash.

Richie Corrigan. Family friend. My mother's lover. Seán Flannery's solicitor.

'Does he?' Anger roiled around my insides.

'We have to consider what your mother might want.'

My anger popped, deflated by the pinprick of her years-long affair with Richie Corrigan.

'As you wish, Judge.'

He scraped a dry hand over his face and up into his hair. 'It's not what I wish at all, Bridget, but we can't be . . .' he struggled for a word to normalise the situation, 'unkind.'

'No more than four times a year and one of us has to be present.' I was scrabbling for control – if I could size and shape something, I could deal with it. However, my usual classification methods weren't protecting me from the pain on my father's face.

'Agreed, I'll inform the nursing home,' he said.

It was wrong, Richie Corrigan exploiting my father's sense of fair play.

'Do you want to go to France to see Beatrice Corrigan?' I kept my tone quiet and devoid of emotion.

'Why?'

'I thought, maybe . . .'

'Tit for tat?' said my father. 'No, there was never anything there. On my side.'

He shook his head and changed the subject.

'How was work?' he said.

This was safe ground for us, but thoughts of my new position drained me further.

'Oh God, I forgot to tell you! I'm now an advisor to the Supers on the Policing Authority. DCS Muldoon asked me.'

The Judge snorted and I cracked a smile.

'The price of getting back to detective?'

My father was not one for sugar-coating.

'Yes, Judge.'

'Graham Muldoon is a canny man – he knows I can help if you get stuck.'

I raised an eyebrow, not at the veracity of his statement, but at his total lack of humility.

'What? What have I said now? It's of use to have a retired President of the High Court at your disposal.'

'True, Judge.'

'Tell me who's on the board?'

His eyes were bright, brimming with affection, but his love was an ambigram revealing itself only in reflection. So it was that my father and I could only connect during the impersonal, the personal too encoded without the mirror of my mother.

'The Honourable Mr Justice Michael Denby,' I said. My father liked judges, sitting or retired, to be given their due. 'Emeritus Professor Sheila Ramsey, Dr Neil Moriarty.'

'Denby's a good man, got a solid head on him. Commercial. Don't know Ramsey, I'll put a few feelers out. Watch Moriarty. He's a career civil servant and as slippery as they come, worked in law reform for twenty years and changed nothing. Not as easy as it sounds. He'll say nothing at the meetings, wait for the minutes to come out, then back he comes when he's nit-picked every document. Any senators?'

I told him of a smug retailer appointed to the authority.

My father chuckled. 'The fellah in favour of upward-only rental contracts? People mightn't find him so charming if they knew how many rental properties in our large cities his holding company owns. He'll be fun.' My father scrunched up his face. 'What was his slogan? Your mother always said he had the best corned beef.'

He was relaxed and it gave me a lift.

'You might go through your mother's reading room, take her some books? She can't concentrate long enough to read, but you've a beautiful speaking voice and she'd enjoy listening to you.'

In times gone by I'd have taken umbrage, understanding the comment to mean I was wasted if not using my voice debating as a barrister in court.

'My intonation's all wrong from years on the bench,' he said. 'Too dramatic.' He sighed, looking old, his store of lustre diminishing.

'Sonorous, Dad. And Mum loved listening to your cases – she would go to your summations, particularly when you were prosecuting. Of course I'll read to her. Should have thought of it before.' A door opened in my tired mind, my unseen mother turning the handle. 'I might read some of her correspondence, the letters from her cousin in Canada, the woman in the convent?'

'Oh yes, Sister Finbarr. Good idea. I'd say the older letters. The nurse says the present isn't as familiar to her but she remembers many things about her girlhood.'

'I'll have a dig around in her bureau. Unless you'd prefer to, Judge?'

'No, no!' He looked scandalised. 'I never went into your mother's reading room. It was private. Even though she's not here anymore I feel it incumbent upon me to respect her privacy.'

He'd become pompous again, as though my mother's

reading room was full of sanitary towels and other 'woman's things' as he'd once called my tampons when he'd happened upon a packet in the downstairs toilet.

The door to my mother's reading room was locked and I put my hand up to the top of the door ledge and scrabbled for the key. It swung open and I stepped into the room. It was the essence of my mother, her amber smell mixed with Amalfi lemon. I stood for a moment and breathed her in.

My mother had documents stuffed everywhere. In a huge rolltop desk were household bills, manuals, Revenue returns and any amount of bank statements. Some I recognised – the old ICS building society – others such as Nasda Holdings meant nothing to me. This was my mother's work correspondence.

In an antique writing bureau with delicate rosewood legs I found bundles of letters tied with ribbon, my own from boarding school tied in pink, my father's fastened in red and packets of other letters tied in forget-me-knot blue. The irony wasn't lost on me. I hoped Mum would remember some of these letters.

I looked for the return address of Sister Finbarr in Quebec, finding a neat pile from her. They were stacked in date order, so typical of my mother, and I pulled the first one out, golden-washed with age. I settled down on a chaise lounge to enjoy it.

'*My dearest cousin, Elizabeth . . .*'

Sister Finbarr's writing was dainty and as restful to look at as her prose was to read. I lay there reading the first packet of letters and saw my mother and her Laois childhood through her cousin's words. A breath crossed my cheek like butterfly wings and my eyelids came down of their own accord. I dreamt of bogs at turf-cutting time, the slice of a *sleán* as it cut through the rich brown peat, taking a single sod with it, and girls skipping towards the workers with a pail full of sandwiches and flasks of tea.

Chapter 15

'You listen to me, Bridget Harney! Christ, I should have known something was up when you asked for this meeting!'

Joe was standing in his new office in CAB, more of a repurposed toilet cubicle. The chill autumn crept in and a pigeon flapped by, looking for a perch on the lipless window. The sound of belling trams floated up. A pleasant backdrop, were it not for Joe rammed up against the wall on his side of the desk, fists bunched and glaring for Ireland.

'You might think I'm off on –'

'But isn't that you all over, Bridge? Hard lessons given but still the same stubborn girl.'

There are few people who will call me 'girl' to my face, but Joe Clarke has the right, given I owe him my place in the Garda.

'I'm not, Joe, but I'm going to investigate this drug seizure. Any leads I get I'll share, my movements will be accounted for and I'll update the systems. I have changed.'

'No, you have not.' He rubbed a hand across eyes whose pouches had pouches. 'You're still running a tout no one knows anything about.'

'Who told you?'

'Your face.' He held up a hand. 'You're secretive, it's your nature, and I won't fault you, but you have to put that informer on the Covert Human Intelligence Sources system, at least have some written record of this fellah. You're dependent on this tout. I'd hate to think –'

'Someone was leading me astray?'

'Or that you're making promises you can't keep.'

A well-aimed blow. Lorraine Quigley dead in a deep freeze was a punctured pattern in my mind, as if a cobbler had hammered it in with silver nails. I was silenced.

'That was a step too far, but I need to know who the informer is, Bridge.'

Silence wasn't serving me, and Joe deserved better.

'Put up the window,' I said.

I sat in the small chair and Joe closed the single pane. He had an air of expectation about him.

'Well?' he said.

'Sheila Devereaux.'

A muscle in Joe's jaw, tucked into a jowl of empty skin, trembled.

'Jesus, Granny Dev herself? The crooked witch? Are you sure?' He waved a hand in the air. 'Stupid. Sorry. I mean, why is she doing this? The oul' bag has been lying to us for decades, covering up for her own sticky-fingered mother. You know her father disappeared after botching a robbery for that gangster Henchico in the sixties?'

'They have form, for sure.'

'Don't joke, Bridge! Sheila Devereux's kids are no better – her daughter ran off at fifteen after she'd had Gavin and her son's serving life in Portlaoise. Why'd she turn Turk?'

It wasn't a politically correct comment, but that was Joe.

'Sheila Devereaux has joined the dots. She's worried for her grandson and Seán. Dealing with the cartels is a death sentence. They're in over their heads.'

'Ah, she's petted Gavin for years and she's not wrong about the cartels. How did she get to you, outside the normal channels?'

'The Judge.'

'What!'

'Dad sentenced Gavin. He had just turned eighteen. The Judge believes he should have gone easier on Gavin, kept him out of Mountjoy. It's the only sentence in all his time on the bench he's ever spoken of with regret. To me at least.'

Joe dipped his head. 'How well she knew to throw that at you.'

'She used the same solicitor who worked Gavin's case to make the approach. He was on the Bails years ago when Gavin was arrested, came with her to the house.'

'Sheila Devereux came to your house? The oul' bitch.'

A smile tugged at the corner of my mouth. 'You never swear.'

'I know, I let myself down and you, but I'll make an exception for Sheila Devereaux.'

'She wants her great-grandchildren to have a chance. Gavin lives in the Gardens. It's Flannery's compound, but Gavin's children are there too. He's in on every deal Flannery's ever pulled.'

'Criminal mastermind,' said Joe.

That got a laugh from me.

'Gavin's as dumb as a box of rocks,' I said, 'but his granny isn't and she wants him out, wants both of them out. Calls them "*de boys*", like they're a pair of scamps.

Said this thing with the cartels would end one way, with her family in coffins.'

'She thinks of Flannery as her family?'

'I believe so, from what she said – he came to her soon as he left State care.'

Joe looked thoughtful. 'Do they want relocation? You'll have to go through C3.'

'Garda Crime and Security Branch? Why does everyone still call them C3?'

'Habit – and same people running the show. Anyway, I've a friend there, worked with her years ago in Roscrea.'

'They don't want relocation – the Devereuxs are enshrined in the East Wall.'

Cogs clicked behind Joe's eyes, his mouth snapped into a wet circle.

'She wants Flannery and Gavin *in prison*?'

'Yes. In a protected wing of Portlaoise, serving some minor possession charge.'

'Jesus Christ, she wants State protection for them!'

'She believes it's the only place the cartel can't get them. When Fuentes are destroyed and someone else starts up, the boys can come out and be safe. And I quote.'

'She told you about the shipment and the Farm?' said Joe.

'Yes. I'm guessing she wanted to bring Fuentes to Dublin, in the hope we'd disable whatever retribution they try to deliver and in parallel charge Seán Flannery and Gavin Devereux, keeping them safe in prison. When the "de boys" are released from prison there'll be no more drug-dealing. Sheila Devereux's word on that.'

Our mouths twisted in a semblance of smiles, but no mirth.

'She said that?'

'And expected to be believed.'

Joe's chin found his hand, the rough palm scratching off his bristled skin. 'Sheila Devereux's had no schooling to speak of, but she's as cunning as they come. Those crime families in the East Wall are bandits, ignorant and violent. And in this day and age it's by choice. They glory in it.'

I was taken aback – the soap box was my usual haunt. 'I'm speechless.'

He smiled. 'Go on, that'd happen! Any chance you'd tell Flannery his beloved Granny Dev is a tout? He'd burn her place to the ground if he knew.'

'Ah here, Joe, talk about taking a joke too far!'

'I was kidding.'

The pinching sensation sliding down my back disagreed.

'The Fuentes shipment was good intel and it bought us kudos with the brass.' I jabbed a finger up to the sixth floor, which accommodated two assistant commissioners and a confederacy of chief superintendents. 'But the whole landscape is about to change as a result of our seizure.'

It was an understatement – we were standing in the vortex of a tornado and at some point we'd have to pass through it.

'Fuentes will send someone, or several someones,' said Joe. 'I'd love to tell you we'll be all over it, but we won't. If we're lucky, some fellah or girl with a record will show up through the National Central Bureau – or Interpol might catch a passport, but it's unlikely."

Depressing and accurate.

'Know what I'd do, Bridge?' Joe gave me a level stare. 'I'd let them have at Flannery and Co. The cartel might have them already.'

'*No!*' It was out of me before I could rationalise. 'You

don't mean that. We know Sheila Devereux's manipulating us but forewarned is forearmed.'

'I say we stand by from the safety of the side-lines.'

'It wouldn't be safe. You know how many innocent lives would be lost. And the likes of the Devereuxs and Flannery would escape unharmed – they'd be told of our plans well in advance.'

'Bridge!'

'You know it's true –'

'What have I told you?' Joe lowered his voice. 'Do you want O'Connor to end you? And I don't mean in the Force.' His face stayed the same, affable to anyone looking in, but the words themselves trembled from rubbery lips.

'Circumstances point in that direction. The only time Flannery hasn't been a step ahead of us was this seizure.'

'You've no proof Flannery's getting information from him.' Joe scowled.

I pushed a damp strand of hair off my forehead. 'Lorraine Quigley told me last year Flannery had an informant in the Garda. Do you remember the meeting we had about Flannery's involvement in Emer Davidson's murder? Who was in that meeting?'

I answered my own question, knowing by the set of Joe's mouth he wouldn't.

'O'Connor, you and me. He was in all the high-level meetings about the seizure in Kilkenny. Tell me, who was in the briefing when MAOC first contacted us?'

Joe sighed. 'Muldoon, me and O'Connor, but that doesn't mean anything, Bridge. The Supers all brief one another.'

I continued, unwilling to be side-tracked.

'Last year, when we thought we had Flannery, O'Connor denied me the Armed Response Unit when I tried to raid St

Martin's Garden. We had probable cause. The second time he gave me armed support, Flannery was ready and waiting. He'd been tipped off. And another thing I know. Neither of us have two ex-wives and four children in private schools.' I couldn't stop myself. 'Kay was lured into meeting Seán Flannery. I'll bet he used his informer as bait.'

Joe was pale to begin with but now he was rinsed of colour. 'Bridget, no more. Not in here.' He looked out his closed window. 'You're going down a dangerous path and for all we know Flannery is manipulating the information you're getting.'

'Flannery's on the hook to the cartel for over two tonnes of coke and prescription drugs. He's risking his life and the people he thinks of as family, to get me? I don't think so.'

'Please, Bridge, take a step back.'

'No, I can't.'

'*Bridget, don't chase O'Connor or the cartels, it's too dangerous, it'll change everything, there's no way back from this.*' He spoke in a slurred panic, a man who believed in the weight of words and that putting enough of them in the right order could change minds. He took a breath. 'The odds of succeeding are negligible.'

'I have to try, Joe. I'll keep Flannery under surveillance until the Fuentes strike, take as many as I can get into custody with Flannery and wring the informer's name out of him. Then charge Flannery with Kay's murder as well as trafficking drugs.'

'Because it's that simple?'

'No, Joe, it's walking a burning tightrope with no net, but what choice do I have?'

He made a reedy sound, somewhere between a sigh and the prelude to a choking.

'Think about this, Bridge. You can walk away or you can start a war. Because make no mistake, these people are personal. They'll target you and everyone you love.'

I said nothing. Joe would spot a lie.

'Your mind's made up. Go to Muldoon. You'll need massive resources for this and an ironclad case. Apart from the Commissioner and the ACs, who would have a heart attack if they were asked to go on active duty, he has the kind of heft you need.'

'The seizure has everyone looking at us and applauding. We'll get extra resources now. We have a chance, Joe.'

He looked doubtful.

'Will you help me?'

'Of course I will, *alanna*, what else would I do? While we're at it, put a listening device in Flannery's car.'

'Flannery doesn't drive. Gavin Devereux does all the driving – they use an old Avensis. What are we going to do? Ask Toyota out in Bluebell if they'd give us a copy of Flannery's key and we'll black-ops the bugging device in at night? Or better yet, we'll pose as mechanics and fit up the car when Flannery brings it in for a service. I'm sure Liam can change oil and tyres.'

'Quite the comedian,' said Joe. 'I find the easiest way is often the simplest. Get your tout to plant it.'

I had to hand it to him.

'If Sheila Devereux won't do it, she's not genuine,' I said.

'We can't use any of it in evidence, but it's a way of her establishing good faith. If she won't do it, any deal on immunity for Gavin is gone. And while we're at it, I want to know what Flannery's up to. Get the solicitor – Richie Corrigan – in here, let's see if we can't squeeze him.'

'He's downstairs.'

'Aren't you the early bird?' said Joe. The merest hint of a smile.

'I'm not sure he knows much about what Flannery's up to. Richie's getting on a bit. I'd say Flannery uses him because he's not as sharp as he was.'

'You could be right, but he might have more information than he realises,' said Joe.

I gave a tight smile.

'Don't stand there grinning. Go and get Corrigan.'

I headed for the lift bank, the idea of Sheila Devereux putting a bug in Gavin's car a light inside me.

DCS Muldoon's secretary was in the lift when the doors opened. A formidable woman in her fifties, she was coiffed and manicured, an old-style personal assistant who got Muldoon his tea in a china cup.

'You look pleased with yourself, Bridget Harney,' she said.

You had to be above the rank of superintendent before she'd use your title.

'Just in good form, Josie.'

'Ms Goddard to you, Bridget Harney.'

She harrumphed and we stayed silent as the lift car descended to reception. I could sing for my next meeting with DCS Muldoon if Ms Goddard took against me. The doors opened onto the too-bright reception. Some architect had shoved a glass box in the old entrance during a renovation, giving the impression the building's mouth was forced open in a ceaseless howl.

Richie Corrigan stood to greet me and I badged him through the Perspex security gates. His glance snagged on Ms Goddard, flushing when I caught him staring.

'There's life in the old dog yet, Richie.'

PART 2

If you look at the drug war from a purely economic point of view, the role of the government is to protect the drug cartel. That's literally true.
Milton Friedman
(Nobel Memorial Prize Winner in Economic Sciences)

Chapter 16

At the start of every run my joints protested, despite my warm-up. There was a taste in my mouth of old pennies and my breath was coming in piston-pumps, but the pace evened out and my body began to remember the routine. The emptiness of running contracted my problems – they never went away but were easier to deal with. Tonight it was my mother – it was my mother most nights. The loss of her presence in the house, milky clouds in her eyes stripping away her memories one by one. She didn't recognise me anymore. I ran harder, my lungs iron-hot and bursting in my chest.

At no point did I have a plan but when I found myself in Waterloo Lane, metres away from Paul's house, I couldn't deny the thought of him brought me comfort. It was late, past eleven, and he could be out having a late dinner or upstairs with someone after an early bird. Caution was not high on my agenda as I rang the bell on his front door, my breath frosting on the night air and sweaty ovals of fingerprints left on his glass sidelights. I gave the bell a second tap and winced as digital chimes jangled again. He came down the stairs two at a time, sleep-tousled and yawning.

'Bridge.'

He wasn't surprised to see me in the middle of the night, dressed in my running gear. He took my chin in the crook of his index finger, pulling my face close to his and kissed me. I fumbled in the door and he closed it with a push, taking my hand and pulling me upstairs to his bed. There was heat and melting skin until we shared the same space. My moan came from his throat and the catch in his breath from my lungs. He trailed figures of eight around my breasts. Our sweat moulded us together. I peeled away only to join him again, hoarding the sensation of being recoupled. My body was dissolving, made of soft paper turning to pulp, a single splinter of old wood showing.

'Do you want me?'

'What?' His voice was amused in the dark. 'This isn't like you, looking for reassurance.'

I didn't have an answer and leaned into him, travelling down his body.

'I want you.' His voice was hoarse.

Chapter 17

The air in CAB's offices had the texture of cottage cheese when I pushed open the doors, the pong of fried food and overcooked vegetables greeting me. It signalled late hours and delivered food. Joe had asked to meet in one of their poky meeting rooms – to be fair, everything in Harcourt Square was poky or overfilled with gardaí. I was delicate after my night-time tryst with Paul, afraid it would be graffitied on my face and was glad Joe had his own news.

'Morning, Bridge!' he said. He was standing at the halfway mark in the doorframe with an excited meercat look to him. 'In here.'

'Easy, Joe. You'll give yourself a hernia with excitement. What's up?'

Joe looked sheepish. 'Do you remember I had a contact in C3?'

'Of course.'

'Well, here's what she got me.'

I crowded in until our heads touched over the small desk, a communion of skulduggery.

A nondescript black box, half the size of a standard android phone with a couple of stubby red and blue wires protruding. Another wire, black and thin, about one and a half metres long. The listening devices I'd researched on eBay were chrome, snazzy-looking and Hi-tech. This was more *Harry's Game.*

'This is it?' I asked.

'And you can take that tone out of your voice, Bridget Harney. This is a top-of-the-range listening device. You'll give it to Sheila Devereux to plant.'

'How does it work?'

'It's hardwired into the car's own electronics so you can get a trickle charge from the car's battery to keep it going. It has a SIM card and two options for listening – first you can dial the SIM card and it will activate the microphone and start listening, or you can have it voice-activated. If using the voice-activation mode, the bug will detect sound, send you a text and you dial in.'

It was practical if somewhat clunky.

'What's the downside?' I asked.

'If there's poor network coverage it won't work and it doesn't record anything, so you'll need to listen in real time or you can use the TapeACall app. The app records calls and you can store the conversations in the Cloud.'

'Get you, Joe, and the Cloud. This spook must be into you.'

Joe shook himself and tried not to look pleased. 'I wasn't always behind a desk.'

My stomach rumbled.

'Hungry?' Joe avoided looking at my bedhead.

'I'm fine. How's Sheila Devereux going to get it hardwired into the car?'

'She won't, unless she's an auto-electrician and last time I looked she had no qualifications to speak of. She'll have to ask Gavin if she can take the car – day out at the cinema for the great-grandkids or something – God knows Gavin's given her enough of them – we can install it while they're at the pictures.'

It made sense and, though I was tempted to remind Joe of my car mechanic wisecrack, I bit my tongue – he was on a roll.

'The main unit has to be installed somewhere behind the dashboard.' He picked up the snake-length of thin black cable with a dot microphone at its end. 'The mic should be hidden behind the roof lining material over the driver's head. It's the best position to get sound from.'

'There's a girl in the Tech Bureau could do it,' I said. 'She's getting married soon and looking for nixers.'

'Grand, use her so. This will put Sheila Devereux in a tight spot and that alone is worth it. Get yourself a burner phone. Untraceable. Don't dial into it from any other phone.'

'Does it have a serial number? Do C3 have any way of identifying the bug?'

Joe shook his head. 'No serial number and all the components are bought for cash in shops that supply the public – they make them up from scratch. This can't be traced back to us. That's the point.'

Chapter 18

She knew she enjoyed going to restaurants and staying in large, fancy hotels. She knew that better than she knew her own name. <u>Elizabeth Harney</u>. She underlined words in her mind based on people's facial expressions, the words were important, anchors in her moth-eaten consciousness.

The days had no meaning for Elizabeth in this place, with its endless miles of carpeted corridors she kept walking up and down, some kind of looping conveyor belt where she saw floating faces. It reminded her of being on the Tube in London going down the escalators and spotting someone coming up on the other side but recognising them too late. The stalled moment between catching someone's eye and recognition was where she lived. The walking helped, but more of the world slipped into the electrical storm of her overloaded synapses. Dark and frightening with single shots of forked lightning to help her steer a path. Her last hope was to keep walking and the destination might reveal itself.

'Your <u>daughter's</u> in the day room – come on, Lizzie,' a nurse told Elizabeth.

She wanted to tell the nurse she had a son, not a

daughter, and she hated being called 'Lizzie'. She looked around for her favourite nurses. The sisters who called her Elizabeth and took her arm, walking beside her when the burden of searching for her son became unbearable.

'Here she is!' said the nurse with the affected jollity of a school matron.

It hurt Elizabeth's ears and she eased herself into a high-backed padded chair.

It was The Girl. Tall, blonde and all angles, with such sad eyes. Elizabeth wanted to ask her what was wrong, but it was impolite to pry.

'Hi, Mum,' said The Girl and pressed a cheek, fresh as an ironed sheet and as sweet-smelling, into Elizabeth's own parched skin. She didn't have the heart to tell The Girl she wasn't her mother. She had an indefinable quality Elizabeth liked, an innocence and an unashamed desire to be loved, despite being crimped by the ordeals of adulthood. The Girl sat down and took Elizabeth's hands in her own. This, Elizabeth had decided, was where the confusion lay. For all the world The Girl's hands looked the same as her own – younger of course, but there was a familiar symmetry in the joints and lengths of the fingers. The deep inward curve at the base of the thumb. Elizabeth got lost in the lines on her and The Girl's skin.

'Mum?' said The Girl. 'You look lovely today. I brought a jigsaw – we can do it later if you want? It's the Bridge of Sighs. You and Dad visited on your honeymoon.'

The Girl's face changed when she said 'Dad', full of love, so Elizabeth knew it was an important word, but it couldn't be her father, could it? Elizabeth's father would never visit her, not after what happened.

She struggled with The Girl's speech, the patterns and

intonations were too quick for her to hold on to, she couldn't make anything stick in her mind, so responses were futile. Her eyes flitted onto the blue box with a picture on the front, and from the dark clouds of her mind came one word: <u>Venice</u>. She looked at the girl and smiled.

The Girl lit up. 'Shall we open it? Put out all the pieces?'

Elizabeth nodded, buoyed by The Girl's enthusiasm and an eagerness she didn't understand, but let it take her anyway. The pieces were pink on one side and on the other were sky-blue or grey stone. She liked the shapes, the sharp corners and the busyness it brought when she had to put them together. It gave the anxiety lying coiled within her a task. She had one foot in this world and the other in a shadowy place filled with crying – it couldn't have been Heaven because she had been taught as a child Jesus lived in Heaven and it was a glorious place. The other place might have been Limbo, where all the unbaptised dead children went. Buried outside graveyards in unconsecrated ground.

'Mum? Are you OK? Nurse!'

They crowded around her, making her more agitated.

The Girl took her arm and walked her to a bedroom she recognised bits of, but it wasn't one of her favourite hotels. The bed, for one thing, wasn't right. This bed had bars on the side of it. And there was a smell of roast dinner.

She sat without complaint on her chair in front of a dressing table that wasn't hers. Her eyes flickered across the silver brush and matching hand mirror. A handsome dancer floated across her mind, the ballroom in the Gresham Hotel and a calf-length blue dress made of duchess satin, her hair twisted into a chignon by that brush. Had it been a birthday? The clove smell of the lily corsage

<u>Vincent</u> had pinned to her dress. Elizabeth was lost. He was so tall. His wavy dark hair slicked back, his eyes when he invited her to dance. Elizabeth swayed with the motion of a remembered waltz and the pleasure of the brushstrokes on her hair. The Girl had a gentle hand.

'That's it, Mum. I love you.'

And Elizabeth loved The Girl. She knew that, despite not knowing her or being unable to make sense of any of the fractured pictures in her mind. They lacked the edges that fitted into one another.

The Girl looked sad.

'Are you sad, dear?' said Elizabeth. Her voice sounded creaky.

The Girl looked confused and put her head down to her mouth.

'What's that, Mum?'

The Girl kissed the top of her head and murmured something she didn't catch. So she tried again.

'Are you all right, dear?'

Something was happening with The Girl's hearing. She rubbed Elizabeth's shoulders and spoke as she would to a child.

'It's OK, Mum.'

Elizabeth assumed something was wrong with The Girl and patted her on the hand. They stayed like that, The Girl brushing Elizabeth's hair with slow, soft strokes.

'I miss Kay, Mum.'

The Girl's voice was all but inaudible and Elizabeth didn't understand the words, couldn't put them in the right order, but she understood the tone. Loss. She was all too familiar with that sensation and reached up to The Girl's face and brushed away a tear rolling down her cheek.

Elizabeth looked at The Girl's reflection in the mirror. Where had she seen her before? She was cross with herself for being of such little comfort to The Girl.

'Oh!' said The Girl. 'I brought these letters from home for you. I can read them to you?'

The Girl took a packet of yellowed letters from inside her jacket and placed them into her hands. She turned the packet of letters over, letting the brushed-velvet texture of the old paper take her someplace else.

'Do you like them, Mum?' said The Girl. Her voice was coming and going, a snowy television signal beamed from the past.

These letters were important. Elizabeth had waited for them. They were an exit out of the rundown cottage and her mother's cold anger.

'Bridget!"

The Girl turned.

A nurse in the doorway had called her.

'<u>Bridget</u>, there's another visitor here.'

That was The Girl's name! Elizabeth tried to hang onto it. She looked around for a pen, to write the name down, but even as she searched she knew that her body wasn't moving, or moved too slow to make a difference. She hurried and the letters dropped from her fingers but she paid them no heed. The shape of The Girl's name was slipping off the surface of her too-smooth mind.

'Mum? Mum! Stay where you are. I'll get them.'

'Elizabeth?' said a lumpy man in the doorway.

His voice brought something forward in her mind. The thought stayed in a display case like a taxidermist's prop, scooped out and lifeless with only the outer skin left, the thought itself gone. Elizabeth's mind was full of these garish husks.

The lumpy man barked her name, the way a savage dog would, and The Girl swung around, anger written in large letters all over her face though she forced restraint on herself. Elizabeth saw it in a gesture she recognised, the way The Girl's hands bunched into fists – she'd seen it before.

'What are you doing here? Dad and I gave permission for quarterly visits and you have to be accompanied by us.'

'Bridget, I wanted to see Elizabeth. She . . . we . . . I miss her.'

The Girl looked ill and Elizabeth wanted to tell her that the lumpy man made her ill too. Elizabeth wanted <u>Vincent</u>, wanted to find the words to tell The Girl that the lumpy man came in when no one else was around, touching her, trying to get her to hold a pen and got mad when she couldn't. She wanted to tell The Girl but couldn't find the words. A sense of dread rose and crashed off the bird-like bones inside her chest.

Elizabeth asked God to tell The Girl to stay.

<u>Richie Corrigan</u>. The name appeared from the smoke of her mind.

Chapter 19

DCS Muldoon rapped on a table. An Assistant Commissioner was in the Drugs and Organised Crime Bureau's squad room. The squad room was packed, detectives greeting one another with a hard handshake or a curt nod depending on the prevailing political winds. What shocked me was my attendance. Joe Clarke had dialled me up and told me to make my way to the fifth floor. The results of Lorraine Quigley's post-mortem were back. I'd sprinted up the back stairs, high knees and high nerves at the grave tone of Joe's voice. I hadn't expected access to this meeting, and it was a bonus I was determined not to mess up.

The AC stood to one side in full dress, face as stiff as his freshly pressed uniform. I could smell the chemical dry-clean of it over the sour musk of twenty people sardined into a room. Paul Doherty was in the Assistant Commissioner's group, but I kept my face turned from him. Liam O'Shea caught my eye and motioned with a jut of his chin to join him and the other DOCB detectives. I walked over to the clump they stood in and was greeted by nods, a shuffle, and a few comments.

'*Howya, Bridge, stand in there.*'

'*Move in to the left, Jimmy, would you?*'

They were quiet after a fashion, the presence of an Assistant Commissioner enough to quell even the most determined entertainer in the ranks.

Muldoon's secretary was in situ – she was his American Express card, he never left home without her.

The Head of Communications, a rising superintendent who had a Master's in political communications from Dublin City University, was inscrutable. She was professionally polite.

DS Niall O'Connor's eyes roamed over the crowd and picked out Liam.

'O'Shea, you start with this.'

It was a tall order in front of an AC, and craven. If O'Connor wanted the post-mortem reviewed, he should have done it himself. We received the report a short hour before the briefing. Standard protocol was to review with your sergeant or the cig on the case and work through it, for however long was needed. Not present it, with the expertise that implied. A sheen of sweat broke out on Liam's bald head.

'Don't worry – any questions land them on me,' I said. 'O'Connor couldn't dislike me any more than he already does.'

Liam looked sceptical and moved off. He parted the town hall of detectives as he walked up to the desk where Muldoon and O'Connor were standing.

'I'll put it up on the whiteboard – you get yourself up to speed in the meantime,' said O'Connor. He fiddled with the leads in an attempt to connect his laptop.

Liam was being set up to fail and I blinked at him,

hoping he could decipher my Morse code and stick with the post-mortem summary, but it was more difficult when an AC was to your back. I eyeballed Muldoon to no avail. His face was blank, awaiting instruction.

Liam began. 'The body is that of a twenty-six-year-old, underdeveloped, poorly nourished female. There is no peripheral oedema of the extremities. There is an area of congestion/erythema on the upper chest and anterior neck. There are multiple areas of haemorrhage –'

'Jesus, move on, man! We're not a First Year Med class,' said O'Connor. He was enjoying himself.

Liam raised his eyes to the group, shuffled his feet on a quicksand floor and swallowed. In the unnatural quiet it was a loud water drop.

'Internal examination. Body cavities. The right and left pleural cavity contain 10ml of clear fluid with no adhesions. The pericardial sac is yellow –'

'Go to the summary, Liam,' said Joe. 'I would say, Detective Superintendent O'Connor, no one from the squad has had more than an hour to examine this report and we should bring ourselves up to speed before including anyone else in the briefing.'

I wanted to clap him on the back.

'Since when, Clarke, are you in the DOCB?' said DS O'Connor.

You could have roasted marshmallows off Joe's face. I'd never seen him lost for words and of course I should have said nothing, but when have I ever?

'This was a joint effort between CAB and DOCB. It was a massive haul – as has been widely reported in the media. DCS Muldoon, I believe DS O'Connor was on the nine o'clock news last evening commenting about it.'

If nothing else, I was going down swinging.

'*What is she doing in here?*' said DS O'Connor. He was bellowing.

It was better than I'd dared hope. A look singed between the AC and DCS Muldoon.

'That will do, O'Connor,' said Muldoon. 'Get on with it, O'Shea. The Assistant Commissioner doesn't have all day.'

It was late afternoon and the winter sun was low in the sky, glancing into the squad room and blinding Liam. I reached for the beaded cord of an ancient venetian blind – it whizzed down the frame of the window and smacked the base. O'Connor jumped and glared at me.

'Lorraine Quigley was killed by blunt force trauma to the back of her head consistent with a wooden bat or plank,' said Liam. 'She sustained multiple injuries to her face and upper body consistent with punches or blows from an individual. After death Lorraine was washed in a saline-and-bleach solution so no trace evidence remains. She was frozen, which slowed down decomposition –'

'So we have nothing,' said O'Connor, his desire to be the big man in front of the AC outweighing his desire to hear the rest of the autopsy.

'There were no toxins present at the time of her death,' continued Liam and I admired his decision not to be cowed by O'Connor.

'Detectives O'Shea and Harney, please move to the seizure,' said the AC.

The room quietened, Liam looked at me and I took my place beside him.

'We received information that a seizure we were tracking via MAOC was already ripped off in Dublin and on its way to Kilkenny,' Liam said. 'We drove to Mullinavat and found an articulated lorry loaded with an international shipping container abandoned in a service station. On further investigation we found what we now know to be two and a half tonnes of pure cocaine and one hundred kilos of prescription drugs, benzodiazepines, Valium, Xanax.'

'Here's the list,' said DS O'Connor, unwilling to be shelved. He brought up a slide with the seizure breakdown.

The AC didn't waste any time. 'Detective Harney, I've read your brief and incident report on the seizure. Do you think Seán Flannery is supplying on an all-Island basis? Is there paramilitary involvement?'

'Assistant Commissioner, I've no proof of that. But it's possible. Flannery's gang are well armed and trained. Any of the guns I've seen are well maintained.'

The AC would get my inference. Some of the dissident republicans trained criminal gangs for a fee and let them use their underground ranges. It stood to reason Flannery would use those dissidents and that was a two-way street. Flannery would be charged a tithe on a shipment of this size.

'The genesis of the cocaine, please,' said the AC.

It was a fair question.

'I believe it's the Fuentes cartel from Venezuela,' I said. 'They're one of the largest cartels in South America with routes and operatives into North America, West Africa and Europe. The purity levels of the cocaine is consistent with Fuentes. Some of the other cartels are exporting coca base to labs in Mexico to be refined into cocaine, but it's not as pure as Fuentes' product. I've been working with Forensic Science Ireland on a geographical signature for the cocaine – and, although it's not foolproof, along with the gang tags on the cocaine we believe Fuentes are Flannery's supplier.'

'A find of this magnitude changes the way we investigate this gang.' The AC took a good look at me. 'You believe this is Seán Flannery's gang and the farmhouse was his production facility?'

'Yes, Assistant Commissioner.'

I wriggled on the hook.

'Seán Flannery's gang will be upgraded to an Organised Crime Group,' he went on, 'along with the other two gangs the state is investigating on an all-Island basis. DCS Muldoon will head the investigation into Flannery's gang. His unit will work across all necessary Garda and Government departments and your forensic work will take precedence. DCS Muldoon will brief me directly on an event basis and I look forward to your first report. Good day.'

The AC and his team exited the room in a series of heel-clicks and swinging doors.

Paul threw an appreciative glance at me on his way out. At times I was a cat dancing towards a dot of light with Paul holding the torch, twitching it with the subtlest of taps.

O'Connor snarled at me. 'You'd better be right about Flannery. If all he's supplying is Mummy's Little Helper, no amount of pull from Mr Justice Harney will keep you in the Force.'

He left in Muldoon and the AC's wake. The shell of tension surrounding the rest of us cracked. Some detectives even laughed.

'Right,' said Joe. 'Tech Bureau are going to love us. Bridge, call the duty scientist you know in FSI and tell her there's a change in the forensic strategy on this case. They'll have to get down to Kilkenny again and map that farm for everything it's got.'

119

'They'll kick off no end,' I said.

Joe supressed a snort of amusement. 'Go on! You're delighted. Flannery's being upgraded to an OCG so the Tech Bureau will have to suck it up.'

Liam didn't give me a high five, it wasn't his style, but he grinned in my direction. 'One step closer.'

'I'll get him, Liam. He'll be on the run now with his largest shipment impounded and his lab out of action. Problem is, we won't be the only ones after him.'

'True. He'll have Fuentes on his tail. Hey, your man Paul is well in with the brass.'

He was looking for car keys or something he'd put down and had his back to me. I was glad he didn't see the heat flooding my face.

Chapter 20

1988

Clarendon House was a Mother and Baby Home and housed forty-five boys from babies to twelve-year-olds. The Home was a Victorian house in a cul-de-sac off a secondary thoroughfare in Drumcondra. With too much grey rendered stone and too few windows, it wasn't to the liking of the parish priest for whom it was built. He gave it and the two acres on which the building stood to the nuns. They were the Sisters of Christian Charity and Education and they intended the house for boys in the long term. The girls in residence were six and seven weeks old, awaiting adoption or transfer to an orphanage if they were not successful in acquiring new parents.

Seán was singing to himself as the boys walked in a line down the tiled corridors to the refectory for breakfast. Sister Assumpta had told him he was lucky to be in such a good home with kind nuns to give him a path to follow. There was a shuffling further back the line where the younger boys were and he heard a sob he recognised as being from his friend Gavin. Gavin struggled a bit when trying to keep up with the others, complaining when his heels had been rubbed to burning from too-tight shoes.

Everything was new, at least Sister Assumpta told him everything was new, and what had Seán to compare it with? He got all his shoes and clothes in bin bags. Some had a clean lavender smell, others not so much. The biggest problem was nothing fit. The nuns took whatever was donated. Once they got shoes from the Dubarry factory and a boy had walked around in navy wellies for six months – they stank but Sister Assumpta had said 'Isn't he covered?'.

Gavin had started to cry in earnest, big whinging sobs, and Seán looked around to shush him. He hoped to see Sister Assumpta, but she was on kitchen duty. The boys walked to all meals in single formation, arranged by age, and with their index fingers pressed into their lips. Seán was eight and close to the top of the line, a few bruisers in front of him, but those boys were men to Seán. He worried Gavin might get into trouble – the nuns told the boys they had nothing to cry about.

A single nun swept up the line, the beads of her rosary swinging in the furrows of her black habit. Seán knew by the ear-splitting silence that she'd stopped. A slap was delivered, not stinging – Seán could grade these things from a flat-handed smack to a knock-out punch. This was nothing, but enough to stop Gavin's sniffles.

The refectory was one of those places where death had lived. The nuns spoke of consumption and the time their sisters had selflessly nursed those with tuberculosis. He knew the nuns had lost sisters in that epidemic. He didn't know what the words 'epidemic' and 'tuberculosis' meant, but he knew anger when he saw it. Whenever Sister Assumpta spoke of it her mouth became wire-thin, lips pushed inwards, and she steepled her gnarled arthritic fingers. She called it 'The Great Sacrifice' the nuns had made for the Irish people. 'People who were sinners.' Sister Assumpta's voice was thunder after lightning. These people were sinners because they believed in the wrong God and yet the good nuns had nursed them. Like those sinners, Seán was a sinner, but his sin was indelible, given to him at birth by his mother, according to Sister Assumpta. No matter how many times he asked forgiveness of God, He couldn't hear him as he was steeped in original sin. Seán was a teabag at the end of the huge crockery teapots when all the tea had been poured out, soggy with sin. Even so, he tried to make God listen.

The refectory was in the basement and had clerestory windows, but the house faced east and the sun pushed as much splintered light and rays onto the boys as was possible during the summer months. They sat at rickety trestle tables and each nun had a row to give breakfast to.

'Seán,' said Sister Assumpta. She put a rough ceramic bowl in front of him. It had a thin green line around the top and a much thicker green line around the centre. Guineys shop in the city centre hadn't been able to sell them as they were rubbish, even for remnants, so gave them to the convent.

Sister Assumpta came down the line a second time with a huge pot of porridge made with milk. Premier Tír Leighin dairies left extra bottles of milk with the daily order – rumour had it one of the farmers in the big depot in Rathfarnham felt sorry for the orphans. She ladled out the porridge. It had a toasted oaty smell and was hot. Seán took a spoon of brown sugar from the bowl, pooling the grains on top of the fluffy porridge, and watched it caramelise. It was his favourite time of the day – the clattering of cutlery, the smiling nuns, the rows of boys slurping and joking. They were allowed to talk during mealtimes if Father O'Mahony wasn't there.

It was rare for the priest to appear at breakfast, as the morning light seared his rheumy eyes. The nuns would stop meals whenever he came into the refectory and everyone had to be quiet. A small knifepoint of a man, he had shiny brown hair and pockmarked skin. This was one of those rare mornings.

Father O'Mahony's cracked blue eyes ranged around the refectory until they found Gavin. He shrank under the priest's gaze yet was brave and never shook. Father O'Mahony's eyes probed Gavin for a weakness and bored into it, all through the prayers of adoration and contrition.

When breakfast was over and they were making their way to the classrooms in the shabby prefabs near the edge of the grounds, Seán passed by Gavin and squeezed the top of his arm.

Gavin's eyes pleaded with him and Seán mouthed, 'It's OK'.

When Sister Assumpta came for Gavin in the evening to assist Father O'Mahony at vespers, Seán took Gavin's place. He was too young, seven, and Seán had been eight for nearly a year.

Later that night Seán pulled his Foxford blue blanket up around his shoulders. Sister Assumpta had allowed him sleep in with Gavin as a special favour. He'd cried on Seán's neck until it was wet, mumbling 'sorry' over and over until the double breaths from his sobbing chest shook both their small bodies.

'Don't worry,' said Seán. 'I'm older than you. I'll keep you safe.'

He pulled Gavin into him and tucked the blanket

around both of them. The blanket had come all the way from Swinford where it was knitted on big machines in the woollen mills. Most of the babies in Clarendon House went to America, so the mill sent down blue and pink blankets to wrap them in as they went on their journey. Seán knew no one had wanted to adopt him, but Sister Assumpta had said he could keep the blanket anyway.

Chapter 21

2019

A couple of days after Lorraine Quigley's post-mortem I found myself outside the cracked stone gates of a convent, made more bleak by a rumpled iron gate across the entrance. I got out of the car and the shrill November cold tore through my work suit. Inside the grounds, work on a housing estate had finished for the day with muddy potholes everywhere. Was there anything as woeful as part-built houses and silent cement mixers in the semi-darkness of winter?

I parked on gravel needing a rake and pushed the doorbell. A rattling of pulleys and bells then a sparse woman in a flowery housecoat opened the door. Her face as florid as her housecoat was floral, a blinding combination.

'I'm here for Sister Assumpta, please? My name is Detective Garda Bridget Harney.' I flashed a smile to go with the badge and she put her hand out to hold my wallet. Why do people always want to handle my badge? Of course I couldn't give it to her, so I held it under her nose, suspecting she couldn't read anything near or far without glasses.

'It's all right, Philomena,' said Sister Assumpta.

She stood in the shadows of the hallway, hers a stentorian voice inconsistent with her stealthy steps. She was a scrubbed-clean woman with a fine thatch of snowy hair pinned under a veil and quick eyes. Less the kind of nun who wanted to help and more the austere Reverend Mother, suited to the buttressed and high-raftered ceilings of the convent. Her voice expanded as a good red wine filled the mouth.

'You are welcome, Detective Garda. Come in.'

There was no warmth, despite her greeting.

She led me to a splendid but severe parlour, and we sat down. Looking around, I judged that the parlour was designed to make the laity feel cowed in an everlasting God's presence.

'You said on the phone this was to do with someone connected to a case you're working on?'

No small talk, none of the famed nun's parlour tea from my boarding-school days.

I tried to soften her. 'Yes, and thank you for seeing me at such short notice.'

She gave a bark of laughter and threw her hand towards the window. 'Well, there's no point in pretending things are normal. Look at what's happening to the place. This is the only time it's quiet.' Her face was wreathed in a manic humour.

I had misinterpreted her opening coldness. She was furious.

'The order sold the convent and grounds to *developers*.' She meant philistines, her last words full of rancour. 'We're to be evicted in three months. To a house in Celbrige. This is what we are reduced to, selling our convents to fund a Redress Scheme for ungrateful wretches we helped.'

It was spoken with such disdain I couldn't let it pass. 'I don't know anything about your circumstances. I was educated by nuns, good women, but there's no denying the wrongdoing in some of those Homes.'

She gave me a look that curdled in my chest, so I changed tack.

'Celbridge is full of old-world charm, good bookstores and you're not homeless.'

She snorted. 'What would you know? Steeped in privilege as you are. Your father a retired judge.'

'How do you know about my father?' This was interesting.

'Oh, you're assuming because I'm a nun I'm not up to date with the world's affairs? All you have to do is look outside to see how imbedded in the world's affairs I am. Bunch of builders knocking down my home and destroying the sanctuary of this place! It's all we have left.' She shook her head at me. 'I don't want money, none of us ever wanted money. All we wanted was peace and quiet.'

Again, discretion should have been the better part, but our countryside was littered with grottos and churches the size of beached cruise liners.

'How many of you are here?' I said.

'So because we are a few old women we deserve to lose our home?'

'No, of course not, but this building is the size of a hotel – you could house over fifty families here.'

She looked at me with the scorn of the righteous to the godless.

Despite her sense of entitlement, I pitied her. 'It must be difficult to lose your home.'

'You have no idea how it pains our community! To leave the refuge of a convent and go to live in a . . . house.

Where do we gather to pray? We have no place anymore in society.'

A marble mantel clock with a glass dome and ivory figures at the centre made square-sounding ticks and frowned at both of us. It was the type of ornament people would have flocked to see in a jeweller's window decades ago. Now it was offensive, an embarrassment that would end up in the rubbish heap or eBay.

'Sister Assumpta,' I was mindful of her pain, 'have you heard of a young woman called Lorraine Quigley?'

She lowered her chin. 'She was the girl you found in a freezer in Kilkenny. It was on the news and in the papers earlier in the week. Terrible.'

'This man is connected with her murder. Do you know him?' I handed her a picture of Seán Flannery.

She pulled a glasses case out from behind a cushion. 'These are the community pair,' she said. The half-moon spectacles sat on her nose and gave her an elegant look.

When concentrating she was a handsome woman, but the dark habit and the veil gave her a sexless quality.

'No, I've never seen him before. Who is he?'

'His name is Seán Flannery. He heads up an organised crime family – although gang might be more appropriate – he has no actual family. Flannery was a product of the church and state environment. I believe he was born in Clarendon House, the Mother and Baby Home, then grew up in St Augustine's. You never came across him?'

'I'm not sure, I will check our records. People don't realise there were thousands of unwanted babies in this State. Before things changed. There were many homes run for orphans by any amount of orders. You don't remember it, but we were in education, healthcare, everywhere people needed help. We did what God asked us.' She eyeballed me, daring my defiance. 'Never forget it was the plain people of Ireland who gave us those girls.'

I had no intention of 'rolling back the years' and wanted her to be more specific.

'Did you work in any of the Mother and Baby Homes? I've checked some medical records and I believe you're a qualified midwife.'

Her level gaze gave nothing away.

'Yes, but I haven't delivered a baby in decades. Many nuns of my time were from good families and we were educated. I moved from Home to Home as I was needed. I lived in our main convent in Glasnevin. Not that it's any of your business.'

She stood up and walked to the parlour door.

'If that's all, Detective Harney?'

'Will you contact me if you remember anything about Seán Flannery?'

She nodded and called for Philomena to show me out.

Sister Assumpta was on my mind as I got into the car. My hands of their own accord tied my seat belt. I turned the car towards Harcourt Square and dialled the listening device in Gavin Devereux's car. The unit connected without a ring tone. I had listened to hours of recordings from the interior of Gavin's car, all of it boring, ounces being discussed and street dealers, and one guarded conversation about 'toys' which meant guns. We knew Flannery's gang received guns from the Fuentes cartel, but it was nothing that would stand up in court and no details as to locations. Gavin was a talker and had a complicated personal life with many girlfriends and a fleet of accompanying children – he spent much of his time ferrying them around pleading and arguing with their mothers in equal measure.

The radio hummed in the background of Gavin's car. He was alone. He pulled in somewhere and the driver's door binged as he stood out with the engine still on. Out of range of the microphone I wasn't catching anything.

I heard the door slam. And then another. Someone was in the car with him.

'I don't know where he is,' said Gavin.

There was an edge to his voice.

'What do you want me to do?' said another voice.

A guttural voice I didn't recognise.

'Find him,' said Gavin. 'He dresses as a beggar sometimes and hangs out on the southside – Monkstown, Dalkey, Blackrock. He can live on the street for days.' A thumping sound of fist against dashboard. 'What the fuck did he think he was doing? Check local Garda stations in those areas. If for some reason he was picked up it'll be for loitering outside a school or playground. But he'd never give his real name and they mightn't realise who they have.'

'OK.' The other voice was deep, betraying no judgement. 'How long is he missing?'

'He's been gone two weeks. I've kept it quiet, but people are looking for him. Bloody razzers tore up the lab, all hell's broken loose with the dealers. There'll be a street war if he doesn't show up soon.'

The wheels screeched as I turned into the bus lane, leaving tyre tracks on the road. Blaring the sirens and full lights on in the grill, I raced back to the Square.

Seán Flannery was missing.

Chapter 22

The sky was whipped ice-cream shot through with grey ripple, cold but dry. My taste buds were watering for warm soda bread pooled with butter and laden with fine-cut citrusy marmalade. It was seven thirty and nothing was going to keep me from the canteen in Harcourt Square.

Amina and I sat at conjoined desks and she logged on to her laptop as I shovelled brown bread into my mouth.

'You and your marmalade!' she said.

A playful smile hung off the corner of her mouth. It was good to see. She'd discarded her niqab in favour of a headscarf when Ashleigh from HR – who I'd christened Bluntface – had unceremoniously told her it was against Garda policy to wear a bedsheet to work. Perhaps she had hoped Amina would complain, act the victim. Amina had shrugged, telling Bluntface the niqab had served its purpose. Bluntface's confusion was comical and Amina hadn't enlightened her.

'What purpose was that?' I had asked Amina.

'For someone to see through it,' she said. 'Everyone else ignored my niqab and by extension me. People who benefit from the status quo feel the most natural way to keep order is to ignore change and isolate anyone different. You aren't like that.'

I had felt ridiculously pleased. It was a curtain pulled back on our friendship. I had longed to take Bluntface down on Amina's behalf, but my motives weren't entirely altruistic. Amina had returned Bluntface's insulting behaviour with a searing politeness and I would emulate it in future.

'You're always eating sweet stuff,' she said now. 'How do you stay so thin, Bridge?'

'It's not sweet stuff, it's marmalade, one of your five a day right there.'

My mouth was packed and she grimaced at the train wreck littered with orange peel.

'Disgusting,' she said.

'Fair enough.'

Amina checked Interpol's systems for postings and outstanding warrants. 'We're an hour or more behind the other police forces – I-24/7 is crawling – there are too many sessions open.'

As Amina continued to talk about IT failings and her challenge in learning the complexities of Interpol online, her hands were busy, full of purpose.

My phone beeped, a text from Chris asking me to phone him, soon as I could.

'Chris?' I said.

'Aye, good of you to call, lass.'

'Well, you said it was urgent.'

'Get yourself somewhere you can talk.'

His usual soft accent was tight in places.

'I am – is everything OK?'

His tone of voice alarmed me.

133

'Right, no easy way to say this, so I'll come out with it. There's drugs in Burgess Data Centre. Kilos of cocaine in a water cooler.'

I was washed up on the edge of my seat. No words.

'Andy the financial guy in Burgess Data Centre found them,' said Chris.

'But how would you fit drugs in a water cooler? Wouldn't people see it?'

Chris gave a mirthless laugh. 'No, Bridge, it's not drinking water. This system cost over ten million pounds according to Andy. It has towers, pipes and ducts, cools the cages and racks where the servers are stored. It's the latest in technology, but the thing is – it's never been operational – although Burgess Data Centre paid for it as soon as it went in. Andy's been on hot coals since the Inland Revenue audit wanted to understand why the cooling system was never turned on. He had a look inside the cooling towers, found bricks of cocaine.'

'Christ!'

I tried to picture Mike Burgess's florid face. All I had was a head of dyed hair and indistinct features.

Amina was listening, gimlet-eyed.

'How big were the bricks?'

'Five-kilo packs. Wholesale,' said Chris.

'Mike Burgess was an importer? How did we miss this?' Bile rose and I put a hand under my breast, cursing my scaffolding-like bra, and massaged the heartburn.

'Looks like it, but given the amount of time we spent investigating Burgess, why didn't we find anything? If he's managing a drug network, why weren't there any traces of it?'

'You're sure about this finance guy?' It was a whistle in the dark.

'He's motivated, terrified he'll go down same as Burgess.'

'Is any of the Burgess Data Centre business legitimate?'

'Aye, Andy says the data centre has real customers, thousands of 'em. Burgess has blue-chip trading partners and a logistics company he uses. It's all above board.'

'How can I help?'

'Not sure you can. I'm on my way out there now with a forensics team.' Chris sounded dismal. 'Maitland will have me for this.'

'He can't. Maitland and O'Connor were involved in the original investigation. They were the senior officers on the case, and we ran everything by them.'

'Aye.' He sounded perkier.

'Does this have something to do with Emer Davidson's murder?'

'Well, if Burgess was importing cocaine on this scale it throws up a whole new avenue of suspects at least. It would give a brief something to bring to a judge's attention.'

'But Anne Burgess confessed.'

'I know, lass.' Chris had a placating tone in his voice. 'But drugs on this scale, we should've picked it up.'

'Can you see Mike and Anne Burgess involved in the drug trade?'

'No, Bridge, no more than you can, but we could both see Declan Swan in this.'

'Where is he now?'

'Don't know. Supposed sighting in Brazil, warrant for his arrest is active. Watch your back – there'll be wigs on green when Maitland gets this information and you can be sure he'll be on the blower to O'Connor the minute I'm out of his office.'

'He's Detective Superintendent O'Connor now.'

'Course he is, the arsehole.'

I couldn't have put it better.

'If I were you, Bridge, I'd get out ahead of it. I'm leaving now for BDC and I've a meeting scheduled with Maitland this evening.'

A strand of tension rolled around my stomach, the way a candyfloss stick moves around the bowl, rising and growing with each swirl.

'What was that all about?' said Amina and her nose twitched.

'You know Kay and I found an arm in a pig carcass last year?'

Amina nodded, her busy fingers still.

'Turned out it belonged to a girl called Emer Davidson, her other arm turned up in Birmingham. This older man Mike Burgess was having an affair with her so his wife, Anne Burgess, killed Emer Davidson. Seán Flannery was called in to dispose of the body.'

Amina's hands flew up to her face. 'How did Seán Flannery know him?'

'Relax. It was legitimate. Flannery crewed for the George Yacht Club in Dún Laoghaire. Mike Burgess kept a boat there and Flannery was his skipper for a summer.'

'And Anne Burgess is in prison?'

'Yes, but we've missed something quite significant,' I said. 'I won't pretend I was wary of Anne Burgess's confession, I believed every word, but I'm not so sure now. Declan Swan, her son-in-law, has absconded and Burgess Data Centre is concealing kilos of cocaine. Different landscape from last year.'

Chapter 23

1998

'In there, look! She's sitting in a window with her diddies hanging out.'

Gavin's voice was off-key with excitement. He and Seán ran down Bloedstraat in Amsterdam's red light district at full pelt. Brandy and Monica sang about a boy being mine from speakers outside a coffee house. Both boys whickered with laughter as they passed semi-naked women in windows lit with neon red. They ignored the men-with-the-money congealed around the base of the houses, the Japanese tourists with their Nikons slung around their necks and the girls with threadbare veins who didn't have windows to sit in.

It was hot and the canals reeked. They were inky-coloured at night and reflected the garish neon, giving a spray of plastic seduction, but the daylight sloughed it off and left the canals their original offal-brown colour. Gavin and Seán tried to move their mouths around the names of the streets, 'Bloedstraat' and 'Oudezijds', the profusion of consonants and double-weight vowels belonging to a different planet and 'the Dam' was light years away from Dublin.

137

'Come on, man,' said Gavin, 'how are you going to celebrate turning eighteen? Get laid or get high?'

Gavin wanted nothing more than this and his excitement, toxic and pollutant, issued off him in hot waves. He spun around, drunk at ten on a Thursday morning in August, on a day that promised to be at least as hot as yesterday's thirty-four degrees.

'This is the life, man! Fucking eighteen and kings of the highway!' he said.

'You're seventeen.'

'Ah Seán,' Gavin was laughing, 'you're so serious. We can do anything we want – no one to tell us what to do, what time to come in 'cos your fucking tea is getting cold.'

Seán looked at Gavin who didn't understand his luck escaping Clarendon House to his grandmother's home at eight years of age. Seán had been left there, moving just before his thirteenth birthday to St Augustine's Home, where routine had eroded free will and lights out ushered in some of the most violent times he'd ever known.

He took out his sheet of paper where he'd written instructions for the trip, a selection of dates and times of flights back to Dublin, for when they'd have to buy a ticket home. He knew a good part of this was meaningless, but he was reassured by the plan. The squareness of the paper, the neatness of his handwriting made everything manageable. In the uncurbed vastness of a world where he had no one to depend on, Seán was calmer if he had instructions, even if they were his own.

'Stop swearing and remember we're here to do a job,' he said. 'We're not on holidays like all these other fools. Our way was paid for one reason.'

'Yeah-yeah – but look at the babes!' Gavin's narrow

finger pointed at the windows, a bottle of sudsy beer in his other hand. 'Fuck, I'm hungry – any chance we get some Rancheros? Or do they have Taytos in Amsterdam?'

Seán's phone rang.

'*Man with a mobile phone!*' Gavin shouted it out loud. 'Is it that Guy-whose-real-name isn't-Guy? He's a fucking copper, isn't he?'

'Shut up!'

The brick pavements were old and uneven, covered in the summer's baked-in dirt and dog excrement.

Seán pulled Gavin onto the Korte Niezel bridge and walked towards Dam Square, telling him to keep quiet. The Nokia 8210 continued its blippy ring and a number pulsed on the green screen in thick-stemmed font. They stood in the doorway of a vacant shop with a dusty window covered in '*Three Lions – 98*' stickers.

Seán put the blue-and-silver phone to his ear, marvelling he'd been trusted with it.

'Hello, Guy?'

'How are you getting on?' said the dislocated voice on the other end.

'Good. We're staying in a place called the Trident. It's off Dam Square. We found an ad for it at Central Station. It's good value.'

Seán had no idea of hotel value, but he wanted to sound sophisticated. They were in a room at the top of a budget hostel. The bed was strange – a double mattress sunken into a purpose-built cavity in the floor, the edges surrounded by cushions. Seán was beyond impressed by this and took a photo with his new camera. He'd get it developed when they were home. The boys had slept in their sleeping bags on top of the bed, unsure if they were allowed get under its striped cover which was tucked into the floor.

'You have enough money to get around?' said Guy.

'Yes.' Seán had more than he needed and was already planning to keep half of it for when he got back to Dublin.

'Good. Go to Daazta bar in Leidseplein and meet my contact Lucas this evening at 11pm. I've told him you're coming, and he'll be expecting both of you. He's going to give you some product and we'll see if you can get it back here. Then we can move on to the next step.'

'OK,' said Seán.

'Don't say much, do you, kid?'

The voice was mocking and Seán hung up. He and Guy weren't friends.

'OK, so what did the *Man* say?' Gavin put emphasis on the word and gave a snicker. 'You know his real name isn't Guy, don't you?'

Seán bent his head a fraction.

'You should tell him we know all about his bullshit,' said Gavin.

'Stop swearing – you're letting yourself down and me down by association.'

'Ah shit, Seán, you're not still on about that?' Gavin reeled, the early-morning drinking taking a toll on his balance.

'Calm yourself – you'll draw too much attention to us.'

Seán knew who 'Guy' was but didn't trust Gavin. It was too risky and of late Gavin had been reckless. Arrogance sticking out of him as far as his puny erection when he pointed to the girls with the fake smiles behind the full-length windows. Seán hated to make eye contact, but his vision snagged on their bare limbs. A window full of fat Arab women made him shiver with disgust.

'*Look at the dumbo on her!*' Gavin was shouting.

'Keep it down and come on.' Seán's head knotted and a thirst to beat one of the Arab girls filled him. Sister Assumpta had warned him against his uncontrollable temper. 'We have to go to this Daazta bar at eleven this evening – we'll go over there now and check it out.'

'Recon!' Gavin drawled in his best *Platoon* voice.

'Shut up, Gavin. You can get something to eat in Leidesplein when we've sussed this bar out and we can take a bit of time for ourselves after.'

They kept walking.

It was important to be clever. Seán had read a book where the main character said life wasn't for people who weren't clever, who didn't have something intelligent to say. Clever people had better, cleaner lives.

'Why did you put us on a boat with those useless psychos?' Seán asked Guy-not-his-real-name, anger fizzing out of him.

'Lower your voice. What did you think was going to happen when I sent you over to Amsterdam? You were there to bring coke back. Did you think you were on a holiday?'

'No, but I didn't think we'd end up sailing some rubbish boat home!'

'Thought you'd be flying home first class, did you?' Guy laughed – more a sneer at what he saw in Seán's eyes.

He had thought they'd fly home, maybe post the drugs back to Guy. He felt foolish standing in the circle of Guy's nasty amusement.

'I had to test O'Dwyer and the route,' said Guy. 'He approached my contact in Holland – the man you met in

141

Daazta bar – with a deal about sailing a private yacht from Rotterdam. So we wanted to test it. Have to say I didn't buy into it. I'd have sworn you'd get pulled in by any number of coastguards but turns out it was fine. What was your take on him?'

The man called O'Dwyer was all mouth. He could sail, but spent his time telling Seán and Gavin about his house in Montenotte in Cork city, and how he was looking for the next thing. In this case smuggling drugs into Ireland through Castletownbere in County Cork.

'It's called being on the ball, lads,' O'Dwyer had said.

He had a broad, muck-savage accent Seán despised. Gavin had called him a presumptuous dickhead and Seán had itched to stick a blade into O'Dwyer's lower back. Seán had done the hard work on the voyage, staying up through the night and navigating the Dover Strait, around by Plymouth and across the Irish Sea. Gavin keeping him company. Seán had enjoyed it but was damned if he'd tell Guy that. O'Dwyer slept most of the time, as had his two thugs. He knew his maps and how to sail, but was lazy. The thugs were Dutch and kept to themselves on the boat, in case anything got out of hand. They had carried themselves with barely concealed violence, a body language Seán knew. He didn't share any of this with Guy.

'It was a good learning experience and O'Dwyer said you were useful. He'd sail with you again. Plus, you had the advantage of returning to the country off the books. As far as your passport is concerned you dropped out of sight in Amsterdam. Don't underestimate how useful that is.'

Seán knew Guy had put him in danger with a group of strangers. He also realised Guy didn't care. He had given the boys quarter of a kilogram to bag up themselves and sell. A terrible excitement rose up in Seán as he watched Gavin cut up a Dunnes Stores bag for the twists of plastic they would put their merchandise in.

'Cut it with Granny Dev's bread soda,' said Seán. He took a packet from a shelf over the counter. 'And her hairspray. Then we'll have crack as well – some users prefer it.'

'You want us to start cooking crack in me nana's kitchen?'

'No, Gavin! If you use hairspray to stick it together it will look like crack.'

'Sound,' said Gavin and set about his work.

After a solid hour, they had product to sell.

'So 250 wraps at €50 a throw,' said Seán. He sounded confident and professional.

'So what will we make?' said Gavin.

'Twelve and a half grand.'

'*Fuck!*' Gavin spun in the air and yelped, his voice rising to canine frequency. 'Can you imagine me nana's face when we tell her how much money we're going to make?'

He snorted and laughed, looking at the baggies with hard, glittering eyes.

'We're not saying anything to Granny Dev and we're not touching those baggies either, Gavin. Those are for mugs who are going to pay us. We get some start-up money then we can buy ourselves protection, get some other lads to sell for us and see where it goes.'

'You're like an auld wan, Seán. Always so cautious. C'mon, let's see where this lot gets us,' said Gavin.

'Don't take it all – twenty wraps each. Put ten in one pocket and ten in the other. Take this.'

It was a kitchen knife. Gavin put it down the back of his

jeans and Seán took a small, sharp paring knife, good for close-quarter fighting – a skill he'd honed over the years together with bare-knuckle boxing in St Augustine's.

They left Gavin's grandmother's house, taking the bus in to Dame Street, and made their way to O'Donovan Rossa Bridge. There were plenty of punters waiting and Seán was edgy with excitement, knowing he was starting into a new, profitable future.

They walked onto the bridge – and a knife plunged into the back of Gavin's thigh and nicked his hamstring, leaving a weakness he would feel for the rest of his life.

'Did you fucking think you could walk onto my bridge with *yizzer* baggies? We saw youse getting off the bus, pair of dumb fucks!' said a voice behind Seán's back.

He had both legs taken from under him and he hit the cement pavement, a boot pressed into his face as hands rifled through his pockets, taking his merchandise. His mouth filled with blood from the pressure and the grooves of the boot's sole suctioning his skin.

'Do you know me? Young fellah? I'm Larry Dunne.'

The pressure on his face stopped and Seán looked at the pinpoint pupils staring out of a mad head. A beast of a man. He flashed the paring knife Seán had brought with him, flicking the blade under his nose. Gavin was screaming out wounded howls, high-pitched and terrified.

'Guy set youse up royally, didn't he?'

Seán's insides contracted. The rain slowed and an iridescent light bounced off the side of one of his eyes. He thought it was his life-light flickering out as the knife point leaned into the white skin of his neck.

'*Dunne! Back away! Touch him and I'll shoot.*'

It was Garda Joe Clarke, his snarling face and gun aimed

at Larry Dunne. The pressure on Seán's neck was gone and he scrabbled his way off the bridge onto the street. People were everywhere, junkies running away with their score, gardaí fighting with Dunne and his gang, pedestrians getting shoved aside. In the melee Seán could see Gavin crouching, a messy red stain spreading on his trousers, a garda standing over him and talking into her radio. Seán heard sirens hacking up the air, so loud his teeth hurt. He hoped one was an ambulance for Gavin.

Chapter 24

2019

'Morning, Bridge. He's waiting for you,' said Ms Goddard. 'I've left a flask of tea on his desk – help yourself.'

This didn't bode well. Kindness from DCS Muldoon's secretary meant I was in for a right dressing-down.

She winked at me. 'Best get it over with.'

Joe Clarke was already seated there when I opened the door.

The atmosphere was frosty, and a saucer of cut lemons flavoured the air. Muldoon preferred it to milk with his morning tea. He sat stirring a spoon around his cup – it scratched the sides, reminding me of a screw being drawn down a ceramic tile. He used a saw-tooth tongs to pick up a slice of lemon and drop it into his tea.

'Sit down, Bridget.'

My backside found the nearest chair. I didn't dare look at Joe. He was ramrod straight, eyes forward. I cursed myself for not going straight to DCS Muldoon the moment Chris had rung me. If I was in trouble thanks to Maitland and O'Connor, nothing I could do would stop that train, but if O'Connor hadn't told Muldoon I might yet have an escape route.

'Do you want to bring me up to speed on Burgess Data Centre? DS O'Connor was in to me early this morning. In receipt of a call from a DI Maitland of the West Midlands Constabulary.'

So much for that plan.

'Yes, DCS Muldoon. Detective Chris Watkiss of West Midlands rang me a day or so ago and –' I twitched, a sleeping dog chasing phantoms, and my voice cut out.

'Take your time, Detective Garda Harney. Get a cup of tea.'

Joe had one ready and passed it to me.

I gulped at the warm tea – apprehension had left me cotton-mouthed.

'We missed something significant when we were investigating Emer Davidson's murder,' I said then. 'We were focused on the family and it transpired Mike Burgess was having an affair with Emer and his wife found out. She confessed to killing Emer.'

'But the case's conviction was sound, isn't that so?'

'The confession still stands, DCS Muldoon.'

My omission hummed in the space, separating my breaths. Joe looked at me, sensing my hesitation, but DCS Muldoon didn't know me well enough.

'There were no connections to organised crime we could see at that time. The only thread was Seán Flannery. Mike Burgess had a legitimate connection to him through a sailing club and contacted him to get rid of the body.'

'But we couldn't convict Flannery due to evidence going missing?'

'Yes, sir.'

I had impregnated a rug with Flannery's DNA and left it at Emer Davidson's flat in Birmingham. Joe convinced

Chris Watkiss to 'lose' the evidence, telling Chris he'd take the fall if anyone ever found out. The distress of this memory made my voice waver.

'You all right, Harney?'

'Yes, DCS Muldoon.'

'Joe, I want you to look at the Property and Exhibit Management System. There's too much evidence kept in lockers, not turned in and lost RFID tags.'

'Yes, DCS Muldoon,' said Joe. Not a flicker.

'Harney, at the time you believed you got the right person and the evidence corroborated that?'

'Yes, DCS Muldoon.'

'So what's changed?'

'Chris and I believe Declan Swan absconded with BDC's money, best part of two million pounds and he's a person of interest in the Kumran 'Shabba' Stephenson murder.'

'What else?' said Joe.

He was right to push me.

'I believe Declan Swan murdered Emer Davidson. Anne Burgess confessed, we don't know why. Chris went to see her – and will continue to work on her – but she's not withdrawing her confession. The chief financial officer in Burgess Data Centre contacted Chris about the missing money and traced it to an account in Brazil, where there was a sighting of Declan Swan.'

'So the whole bloody case *is* unsound?' said DCS Muldoon, fist bunched on the table. 'You don't do things by halves, Harney. DS O'Connor said drugs were found.'

'Burgess Data Centre had an expensive cooling system installed, which was never operational and turns out the towers were hiding kilos of drugs.'

'Down the rabbit hole we go. What's happening now?'

'We're not reopening the investigation into Emer Davidson's murder, we don't have enough evidence, but Chris has opened an investigation into Burgess Data Centre. It's a financial forensic audit to understand where the transactions lead and what connection there is to organised crime. Amina Basara from our division is helping.'

'Good,' said DCS Muldoon. 'Keep Joe updated. I'll speak to DI Maitland myself. That's all, Harney.'

I was dismissed. Joe hadn't said anything but having him on my side of the desk was a comfort. I pulled the door to the catch as I went out, and stood to one side as the secretary's pod was empty.

'What's O'Connor's issue with her?' said DCS Muldoon.

'Loyalist cases early nineties. O'Connor coerced suspects. Justice Harney tore through him. Wanted him removed.'

Ms Goddard returned, clutching a batch of archive files.

'Eavesdroppers rarely hear good of themselves, Bridget Harney,' she said.

I scuttled away, my face brick-red.

Chapter 25

1998

Seán sat on an old Vespa some thick had left outside the corner shop near Alexander Terrace in the East Wall. Fools who lived in the new apartments in the Irish Financial Services Centre wanted some local 'colour' and came down to the corner shop for a morning rasher butty. Well, it had cost this thick his scooter. It was a warm autumn day, but the wind cut Seán's face and his eyes streamed as he rode out to an almost middle-class suburb of South Dublin. In the days after the drug bust on O'Donovan Rossa Bridge, Gavin's grandmother had come looking for retribution. Gavin had been patched up in the Mater Hospital then put on remand in St Patrick's Institution for Young Offenders. The idea of Gavin in prison, even one as soft as St Patrick's made Seán's guts gurgle with yellow bile. He gripped the Vespa's handlebars and the sharp edges of his knuckles stretched his skin. He was on his way out to Guy's house, determined to get answers, not only for Gavin's grandmother.

Guy lived off the Knocklyon Road in Idrone Close. Knocklyon was beige to Seán's eyes, didn't have the working-class bite of East Wall or the prestige of South

Dublin, despite being located on the southside of the city. What it had was bland aspirations and culchies who had moved to Dublin for a life they never got. Guy's house was a detached dormer bungalow of surprising ugliness though Seán didn't consider he knew much about architecture. Still, he saw the intelligence behind the house and the location. O'Dwyer had told him Guy was worth millions, had paintings stashed away and gold bars in a Swiss bank. He was wealthy and hid it.

Seán had followed Guy to work and home on many occasions, borrowing a motor bike from an ex-resident of St Augustine's who worked in a chop shop. Despite Guy's line of work, he wasn't observant. When he clocked off he was a street stiff, same as everyone else, on the conveyor-belt home. Too wrapped up in the thought of his dinner to notice a tail. Seán believed in the most direct route possible to whatever he wanted. He didn't like Guy, but he admired his subterfuge, hiding his money and living well below his means.

It was a Saturday and Seán figured Guy would be at home. On the way out to Knocklyon he decided to leave the stolen scooter near Guy's house. The idea appealed to him. The gardaí would find it at some point and might cause Guy a moment of panic when some of his pals gave a *ding-dong* on his front door. Seán parked it beyond the house and looked around.

The usual work routines were suspended, and children ran everywhere with soccer balls, dressed in team colours and shouting goodbye to waving parents on the doorsteps. A breaker of anger threatened to drown Seán, a block of emotions he had no name for pulled at his feet as though he were cemented into it and thrown off a pier. His footsteps slowed, his breathing shallow.

Guy's wife brought him back to the present. She was good-looking in a blowsy way, but her mouth was a red line of discontent bleeding outwards. Seán knew if Guy saw him outside his home, he'd be furious. He took cover behind an obliging hedge and dialled Guy on the Nokia he'd given him for the Amsterdam trip. He picked up after the fifth ring.

'I'm outside your house – yer ball and chain is standing waving at some neighbours.'

He listened to Guy's wife's nasal whine.

'She's saying something about Knocklyon United?' said Seán.

Guy appeared at the top of his driveway and turned towards his wife, said something Seán didn't hear, and walked towards him with a face full of sunshine.

'You'll be taking that fucking stolen scooter with you when you leave, Seán. And you'll be leaving soon.'

The words fell from his cardigan-wearing-Saturday face, a genial smile as though Seán were some local teen offering to mow his lawn.

'You set us up. Me and Gavin. He's in prison now and you did nothing. What's to stop me from going to some of your pals and snitching?'

'Nothing, Seán, except you haven't. That tells me something. You're in it for the long game, which is intelligent.'

'Why did you tell Larry Dunne we were bringing our gear to the O'Donovan Rossa Bridge?'

Seán hated the hurt he heard in his own voice. It wasn't for himself – it was for Gavin. Gavin hadn't been to St Augustine's, didn't have the skill set to survive prison.

'We needed to get rid of Larry Dunne. He's a liability, a junkie, and sells product on street corners in full view of the gardaí, brings too much heat on everyone. This way he's behind bars. I'm sorry about Gavin, but he'll be compensated when he's out.'

He stopped speaking and looked right into Seán. 'You watch out for his granny. Sheila Devereux's a tough woman.'

Seán wanted to spit in his face – nothing was scared to Guy – so Seán settled his face and looked like he couldn't imagine a better way to spend a Saturday morning.

'I want to do something bigger, Seán. We have thousands of miles of unprotected coastline. I can make you rich and important. Are you listening to me?

'I don't want to be important.'

'All right, invisible then. Bags of money and your own pigeon loft, that's what all you greasy little East Wall degenerates aspire to, isn't it? Don't go to the horse races, no sir, you like to race pigeons. You could be the Aga Khan of East Wall!'

Seán wavered. He distrusted Guy. A memory of sitting in the Home's refectory came to him. The nuns had hung flypaper over the tables. Attracted by the kitchen smells, the flies found a way in but got stuck on the sticky coils of paper. He remembered them, with their wings pinned to the brown ooze, hairy legs waving in distress.

'Can you shoot a gun, Seán?'

He shook his head.

'What good was going to St Augustine's if you can't handle a weapon?' said Guy.

'You want to arm the nutjobs in St Augustine's?'

Guy threw back his head and gave a showy laugh, despite the fact the close was empty but for a few faraway knots of women talking, the family cars packed with kids gone.

'You know your trouble, Seán? No sense of humour.'

Seán ignored him, but Guy spoke into the silence.

'I want you to learn how to shoot a gun, clean it and be professional around firearms. There's a couple of men in Monaghan have an underground shooting range.'

'Underground?' Seán hated tight, enclosed spaces.

'Has to be. It's lined with old tyres to muffle the sound. The Provos use it but of course they won't be using it as much now, with the Good Friday Agreement.'

Guy clapped at his own humour, but Seán didn't join in – anything to do with Republicans frightened him.

'You'll go and be trained.'

'Are you going to get them to kill me?'

'No, Seán. We've known one another for a long time. You're more useful to me alive.'

Scant consolation.

'Now fuck off back to the East Wall and your pigeon club. You'll need a well-trained bird for when Gavin winds up in Mountjoy. And don't come here again or follow me home. You do that one more time I'll have Gavin chivved in prison – do you understand that, you cretin?'

Seán walked away, trying to mask his unsteady legs, suddenly aware he was not the observer but the observed.

Chapter 26

2019

I flicked on a table lamp and read Richie Corrigan's idea of a love letter.

'*You must try harder, my darling. You're so close, 90 or 95 percent, so keep going. I will always keep my part of our bargain. Your ever-constant friend, Richie.*'

Was he grading my mother? His father had collected subs for Our Lady Crowned Credit Union in a poor area of rural Ireland, calling in on his neighbours in the evenings to collect punt notes they could ill afford and taking a cut before he handed it over to the credit union. No surprise his son would measure and weigh everything, including love. Richie had cuckolded my father and inserted himself in our lives at every turn. Showing up in the nursing home was a kick to an already grazed cut. But my mother had loved him, and perhaps still did. I couldn't tell. Yet one pile of his Basildon Bond Blue letters was tied with kitchen twine, the type my mother used to truss up chickens for the oven. It must have been a deliberate choice.

We had driven her to the nursing home four months ago. She had wanted to make our forsaking of her easier and smiled when we deserted her. It was a plastic bag over my head. I put the letters down, winded at the memory, and took deep breaths, lifting my chest against the bank of tears that would never leave, could never be cried away. Mum had got some comfort from the sight of Sister Finbarr's letters so I would bring in more correspondence. It was invasive, riffling through my mother's private affairs. Her life, so precious and ordinary, fanned out on the floor in old bank statements, prize bonds, recipes and letters.

Dusk moved to darkness and I flicked on the main light in my mother's study, the brightness hardening her absence, giving it a shape.

Richie's letters told her she was fortunate to have him as a friend, after her parents cast her off. He hadn't judged her, instead he'd secured a place in a hostel near Stephen's Green. They might walk there on Sunday after Mass in Newman University church. He told her about when he first came to Dublin and worked in Haughey Boland in the fifties. He wrote of how well he was doing in the bank and that his mentor Mr Traynor was advising him to study law at night. He was looking at houses in Donnybrook and advised her to reconsider his offer. He had no objection to their age difference, so what objection could she have?

His tone was imperious yet wheedling. The letter was dated 1981, the year of a princess bride, yet there was no romance I could read in Richie's letters, or passion. The floor was carpeted with his correspondence, his ardour lay in volume. My hand found another parcel of his letters, dated some years later when my mother was married and I was born. They were written on a more expensive thick white paper. His tone was more confident in these letters, less smarmy, but I couldn't imagine these letters would bring any comfort to my mother now.

Darling Elizabeth,

I write from the desk of my new practice in Fitzwilliam Square. I would have to say working with Des was the most enlightening and lucrative time of my career, thus far. His support was invaluable to me as I set up my own legal practice. Fear not, I won't parade around in a black gown, a dancing crow, as Vincent does. I am not a frustrated actor and will work with people who need my help. As you know, I have always wanted to study Law and would have done so years ago if my parents had the money to send me to university.

I cannot tell you how I wish things were different. How I wish you would have taken another course of action. But we don't need to tell one another about missed opportunities.

You expressed a view in your last letter that your husband might not appreciate our correspondence and that the time had come for us to part ways. I disagree but would urge you to keep our friendship secret from Vincent. His colleagues speak well of him, but I have never found him amiable. I hope he treats you with decorum. He will have me to reckon with, if not. You know there are secrets and people depending on me – no one else can protect them. Never worry about that, my darling. I am constant but you must do your part.

I would like to meet during the week – you can come to my office.

Your most faithful friend,
Richie

Chapter 27

The residue of drugs in Seán's system made him nauseous. They'd bound his hands behind his back with cable ties, similarly his feet, and injected him with Propofol, but Seán had never taken drugs and had no tolerance for narcotics. Each time he was injected he passed out for longer than expected and was weak when he woke. They downgraded him as a threat, leaving him in an apartment with a pothead to stand guard.

He had woken to early morning light and quiet, calling for his captor. When no answer came, he realised the man had gone on his regular trip to the shops. Seán had timed these trips and knew he had four hundred and eighty seconds maximum. He got off the bed and began to do high-knee jumps, the ties on his feet helping to keep his knees together. With each jump he pulled his elbows forcibly up and out into chicken wings. The cable ties bit deep into his wrists with each jump and after the fourth he could smell his own blood. He increased the pace of his jumping and the cable ties snapped.

He found a blunt knife in the kitchen and inserted it into the plastic lip mechanism holding the cable-tie tracks in place and popped it, freeing his feet.

Then he waited.

His captor's neck snapped back as Seán elbowed him savagely in the face as he came in the door. No doubt he had broken the cartilage between the man's nostrils and the pain must have been searing. He lay semi-conscious on the ground. Seán wouldn't have hesitated to stamp on his head, but the drugs had made him unsteady on his feet. He ran out the apartment door and skidded on the milk his captor had dropped. The burst two-and-a-half-litre Tetra Pak lay on its side leaking. He stumbled along the corridor, the smell of cooking oil and hot spice hurting the back of his throat. He didn't know where he was but he found a stairwell and took the steps two at a time leading into a painted foyer. He made for the apartment-block door and exited into harsh daylight in a city he didn't recognise.

A shop window caught his reflection. A madman with hair standing on end, bloody wrists and bare feet. People shied away from him. Seán didn't wait. He crossed the plaza-like square. It was too open and populated. His legs pumped. Broken glass, rough pavement and small stones cut his feet to shreds, but he couldn't stop. On and on, into a side street then a smaller alley where he crouched in an apartment service area. Mouth-breathing in the rank smell of organic rot coming from brown bins. He couldn't keep running. He was too conspicuous and would draw police attention. He burrowed down behind a bin and closed his eyes, listening for voices. The gusts of wind lessening the smell of the bins brought sounds from nearby streets – the voices were busy and babbling in a language he thought could be Spanish. He knew his captors were Africans in the hire of the Fuentes cartel and wondered if he was in Caracas being prepared as a tapa for the cartel bosses.

He scrounged around in a blue bin and found a *MARCA* newspaper. It looked Spanish rather than Venezuelan from the football results. The paper calmed him. So he was in Spain and in a big city, but which one?

He opened the drawer of what looked like a clothes recycling bin and pulled out clots of material. Jackets, shirts and coats, everything had a hard sheen of dirt, but nothing to put Seán off. He pulled on a coat and found formal patent shoes with holes on both inside seams and put his bare feet into them. His blood squelched against the inside of the shoe. He limped when the pain built to a pointy heat as he moved down the alleyway, but Seán could put his mind elsewhere when pain came calling.

He made it to another street and found a name on a building. Carre or Calle something-or-other, the letters not in any order he could remember, so he tried to latch onto one word but failed. The buildings were old, graffiti at ground level cheek by jowl with boxy cafés and their tired outdoor seating. He kept to the shadows, searching for a busy parent with an open bag, or harassed businessperson mid-call, but this was a neighbourhood with watchful inhabitants. He was jittery and as near his end as he'd ever been.

A door opened and an elderly woman encumbered with a spiky-looking stroller and a raucous toddler emerged. He would not get another chance. Seán ran at her, full force. He whipped the bag off the buggy handles, knocking down the old woman and child in the process and took off up the street. He could hear the roars of indignation but kept going, swerving around corners. It was like running on knives. He threw off the coat to make himself less recognisable and kept going.

After ten minutes of dodging into lanes at full pace he was breathing hard and in danger of passing out. He slowed and ducked into a side street, shielding himself as he dumped out the contents of the bag. A tattered-looking purse yielded gold: twenty euros and a phone card. Still limping but forcing his legs to straighten, Seán walked in left turns, no thought in his mind other than finding a phone.

Outside a grubby grocery shop was a battered brace of payphones. First one was coin, rare as hen's teeth – in any other circumstances it would have made Seán laugh. The second took phonecards and his stolen card put up ten euros on the screen.

He dialled Gavin, desperation and disbelief at his own circumstances threatening to undo him.

Gavin picked up on the third ring. Suspicion in his voice. 'Who's this?'

'Gavin!'

He tried to say more but relief strangled the words in his mouth.

'Jesus, Seán! Where are you? Are you OK, man?'

'I was taken from the Gardens by a bunch of niggers working for Fuentes.'

'What? How? Where are you?'

'I'm in Spain, but I don't know what city.' He looked around for street signs, saw one and started spelling. 'Where's C-A-R-R-E-R D-E-N R-O-BA-D-O-R?'

'OK, hang on.'

'Take the number as well – the money on the phone card is running down.'

Seán threw out the number, the fear thawing a fraction with the sound of Gavin's familiar voice.

'Seán? Google says you're in Barcelona.'

'Money's nearly gone. Call me back.'

Seán waited for the phone to ring. He sagged against the Perspex hood of the phone booth, his mind and muscles exhausted. The downswing of adrenaline left him in a haze. His hand was on the blue plastic of the handset when it rang, the vibrations thrumming against his palm.

'Gavin?'

'Seán, are you OK? Are you injured?'

Seán let out the breath he hadn't known he was holding in.

'I've made a mess of my feet but I'll live. I need to get out of here.'

'What do you want me to do? I'll send money over by Western Union –'

'No,' Seán cut across him. 'I'm standing here in clothes I took out of a recycling bin. I have no identification, nothing.'

'Go to the Irish embassy –'

'And have them arrest me? Are you well?'

'What would they arrest you for?'

'A body found in the Dublin Mountains.'

'That was you? It's in the news? Jesus, Seán, what's going on?'

'Stay calm, Gavin –'

'Why would Fuentes have taken you? We can pay them back for the drugs we lost.'

'Can we?'

His current predicament began to make some sense to Seán.

'Fuentes spent millions building up that company *Aceite de Oliva Barcelona* – they let it run for over four years before they started shipping gear through it and they bought a new shipping route through Guinea Bissau. The seizure in Kilkenny jeopardised all this. We don't have the money to replace that.'

'Does Guy?'

'I doubt it – but find him and tell him to get me someone in Barcelona. He has contacts everywhere.'

'Do you trust Guy?'

Seán let out a hot bark of laughter. 'Not on your life, but you'll go to him and put a gun to his head. Don't leave him until I'm home. Tell him you'll kill him and every member of his family unless I get back safe.'

'Yeah,' Gavin sounded relieved, 'I can do that.'

'I know you can, Gavin man. Get Guy and call me back in an hour.'

'OK, Seán. This number in an hour.'

For the first time since his kidnap, Seán could see a way out that didn't involve him dying.

Chapter 28

'Bridge!'

'Yes?'

I didn't recognise the voice, but the urgency in the caller's tone had me off my chair, making for the corridor. Amina raised her sculpted brows at me as I went, the other CAB gardaí carried on with their own work, unperturbed. Our office had all the atmosphere of a bus station with everyone bar Amina and me hot-desking. We refused.

'Bridge, it's Yvonne.'

Yvonne, the duty scientist in Forensic Science Ireland who had helped me identify the severed arm in the pig carcass. She'd had a temporary contract and had wanted me to put in a good word for her last year. I had – she was more than competent – and it would appear to be yielding dividends.

'Hi, Yvonne! No number came up.'

'It's the new switch, no more caller ID. Are you somewhere quiet?'

'In an empty corridor.' I checked both ends. Nothing.

'The man with the broken neck found in the forest near Stepaside.'

'Yes, it's being handled out of Rathfarnham Garda Station?'

'That's going to change. It'll be over to you lot in a day or so – you know how things move slowly here.'

'To us?'

'Seán Flannery's DNA's all over the dead man, around his neck, blood on a nearby stone, skin under the man's fingernails. I've done all the testing and matched the samples. I'm not supposed to tell you yet and if anyone knew I was giving you the heads-up I'd be in a world of trouble. But it's Flannery and you're tracking him. We got lucky – some Coillte workers found the body under a pile of logs in an area of forest they were chopping.'

Yvonne was still speaking, but I'd stopped listening. My soul was soaring. Untethered hope. Seán Flannery had make a mistake. In all the years I'd followed his oblique presence I'd never come close. Until now. Irrefutable forensic proof of wrongdoing.

A squad room disgorging detectives brought me back to reality. I cupped my hand over the phone's speaker and crouched in a closed doorway.

'Yvonne, make sure you bring this to Detective Chief Superintendent Graham Muldoon, do you hear me?'

'OK.' She sounded somewhat unnerved. 'Isn't he a bit senior? Would DS O'Connor be a better option?'

'No! Under no circumstances bring it to him. Give it to Joe first if you have to and he'll pass it on, but your protocol dictates information on an OCG goes to the most senior officer investigating. You won't get into trouble giving it to Muldoon, trust me.'

'All right, Bridge, but you know it won't go from me? It'll be our head of department.'

'Then send her an email advising her to send it to DCS Muldoon.'

'All right.' Yvonne sounded doubtful.

No way would I give DS O'Connor the chance to lose evidence or warn Seán Flannery. I would find him and bring him in. A dead body in the mountains. Small wonder Flannery was hiding. I closed my eyes and pictured leading him, hooded and cuffed, into the Special Criminal Court. It filled me with a prickle-edged joy.

Chapter 29

Liam and I made our way to the Daintree building. They made paper and woodcuts for old-fashioned printing, and huge swathes of handmade paper sheets hung on washing lines billowing in the courtyard breezes. It was a scant five minutes' walk from Harcourt Square, and had the finest cake and coffee shop of anywhere: delicate sponge cakes, tiny orange-blossom-and-caramel macaroons. It wasn't a place I'd associated with Liam. He was more of a chicken-fillet-roll-standing-at-the-counter-of-the-Ritzy type man.

We walked up to the café. They had a moist coffee cake with swirls of buttercream icing you'd give away your firstborn for. If I had a firstborn.

'What'll it be?' said Liam.

'Americano and slice of coffee cake, please, Liam. But, tell me, am I dying?'

'Why? Because I'm being nice to you? We're all dying, Bridge.'

'My philosopher! Blob of fresh whipped cream with the cake, please.'

He got to the counter in four strides. The woman serving gave him a shy smile and cut him a wedge of cake.

He arrived back to our table with a tray. 'There you go,' he said to me as he sat down. 'I'll have a bit too – she gave me a load.'

'No, sorry, Liam – I'll go up and get you a piece, but I don't share coffee cake. Can't do it, my dude.'

He grunted and ignored me, hacking into the sweet cake with a fork that looked like a toy trident in his hand.

'No wonder you come here so often – this is good,' he said.

'I'm not here that often.'

'You get takeaway all the time! Never seen a woman with a sweeter tooth.'

He spoke between mouthfuls, his enjoyment evident, and I took a bite. The sweet coffee flavour sat on my tongue and the sugar made straight for my cells.

'How do you stay so skinny when you eat so much cake, bread and marmalade?'

'I do not and I'm not skinny! I'm strong and healthy, plus I run most nights.'

'Is that safe?'

I shook my head. 'Not safe for my mental health if I don't. And they can't catch me – I'm going too fast.'

'I believe you – one of the lads at the training centre said your scores are off the charts. But be careful, Bridge. You wouldn't know with Flannery and his mob, if they saw you had a routine.'

'It's OK, Liam. I'm not complacent and go a different route every night, but I like the quiet and the dark.'

I was a loon saying that out loud.

'Doesn't surprise me you're nocturnal. Mind you, it's nice to have a bit of space. I miss the fields back home and going out to puck a ball. This city crams in on you. Pokes you when you're not looking.'

It was the jostling people determined to get their pound. 'The city's changed in the last few years,' I said. 'You can taste the greed, everything is *me*.'

Liam finished off the last of the slice, a few crumbs loitering on the side of his goatee. He flicked them away.

'Seeing as we're chatting,' I said, 'what's Joe's connection to Muldoon? Why did he take Joe into CAB so fast?'

'And why did you have to jump through hoops and get stuck advising the tributes?'

'I can wonder, can't I?'

'You're an inquisitive thing, Bridget Harney. Why don't you ask him yourself?'

'Because I don't have that kind of relationship with Joe – ours it too formal, mentor and protégée vibe. You and he gossip all the time.'

'Discussing minor county football is not gossiping, Bridge.'

I put a hand up, resigned to having my question unanswered. Liam was being a twat.

'They go back years. Joe's mam was Muldoon's cleaner. Joe's father died when he was twelve or so and his mam went out to char.'

My heart sank. 'I didn't know Joe's dad died when he was that young.'

'Joe doesn't talk about it much. Died of colon cancer. Happened before you and I were born.'

'Even so.'

I couldn't picture a young Muldoon – there was nothing of the boy left in his face – but Joe was another matter. He was there, with his big round laughing face.

We sat for a bit, each of us in our own space, a twinge

inside me for a boy growing up without his father.

'Is everything OK, Liam?'

'Oh yes. Are you under a lot of pressure at the minute? O'Connor's on your back about Flannery?'

'Isn't he always? We've linked him to the body in the Dublin Mountains, but struggling getting an ID for the body – just takes so long.' My voice was pot-holed with frustration.

'And the drug seizure? Any leads who got it out of the Port so fast?'

'Nothing yet.'

'So dead ends all round?'

'For the moment,' I said.

A pause.

'How's your mum?'

'Not so good,' I said and stood. 'Another coffee?'

I didn't want Liam to see how thin my skin was. Underneath I was standing on a crumbling white cliff edge.

Chapter 30

2003

Gavin got out of prison on a grey March morning at eleven, in keeping with the Governor of Mountjoy's procedures. He hadn't wanted to be collected, hadn't wanted anyone standing on the North Circular Road with a cheery smile and conversations about how well he did his time. He knew how well he'd performed in prison. Still, his grandmother was there on the side of the road, waiting.

Sheila Devereux was a barrel of a woman on spindly legs and always wore a baggy coat, no matter the weather. Seeing her there, as though she had popped out for a sliced pan, was an unceremonious end to Gavin's six years in prison. Over the last 2,190 days he had been told when he could eat, when recreation was allowed, when he could go to the gym, when he could sleep. He stood in the shadow of Mountjoy, misplaced. He smelled of prison – boiled vegetables and bleach – an aroma even diesel exhaust fumes from passing cars couldn't rid his nostrils of. One of the men he had walked out with ignored everyone else and ran down the road, a dog pulled by the scent of rotting meat. The other two looked at Gavin, waiting for some sign, which he didn't bother to give them.

Gavin's grandmother called to him.

'Hello, Gavin love!'

'Hi, Nana,' said Gavin.

There were no shows of emotion from either, but her eyes looked into Gavin's, trying to find her grandson in this new version of himself.

'You've put on another bit of weight since I saw you last month.'

'It's muscle, Nana.'

She cocked an eyebrow at him. 'I used to meet your grandfather here – well, not in this spot. The prison was smaller then. I can't believe how much building is going on, cranes everywhere. You won't recognise East Wall – the financial thing has eaten up half of it. Some would call it progress.'

She looked frail and her aging was strange to him, a deliberate cruelty of life moving forward while he'd lived the same immutable moment in prison.

'Did you see your father?' she asked.

'Yeah,' said Gavin.

'And?'

She stopped walking, her head to one side, reminding him of a turkey, gobbling for choice titbits.

'He's at war with the world,' he said. 'Been banged up for nineteen years and not getting out any time soon either. He's barrier-handled wherever he goes.'

'What's that?'

'Screws have riot shields, make a circle and put him in the centre – then they walk.'

'That's new,' she said.

Gavin saw her put it into a memory bank, to bring out when she sat on the steps of the nearby flats, drinking with her friends.

'He told me to stay away from you.'

'Did he now?' said Sheila.

They moved off and she gave a smoker's chesty laugh. 'Fool of a man half killed a guard. Hope the bitterness consumes him. I knew you'd see through him. I wrote to your mother. Told her you were getting out.'

She waited for his reaction, giving him a sideways glance.

'She's in Australia now and thought you might fancy a spell out there?'

'Would I get a visa, Nana, fresh out of the Joy?'

'Do you think she's there legally? Ways and means, Gavin. If you want to go say the word.'

Gavin moved his hand to his chin, amazed at the hope in his grandmother's voice. 'This would be the *wan* put me in a Mother and Baby Home and left me there for the first eight years of my life? You think I'd be making my way over to her, do you, Nana?'

Sheila batted the air. 'She was on the bad thing then, Gavin. You can't judge her. She's clean now. And didn't I come and get you off the nuns soon as I knew?'

'You did, Nana. Soon as she told you.'

They lapsed into silence, Sheila having to double-time to keep up. Gavin was a stranger to her with his prison-gym body and all the teenage gabble gone from him, burned out by a light hotter than her cigarette tip. She fumbled in her pocket and brought out a single, sticking it to the wet membrane of her bottom lip. A match flared.

'Want one?'

Gavin shook his head. 'Still smoking singles, Nana?'

'Cost a bloody fortune with all the tax now, so I'm back buying ones and twos. None to be had at the market. Guards raided the fellah I buy from.'

They kept walking, passed the Mater Misericordiae Hospital – inmates were brought there if the prison hospital hadn't the expertise to cater for them. Gavin touched his side where a white lumpy piece of tissue reminded him of emergency surgery after he was shanked in the yard.

Had his trial been scheduled one month earlier his imprisonment would have been different. Gavin had turned eighteen while on remand in St Patrick's Institute for Young Offenders. For his birthday the Department of Justice transferred him to the adult male Cloverhill Prison, and he had the misfortune of appearing in the Central Criminal Court alongside Larry Dunne. He was tried as a member of the Dunne crime organisation by Mr Justice Vincent Harney, a justice making a name for himself in the State's fight against organised crime. Had Gavin been seventeen at the time of his trial, he would have been tried as a minor, in the in-camera world of the Children's Courts – shorter sentences and back to Saint Patrick's Institution for Young Offenders, a softer landing. Instead he was sent to 'The Joy', where the Governor described the spiralling threat of gang violence as unquantifiable.

'You didn't snitch, Gavin,' said Sheila. 'It'll give you your place in the outside world. Men will know you can be trusted, and they'll approach you. Wait and see.'

She didn't say she was frightened of the changes in Gavin. She knew prison men, her family was littered with them, and much as they looked hard when they came out, sometimes it was for the better. Her uncle had come off the drink in Mountjoy thirty years ago and never taken a drop since, but Gavin was different. Something had been obliterated during his time locked away and in its place a thing with thorns had grown.

'It should've been Seán Flannery in there, not you,' said Sheila. 'You went down for six years because of those baggies. Not to mention those godless Guards, may they die roaring for putting you in with the Dunne gang as an accomplice.'

'That was the Judge's doing, Nana.'

'Bastard.'

She quietened. The pressure of her mind working filling the air around them. 'But the road is long where he's concerned. How is Larry Dunne faring inside?'

'You know.' Gavin shrugged. 'He's a Dunne, being waited on hand and foot.'

'The fucking Dunnes, God forgive me for swearing, but Larry's the runt of the litter. Pure fool they let roam around the city when he'd be better with a bullet in his head.'

'I'll know for next time, Nana.'

Sheila snorted in agreement, then a sharp fear poked her as she understood Gavin's meaning. The last thing she wanted was a war with a family as violent as the Dunnes.

'No, Gavin, leave the Dunnes alone. I spoke out of turn.'

'Where's Seán?'

'I wouldn't let him come with me. The drugs were his idea and he ran off like a yellow streak of piss when the Guards came. We should shop him to the Dunnes, they'd soon –'

'Stop, Nana – we're not snitches, and I've heard this at every visiting time for the last six years.'

'You only let me visit you once a month.'

'Them's the rules, Nana.'

'Do you think I came down in the last shower? I've been visiting that prison since before you were born. You're allowed two visits every four weeks. Who did you give the other visit to? It wasn't Flannery. I'd have heard if it was him.'

Gavin said nothing but ran his finger around the inside of his shirt collar. It was too formal and constricting. His biceps strained against the brushed cotton of the shirt and the suit jacket wouldn't button over his chest.

'Sorry, love, the suit I sent in is a bit small. Got it in Clerys. Wonder if they'd take it back.'

She was laughing. Gavin knew his grandmother shoplifted the clothes, getting a small pleasure at the thought of the screws handling stolen goods.

'You know Flannery owes you – he has a few quid now and I know people – your family – who can make him pay up,' said Sheila.

He was ever surprised at his grandmother's vitriol towards Seán. No one knew where Seán's mother came from, but it was assumed he was part of their community. An enclave of criminal Dublin for decades, family feuds, robberies and beatings on a regular basis, but they never turned against one another. However, his grandmother had set her face against Seán.

They walked with distance between them, wary of one another. Sheila was the first to reach across.

'It's good to have you home, son. Be nice to have some company in the house. I'm sick of Flannery hanging around outside, asking me how you are –'

'It's the last time I'm going to say it, Nana. It wasn't Seán's fault. There was no reason for the two of us to get pinched.' Gavin held up his hand to stop her speaking. 'And I owe him. I will always owe him.'

Sheila grunted then threw up her head before speaking, a nervous tic. 'So you've said, although you've never said why.'

'Is Seán at the house?'

'Yes, I let him in before I went.'

'Where's he been staying?'

'Some place on Castleforbes Road, down a little terrace, nice enough though. Where would he have got the money for that?'

Gavin shook his head, refusing to be drawn.

Sheila took it as invitation enough and nattered about her neighbours on East Wall Road, their comings and goings, who was picked up by the gardaí, who'd had a baby, who had more money than they should.

Gavin let it wash over him.

Seán waited in the small galley kitchen. The old linoleum had lifted at the edges but was carbolic-clean. He'd set out the foldaway table, dressed it with a tablecloth and Sheila Devereux's best china, sugar in a bowl not the bag, and fresh cream doughnuts from the corner shop. Gavin wouldn't want cake, but it was a gesture. He stood in the middle of the kitchen and counted aloud, the sound of his own voice keeping him from overthinking. He and Gavin had communicated once at the start of his sentence, a single letter where they agreed no further primary contact. Let the gardaí believe the association had ended. They communicated through an intermediary. Seán had organised a girl to pose as Gavin's girlfriend and she delivered messages. Seán hadn't heard Gavin's voice in six years.

Through the girl, they worked on their future plans post Gavin's release. Seán had made new contacts and would buy direct from Fuentes cartel via Amsterdam. Dublin street cocaine was twenty-percent pure at best. Seán was going to deal at forty-percent pure for wholesale and thirty-percent at street level. To keep his levels this pure he'd need an army of enforcers. To find those enforcers Seán had supplied Gavin with drugs when he was in prison. Many of the inmates had people throw packets over the wall while they were in the exercise yard but the screws found most of these. Seán had used a racing pigeon he favoured and she'd dropped small cannisters in to Gavin, never a huge amount of product, but enough. And Seán could supply any pills to order, steroids were the most popular. Gavin would give these out to any man he wanted to recruit.

Seán heard the key turn in the lock and an echoing twist inside his chest.

'What's up?' said Gavin.

'Yeah,' said Seán.

'C'mon.' Gavin stood in the doorway, beckoning Seán out into the street.

They left Sheila open-mouthed in the doorway.

'Cakes on the table for you, Granny Dev,' said Seán.

Gavin strode in the direction of the Port. 'Can't be inside or anywhere. Need to look at the sea – come down the Basin with me?'

They walked toward the Grand Canal Basin, built in the 1790s by the Lord Lieutenant of Dublin as an area to dock pleasure boats – that hadn't worked out so well and the Basin was known as Dublin's 'forgotten pond' for centuries. In recent times property developers had moved in.

'Building apartments and such down there now,' said Seán. He noted Gavin's long strides. Gone was his childhood friend, in his place a rangy man with a permanent darkness to his eyes. Seán had no sense of loss, rather preferring this hardened man, who no longer needed anyone's protection.

'Got what you needed.'

'Yeah?' said Seán.

'Army of blokes coming out over the next six months. At least fifteen. So you'd better have that fucking supplier lined up. And don't tell me I'm letting myself down by swearing or you'll be eating your teeth.'

Seán smiled. Prison had been Gavin's university.

Chapter 31

2019

There was a fusty, stale taste in my mouth. It was Wednesday and that meant crisp tacos in the canteen. I pictured the freshly made guacamole. Anything to keep from analysing the emotions surging off Paul. We walked to the coffee cart. He was plumb straight in a pinstripe suit complete with Windsor knot and Garda tie pin. I hadn't seen one of those since I graduated from Templemore. Over the last months I had come to the painful realisation I didn't know much about Paul. More often than not our social life was unscheduled – a coffee in work, drinking in Dicey Reilly's at the end of a long day, or my knocking on his door in the middle of the night. Whether it was his charm or the intimacy he could create, on each occasion I'd overshared without it being reciprocated.

We walked in silence. I had no words to crack the glass between us, every *bon mot* in my mouth tasted banal.

'You're quiet,' he said.

'Don't know what to say.'

'With me?' His eyebrows moved up and bracketed his face.

I walked with my head tilted towards the afternoon sky,

low winter sun illuminating a tuft of clouds.

'Listen –'

'Look –'

We spoke at the same time, a Safe Cross Code of confusion. I laughed and he gave a tight smile.

We'd reached the coffee cart and had something to occupy ourselves with, memories of another time in the hot June sun came back to me, of Paul doing all his tricks to make me smile. Not so today.

'Two Americanos,' he said.

I fished in my pocket for shrapnel and slung out enough coins to pay for us. My movements were jerky and the nail on my middle finger was still tatty from tearing it on the car door with Liam weeks ago. I curled it away, holding the coffee cup self-consciously. A premonition made me want to stall him, tell him there was no need for this conversation. Leave me that feathered thing in my soul.

The expression on Paul's face was formal, buttoned-up and tolerating no familiarity. He turned towards the station and we walked back in double time. He had worked out how long our conversation would take and the premeditated nature of his action chipped away at my confidence.

'I asked you to meet me to make sure everything's OK?' he said.

'Yes, if it isn't I'm not aware.'

I pulled out a shop-worn smile. For a moment wanting to tell him the truth, that my mother fading from sight was tiny rips on an already tattered page and the brutal combination of Fuentes and Flannery terrified me.

'You're distant,' he said.

His shoes had the crisp click of new soles and he had a sweet sea-salt smell of some expensive aftershave.

181

'Still, I suspect you're right. I wanted to make sure we were OK about the last time we slept together. I value your friendship and don't want to use you. I'm not sure we're a match, relationship-wise.'

He spoke to the air and faced forward. I put one foot in front of the other, but the ground beneath me was flimsy and unconvincing. My mind threw up legions of arguments to contradict him, but they backed up behind my teeth, choked off by his glittering hard smile.

'I understand that,' I said.

I had a lingering suspicion when a man told you he valued your friendship it was because he didn't fancy you. The girl part of me, the small people-pleaser from my youth, wanted Paul to find me attractive. I didn't like that girl and could be unkind to her.

'It's not going to help our careers, that's for sure,' I said.

He looked at me and I had no idea what was going on in his head.

'You're right to be so ambitious, Bridge. And we've violated a code about fraternisation in the handbook.'

'Oh well, we can't have that!'

We were at the front door of Harcourt Square and he gave me a smile-wave combination as he rushed for the stairs in five long strides. I was uncomfortable with the strength of my physical attraction to Paul, finding myself slipping into easy chemistry rather than the effort and time of meeting new people and finding a proper relationship. Still didn't stop the hurt at the relief in his face when he thought I wasn't looking.

Chapter 32

2005

Seán wore oxblood leather slip-ons and a smart suit straight from a high-fashion low-cost retailer that boxed above its weight. He didn't waste money on something he couldn't wear daily, but his look today was important. He had to fit in, an office worker, one of the drones on his way to the colony. He pulled the collar of his suit jacket up against the cold wind whipping down Anglesea Road and passed a hotel, its flags flapping out a Morse code of distress in the icy March breeze. He made his way towards Donnybrook, a car horn blaring at some hapless driver thrown by the oblong and obelisk masquerading as a roundabout. Seán skipped through the traffic and crossed the road. Knots of genuine bank clerks and office workers made their way to buses, with convivial banter as they recognised one another. Seán wasn't familiar with social friendships. Now well into his second decade, he compared himself to Gavin and his mob of friends. Apart from his years in prison – and, even then, he'd made plenty of friends – Gavin always had a bunch of lads to hang out with. Sure, Gavin's crowd had pared down over the years, until the hardest wood was left, but Seán had one friend only. Gavin. He'd cut himself off from others when he knew what he was – the black beat of his desires lay under his consciousness and the hunger rarely left him.

Seán doubled his steps to refocus his mind. He was making his way to St Matthias's parish hall, where he'd been a fixture at the early morning Narcotics Anonymous meeting for over three months. He'd met a girl too, though she was more of a woman.

The endless NA meetings he'd attended over the last year rose in his mind's eye. Sometimes he'd gone to seven or eight in a single week, more than one a night. A manic quality to his behaviour that let him fit right in. He was weary from it. As someone who never took drugs he had no sympathy for junkies, but he needed a recovering addict. Once they relapsed there was no telling what he couldn't get out of them. Seán needed a chemist, someone with specialised knowledge who could guarantee the purity of his cocaine. He'd heard cocaine cut with blood-thinners, like Warfarin, gave a quicker high, brought the social drug-takers to dealers in droves. If he wanted to be the supplier's supplier, he needed his own pharmacist. Seán wanted off street corners, to be nothing more than a shadowy figure.

The sky over Montrose dangled grey strings of rain and Seán jogged, keen to get his seat before he got wet.

The meeting opened with a non-denominational prayer. It was a Church of Ireland parochial hall and he had chosen this group after so many failed attempts. He bypassed the table with the NA literature. His could paper his house in St Martin's Gardens with all the leaflets he'd taken over the last year. He sat down on a row with some seats taken, making sure he was beside a vacant chair. If she wasn't here today, he'd come back tomorrow. These NA meetings weren't packed but had regular attendees. He steered clear of meetings in Ballyfermot, Finglas and Clondalkin, knowing all he'd find there were broken-down users one fix away from being back on the gear. He was looking for professionals, well-educated generation Y who were fighting their habit hard and hiding it.

At first he'd tried the meetings in Lower Abbey Street, Gardiner Street, out as far as Coolmine, expecting to find neo-yuppies away from their homes in Howth and Dalkey, but all he found were cowering hipsters dotted among some of society's most abandoned. It was depressing. He had searched Dublin before finding this good, puritan group. The moment he had walked into the hall he knew he'd find his prey here. The neat but not showy suits and dresses, the smell of baked scones from the vicar's wife, warm strawberry jam and Brown Betty pots of tea told him he was in the right place.

Now Avril Boyle sat beside him.

'Sorry I'm late, I missed the opening prayer,' she said.

At some point she would have been fresh-faced and new-pin neat. Not now. Addiction had desiccated her, taking vitality, leaving her short of confidence and bowed. Her nutbrown hair was clean but had lost its shine from years of injecting between her toes. Her father was Boyle Pharmacies, travelled to his five branches throughout the country and prided himself on knowing his customers by name. He saw himself as a fair man but was in fact an arrogant bastard. At least according to his daughter. She had told Seán of her older brothers, each installed in a Boyle mega-pharmacy and she'd been given the small shop in Ringsend. How she was lonely and had never wanted to work in the pharmacies. She hated retail. Seán hadn't blamed her. He was never surprised at the amount of chemists who took drugs. After all the fun in college, to be stuck in a pharmacy doling out pills day in day out and working newsagent's hours. They needed relief after that reality.

'Nice to see you here,' said Avril. She gave a short laugh somewhere between a cough and a giggle.

Seán turned to her, as if seeing her under a microscope, saw the broken vessels in her nose and the sweat beading on her hairline. He'd found with women the less he said the better it served him. Nature abhors a vacuum. His story for Avril was part truth, he'd grown up in a Mother and Baby home – and part invention, he worked in the Irish Financial Services Centre as an accountant and had developed a drug problem because of the pressure in work.

'Addictive drugs work on the mid-brain,' Avril had told him. 'That part controls the release of dopamine. Addiction isn't the drugs, that's the side effect or symptom. Most addiction is brought on by chronic stress. Like yours.'

Of course she had assumed he was middle class – not a tosser who wanted a high – that was for the working class. There were medical reasons for middle-class addiction.

The meeting moved on, dreary and talkative. Some of the addicts had a nasally tone he associated with his high-end customers, the eco-Hibernians who would take molly, bars and coke but wouldn't touch a cigarette or a bag of chips. Seán zoned in on Avril and complimented her dress, giving her small smiles throughout the group's testimonies. He tuned out the pain in their voices, he had plenty of his own.

At the end of the meeting he asked could he walk her to Sydney Parade DART station.

'Will we go and get our usual coffee?' he said. 'Leave the folks here to the tea and scones?'

Avril smiled and fell into step with him. The coffee concession was good and they would get their respective DARTS after a quick chat. She to Sandymount and on to the shop in Ringsend, he – lying – to Connolly and the IFSC.

Seán insisted on getting the coffee each time.

'Seán, you're spoiling me,' she said.

'Yes, but you're smiling. Anyway, it's nice to have a chat with a beautiful woman.'

Avril flushed an ugly red.

Seán was microdosing her every time they got coffee, a tenth of an actual hit – tasteless and working on the cellular level, it didn't give a high – more of a softening at the edges, but for an addict it was a path back to enslavement. Avril attributed the new calm feelings to her progress at NA and her friendship with Seán.

Chapter 33

2019

The motorway northbound was wedged with cars and we were moving at fifteen kilometres an hour. This was the type of traffic I expected in the rush hour on the Ring Road in Birmingham, not on the way to Dublin airport at ten in the morning. Two cars had pranged and blue lights pulsed, a Roads Policing unit moving the cars onto the hard shoulder. I left them to it.

My mind had turned on me during the previous night's sleep, images of Paul Doherty dismissing me, Seán Flannery dumping Shabba's hacked-up body at sea and laughing behind our backs. It had left me clinging to the toilet bowl in the early morning. I was edgy. The echo of the dream repeating unsettling my stomach. In the car I switched on the radio to occupy my mind and dialled Chris's number. He didn't pick up, but the fact it was ringing told me he'd landed. We'd arranged to meet at the back of the short-term car park in Terminal 1.

When I pulled in he waved and dashed over to the car, agile for a large man. He was cleanshaven and had a rucksack slung over one shoulder. Chris wasn't the bowler hat and briefcase type.

We were out of the airport and heading southbound on the motorway quick smart.

'Good to see you, Bridge, and I'm grateful you could collect me.'

'As if I'd leave you getting a taxi or the bus, Chris Watkiss.'

He gave a schoolboy grin, a most endearing feature.

'How are Swapna and the girls?'

At the mention of his family Chris split with pride and fumbled for a recent photo.

'The girls look great, Chris.'

'They're great lasses. Got a lot on your plate, little 'un?'

The rich inflexion in Chris's voice was unexpected balm.

'I'm a bit overwhelmed.' I surprised myself and the admission brought heat scorching to my face. 'Sorry, that's too dramatic –'

'It's fine. Hard yards at the moment in Birmingham with Maitland, for me an' all. Amina tells me Flannery's missing and you might as well be plugged into your Garda system. What's it called?'

'PULSE.'

'Says you're like a ruddy cyborg!'

I laughed. 'No, but I have alerts on any system I can get into and Interpol have issued a Red Notice for Flannery, but they haven't found anything. I'd say he's hiding.'

'Will you find him if those cartel boys have him?'

'I'm not convinced they do.'

'Don't mind me saying, Bridge, but you're wound pretty tight.'

The knotted face in the rear-view mirror was mine.

'I don't want Flannery to get away. I'm well over the threshold test for evidence. He's heading for prison.'

'Aye?'

'Body in the Dublin Mountains, Georgian national came over illegally on a trawler to Dublin. He doesn't appear to have any organised crime connections. A loner for hire.'

'How do you know he's illegal?'

'Interpol traced him to Holland – he used his Georgian passport – we're not dealing with a criminal mastermind here. Ireland isn't in Schengen –'

'Neither is the UK. Mind you, we're in bloody nowt lately. I'm leading the charge for an independent North of England.'

We both laughed and the strain reaching out from Chris slackened a notch.

'We believe the Georgian met some like-minded individuals in Holland who brought him to Dublin and he fell foul of Flannery's gang,' I said. 'We don't know exact details, but it's a working theory.'

'And Flannery killed this Georgian guy?'

'Yes, judging by the evidence – his blood and DNA were all over the body. Tyre marks from a van that was later abandoned in East Wall.'

'Sloppy. Not like our man Seán.'

'It's the pressure of the having the Fuentes cartel breathing down his neck.'

'What if the cartel's kidnapped him? Because of the seizure?'

'I'm not sure. If the cartel wanted retribution they'd have shot Flannery in his doorway. They have form.'

Chris blanched. 'They've murdered people in Dublin before? Fuentes?'

'Yes,' I said. 'Couple of years ago Fuentes sent over an

Estonian hitman for a particular individual. They don't leave corpses dangling from electric wires – as I said, they're more of a crook-dead-on-his-own-doorstep type of organisation. Flannery's well aware how Fuentes operate and he's hiding. Something went wrong in the Dublin Mountains.'

'So Flannery might try to flee the country? Would he go looking for his old mate Declan Swan?'

My mouth curled up at the thought of Swan. 'Nothing's impossible, but I wouldn't have thought Swan would be Flannery's first choice. Tell me about Burgess Data Centre.'

Although Chris wasn't a man for ill-concealed tension, he was tetchy and wore it around the edges of his mouth. He was here for a reason and it wasn't Flannery.

'I'll come to it straight, Bridge. You've been neglecting the BDC case. Amina's struggling.'

My mouth formed an O. Traffic slowed enough for me to open a window and let some air into the stuffy car.

'BDC's serious. We've found kilos of narcotics in those water coolers. Two hundred to be exact.'

'What! Why did no one tell me it was that big?'

'Well, I'd imagine Amina tried, but you're obsessed once you've got Flannery's scent in your nose. Plus, she's tearing her hair out trying to figure out BDC's business processes and financial transactions. This has cartel written all over it to me.'

Once the spectre of a cartel rears its head, bystanders rush to lay all ills at the cartel's door. Public prosecutors are particularly susceptible to this pinning of unsolved crimes on a likely cartel – it keeps their overall conviction rate solid.

'I haven't had much experience with cartels,' I said.

'Lass, you're the one in the Drugs and Organised Crime unit. I'm a plod in West Midlands and over my head.'

'No, you're not, Chris. You are a superb detective. We investigated a murder together. You're good police, but we think of cartels as bogey men. Despite popular opinion their reach is limited. And they never leave drugs lying around or piling up – they'll burn them if they have to. There was a drugs-haul twenty-four hours ago in Hamburg, of over four tonnes, close to one billion euros street value. It was on a Uruguayan ship. The crew were trying to burn it before the trawler was boarded – some of them were shot dead.'

'You're joking!' said Chris.

'I wish I was.'

'Were it on the media?'

'Not yet, I got it on an Interpol alert, but it's only a matter of hours before it's in the public domain. Hundreds of duffel bags stuffed with cocaine. Some customs official won't be able to resist a picture on social media. Intel puts Fuentes in the frame and a new route via Hamburg, but Fuentes don't do anything by halves. They'll have used this route for months, testing it. Of course, they'll dump it now, but we've no idea how much product they shipped through it before we caught them. I'm guessing tonnes.'

'Could Fuentes be the source of Burgess's kilos?' said Chris.

'Yes, they're one of the biggest suppliers to Europe at this point, but they don't deal in small loads and two hundred kg's is small to them.'

'I take your point. Burgess is down the food chain, but why's BDC full of narcotics? Someone was bound to find it at some stage.'

Chris pulled his seat belt out to give his stomach some room.

'I'd say Mike Burgess and Declan Swan were importing from Flannery. You remember Mike gave us a story about meeting Flannery in a yacht club? I'm not saying it wasn't true, but there's more to their relationship. When Burgess was sent to prison and Swan absconded, there was a vacuum. No one was left to dispose of or distribute the drugs.'

We'd arrived in Harcourt Square. The car doors let out arthritic creaks on opening.

'God Almighty, you need some new motors here.'

'It's rented. Avis have Garda squad cars now.'

Chris harrumphed, but cutbacks and inconvenience were nothing new to any police force.

We made for the station, a cadet-blue sky above and bracing cold below. Chris stood outside for a moment longer, slaking his need for fresh air – there wouldn't be much of it inside.

We made our way up to Amina's desk.

They shook hands and Chris waved away an offer of refreshment.

'No, thanks, Amina. I've been sat on a Ryanair flight drinking tea – any more and I'll be waterlogged. So we'll get straight down to business, if that suits?'

'Of course,' said Amina. She piled folders of printouts into her arms and moved towards the glass meeting room in the middle of our floor.

Three gardaí were already in situ.

I halted. 'Looks like there's a meeting in progress.'

'Don't worry,' said Amina. 'I booked the room online and I have the confirmation printed out.'

She walked into the meeting room and we followed.

With a smile and quick hands she piled up the men's documentation, moving them out of the room with gentle conversation and the ease of a high jumper arcing her body over the bar. A thing not everyone could do.

We took our seats, warm from the previous occupants, and Amina fired up her laptop.

'Right,' said Chris. 'I haven't done much of the finance stuff as it's not my area, but I'm good on the ground. After what Andy in Burgess Data Centre told me, I did a bit of digging around, spoke to employees in the warehouse and on the tech desk. Not much from anyone other than a wary silence, but I got a lad on field support and he was a mite more chatty. BDC have a small field-service business.'

'About £370,000 in revenue annually,' said Amina.

'Which is a tidy sum, but they've around eight field technicians,' said Chris.

'Seems a lot of staff to support – unless it's a lossmaking unit?' I said.

'Aye. My contact says he and a couple of other lads do all the onsite work, drive to the client location and fix cabling, motherboards, whatever it is they do. He was a bit cagey at first, He's got a nice business in refurbished laptops. Sells 'em privately and works on 'em in BDC time. When I told him I'd no interest in his nixers, he warmed up. He's aggrieved that two of the other technicians don't do much work. They've got the uniform, tools and use their own vans, but they never take customer calls or do site visits. They used to trundle off on a daily basis, but my lad never knew where they was going. Said the place was like Paddington Station until Burgess went to prison, now it's a morgue.'

'So what's going on?' I said.

'Amina tracked these two employees,' said Chris. 'They're contractors and ex-employees of Burgess Gas Networks – ring any bells?'

'The business Mike and Anne Burgess sold years back that made them all their money?' I said.

'Yes! It was a gas-appliance fitters and service company and much as it made good money, Amina here found out Burgess only got three million for it when it were sold to Centrica. Don't get me wrong, I'm not going to see that kind of cash in my lifetime but . . .'

'But the Burgesses lived well beyond that,' I said. 'The house in Dalkey must have cost over two million, never mind the yacht and their main home in Newton-on-Severn. Where did they get the money?'

'I tracked down the ex-gas networks technicians. First lad wouldn't say owt other than he were on long-term sick leave. But second man is getting on a bit, told him I'd see him in prison for obstruction if he didn't tell me what was going on.'

Amina stifled a cry, but it was a good strategy and I'd have used it.

'What did he say?' I said.

'Mike Burgess was supplying street dealers for years. Rumour had it he bought off an Irish bloke. He used the field-service team in the gas-networks business to drop off the drugs. Burgess had about thirty gas-installers going at one point – about eight delivered drugs under the guise of servicing boilers. When Mike Burgess sold the gas business and set up Burgess Data Centre, he kept this man and the man out on sick leave as contractors. But the business was different – less drops and bigger consignments. Five-kilo blocks to a designated parcel motel. He said it were never violent and paid well. When Burgess went to prison, he and the other driver left. Neither wanted to work with Declan Swan – he couldn't be trusted.'

'So Swan was in on this? Will your driver testify to that effect?' I said.

'No chance, Bridge. First off I coerced him, so what's his testimony worth?'

'And Anne Burgess is still maintaining she killed Emer?'

'Aye, no budging her. I don't understand it.'

The idea of the Emer Davidson's murder being opened up again and at a minimum facing a major crimes review wasn't a happy prospect. There was no way I'd have time to pursue Seán Flannery if a case I'd investigated was re-opened.

'Amina, need you to crack the financial records open,' I said. 'If Burgess was buying off Flannery there'll be money being laundered somewhere. If we can find Burgess's cash, we'll be able to find a link to Flannery's money. When we can freeze Flannery's money it will flush him out. He's dropped out of sight and it must be costing him a fortune.'

'Aye,' said Chris with a side serving of doubt.

'I'm starving and wrecked,' said Amina. She yawned and showed us the fillings in her molars.

I'd lost my audience.

'Me an' all,' said Chris.

I waved away the offer of a takeaway, wanting to stay and work through Interpol alerts and the financial summaries Amina had prepared for me.

My energy was flagging towards the close of the day, but I insisted on taking Chris to the airport. He was quiet on the car journey. I used the Port Tunnel, muggy and confined but faster this time of the evening. We were sitting in a companionable silence which made Chris's explosion all the more unexpected.

'You can't keep running Amina this hard!'

'*What?* I'm not. At least I don't think . . .' Confusion fought with disbelief.

'You are!' Chris gave a cut-off breath of irritation. 'This is you all over, Bridge. Pushing at everything until it breaks. You push yourself and it works, but Amina's floundering. You need to get her warrants and accesses she can't get – so much of what she's doing is under the radar and she's terrified she'll get found out.'

'So why hasn't she said it to me?'

I wasn't sure what upset me more, Chris's tone of voice or Amina not confiding in me.

'She doesn't want to let you down.'

'Chris, that's daft!'

'No, it's not! You're a hard taskmaster and when you've got the bit between your teeth you can be blind to everything around you.'

I stayed silent for the rest of the journey, processing what Chris had said.

As he headed for Departures I reached over to give him a hug, but he stepped away. A stinging sensation in the space between us. The idea of falling out with Chris was unbearable.

He saw my upset and his shoulders sagged.

'You've nothing to lose, Bridge. The rest of us have.'

Chapter 34

I had been dreaming of noise. It was a dream I'd taken from childhood. A pitch-black square of a weightlessness full of eerie warbling, so loud it thrummed inside my head as though my skull were a bell, hit with a clapper. I sat up and waited for my room to come into focus. It was the small hours of the night when everything and everyone found natural rest. Unlike me. November was a dark month but, even so, light leaked from the lamp in our garden, giving my curtains a hem of amber. I struggled out of bed, my movements slow, my body swollen.

And my period late.

In my bathroom cupboard was a first response pregnancy test. I had bought it in a chemist's on Baggot Street, deciding not to use one near Harcourt Square. I had wanted a baby for longer than I could remember, but I'd never seen myself as a single parent. I wasn't concerned about the chattering classes or unkind remarks, but the enormity of doing it on my own. My mother was ill and couldn't advise me, my father – although a good man – was distant and I had struggled with his exigent parenting. Quicksilver beads of sweat ran down my back. My bathroom had a light-switch cord hanging down from the ceiling and forever put me in mind of a disabled toilet. I felt less than able-bodied as I dithered, wanting this cup to pass. Finally, I grabbed the test. If I was pregnant I was pregnant, and there was no point in waiting until I had my morning pee.

The underfloor heating tickled the balls of my feet as I sat, propped forward on the toilet trying to keep the litmus end of the stick in a stream of urine, and soaked my fingers. I replaced the cap and sat on the loo, legs akimbo and knickers slung around one ankle. Hope and fear twisted themselves into flesh-coloured knots inside me. I didn't see myself as mother material, I wasn't good enough. My mind flicked up a showreel of failings faster than any play button: Kay dead, her children left motherless, Lorraine Quigley forever frozen, full circle to Emer Davidson's dismembered arm.

I looked down at the two blue lines bisecting the small white screen. Pregnant. White hot panic.

I pulled up my pants and went to my mother's bathroom cabinet, pulling open the mirrored door. She had pill bottles of every description – pain killers, sleeping tablets and anti-psychotic drugs.

I stood there looking for a long time.

The dog let out a single bark. I was halfway down the stairs when he settled. I dialled Liam, despite the late hour. He answered on the fourth ring.

'Bridge! What the . . . are you OK?'

'Yes.' My quietness was born of despair rather than composure.

'Then why are you calling me at – four o'clock in the morning?'

A rustling of sheets floated down the phone, a sleepy voice asking Liam who was calling. A giggling *shush*, and the gentle sounds of intimacy.

'Sorry, Liam, mis-dial.'

I needn't have bothered with an explanation. He'd already gone.

Sleep wasn't coming back. A night light in the hall guided me into my mother's study. I had boxed all her letters by year and now I pulled out the pile from Sister Finbarr in 1984, the year I was born. My mother's hands had touched these letters when she was happy and strong. It helped the yammering in my head.

I chose a letter which Finbarr had written shortly after my birth.

Dear Elizabeth,

Go to confession, my little cousin. It's not to enumerate your sins. God knows us, faults and all, but the sacrament itself will give you healing. Give any pain or guilt you feel to God. Let Him carry it. He wants to carry it for you, He wants you to live a full and happy life. Glory in your new baby girl. I pinned her photograph to my notice board. She is beautiful – and those little fists, all wrinkles of fat and love. You deserve to be happy and love Vincent so much and he's a good man. Can you not trust him with the truth? You were so young, and I suspect didn't know what was happening when you conceived. The Kelly boy left for America before he knew you were pregnant, but it wouldn't have made any difference. He wasn't the type to come back.

You wrote that Richie Corrigan traced the baby

you gave up for adoption. I didn't realise you were still in touch and now understand the source of your worry. You need help with a man like Corrigan. He has darkness in him. Please tell Vincent. With his connections I'm sure he will be able to help.

I blame myself for leaving you, but when the Reverend Mother asked me to go to Nova Scotia I jumped at the chance. God forgive me, I wanted adventure. However, I left you, my beloved cousin. With no sisters for either of us, we were as tight as a cross-stitch quilt. I hope you feel we still are. I do. I will do anything I can to help you.

Your loving cousin
Aileen

She hadn't written 'Finbarr' which was her usual sign-off. The letter hurled me into a cold sea of shock. A child? A sibling? I sat at my mother's desk, on her chair, looking down at the dove-grey carpet banded with a brown stain. It spoke of a cup, fallen from a hand, years ago.

Chapter 35

Snatches of conversation floated out from the DOCB squad room. I was on the corridor looking for scraps of information and hoping an ex-colleague would give me access to their touts, if any of them had spotted Seán Flannery. My own sources of information were dry. I was relying on the bug in Gavin Devereux's car, which was worse than useless since I'd heard about Flannery being missing. I'd listened to hours of mundane rubbish and Devereux family squabbles.

The squad room disgorged, and I was surprised to see Paul Doherty among those exiting. He was shielding the commissioner and other superintendents chattered in his wake, as did notetakers with clipboards.

I slipped into the squad room unnoticed.

Detectives were stretching, knuckles and knees clicked.

'That Doherty's a right lick-arse,' said a voice I didn't recognise.

Laughter.

'Bridge?' said Joe Clarke.

A few startled looks and flaming faces.

Joe gestured to one of the incident rooms lining the back wall and we went in.

'Sit down,' he said. His liver-spotted hand touched his hairline to smooth back a few grey strands.

'Everything OK, Joe?'

'Yes and no. The Hamburg seizure's a nightmare, four tonnes of narcotics – there's coke bleeding into the country for the Christmas rush. Do people have no sense or realisation where this crap comes from? Social drug-takers my eye. They're the most lucrative market for these godless gangsters. Young fellah kneecapped this morning in Clondalkin – they threatened to kill his mother if she didn't pay off the debt. And this isn't new.'

Joe was mad, but it was windy swagger – underneath we were both diminished in the face of such a vast haul, the thought of it on our streets.

We sat in silence for a time.

'You wanted to see me?' I said.

'Yes. Bridge, this fellah Watkiss is causing all sorts of problems.'

'Chris? What's happened?'

'He's blaming you, saying your obsession with Flannery being involved in Emer Davidson's murder made him miss the narcotics in Burgess Data Centre.'

I was so floored words failed me.

'You like him and he's a pal, but he needs to stop giving his DI Maitland ammunition to give O'Connor,' said Joe.

My eyes darted back and forth, searching for an explanation of Chris' behaviour.

'Doesn't sound like Chris,' I said. 'He's a good copper. But he was a bit annoyed about the BDC case last time he was here. Said I wasn't giving it enough time.'

'But that's *his* case! Why are we working on it?'

'Looks like Flannery was supplying Burgess with drugs.

Amina's doing all the financial work on it. The data centre's financial records are complex for no good reason –'

'This isn't our jurisdiction!' said Joe.

'Well, if Flannery's involved it could be, and if we can find Mike Burgess's money I believe it will lead us to Flannery's money.'

'That's too tenuous a link for us to allocate resources,' said Joe. 'I don't like this. Chris Watkiss should be doing this from his end with his financial-audit resources – not using ours then complaining to his DI!'

Joe had a point and it stung.

'You sure it's not O'Connor using Maitland as a Trojan Horse to get at us?' I said.

'No such luck. I've had Maitland on the phone and he's a right overbearing git. Go and ask Amina how much time she's spent on this and if it's more than twenty hours tell her to stop. Next time O'Connor comes at me with this Maitland stuff, I'll land Chris Watkiss in it up to his neck.'

'No, Joe, please don't do that!'

'You'd rather Watkiss buries you with O'Connor? Because that's what's happening.'

'I know,' I said – but I didn't. The unpleasant nature of what was happening gave me prickly heat. 'Give me some time to look into this, will you?'

'Hours, not days, Bridge.'

I left at a run to find Amina, worry tearing up my gullet at the thought of Chris against me.

Amina sat with her legs crossed at a circular desk in the middle of the open-plan office. She was surrounded by printouts and was tracking columns of numbers, up and down with her biro nib.

'Amina?' I said.

'Yes?' A small, distracted smile.

'Can we get a coffee?'

She looked up. 'Sure, why not?'

We walked out of Harcourt Square.

'You know I don't drink coffee, Bridge, don't you? No wonder you're jittery with all the caffeine you consume.'

I touched my palms together and steepled my fingers in mock dismay. 'I'm an addict.'

We walked at a brisk clip for the pleasure of it, down Harcourt Street and on to Stephen's Green. Through the gates and into the park itself, bare branches latticed against the sky.

'How did you get on with Chris last time he was over here?' I said.

'Fine, why do you ask?'

'Do you like him?'

'Yes.'

It sounded qualified so I waited, let the quiet set. Talk about underestimating Amina – she matched my silence grain for grain until there was a hill of sand between us.

I caved first. 'Anything else about Chris?'

'I don't know him as well as you do. We don't have a history and he's polite to me.' Her hands flapped. 'Please don't think I dislike him, but he's a great delegator. He hasn't done any work on Burgess Data Centre other than field work. He doesn't understand the financial side at all, doesn't grasp how vast it is. I'm searching transaction by transaction.'

'I get it, but not many gardaí would have your level of knowledge or expertise.'

'I have no expertise, just Leaving Cert accounting. I've

had to learn on the job. Chris doesn't get it at all.'

'He's an old dog – hard for him to get into the digital era. But you've done all this with school-level accounting?'

'Yeah. Could you look less shocked, please? You're embarrassing yourself.'

'Sorry.'

She gave a cheeky grin. 'But your man Chris is great for saying 'get back to me today'. I'd say Chris overuses admin resources in Holloway too.'

'How do you know?'

'Said so, but not in so many words. He said Maitland is on his case because he wants Chris to retrain. I'd say his back is to the wall, Bridge. He told me BDC is a big case in West Midlands. To us it's a cog in the larger story, but it sounds like this could make DI Maitland into DCI Maitland. Did you know Chris is over thirty years in the police force?'

'No! Did he tell you that?'

'Yes, and he thinks he's too senior to be "digging around int'" records.'

She did a good West Midlands brogue.

'Don't judge Chris,' I said. 'He's a good egg, but his strength is in common sense. Not something to be underrated. Maitland is a pal of O'Connor's from way back and a piece of work.'

'It's nice the way you stick up for Chris,' said Amina.

She was trotting beside me on the outer ring of the park, as I strode past Ardilaun Lodge and towards the Grafton Street entrance. The city was busy mid-morning, the sounds being caught by the evergreen bushes in the park and whittled into murmurs. It struck me, as we walked through the park, how difficult it was for Amina. Since she had stopped wearing her niqab weeks ago in favour of a regulation hijab, she must have felt unprotected and ordinary in everyday clothes.

'Chris mentioned something to me last time he was over, about you feeling overburdened?' I said. 'Are you struggling to get access to systems? Can I help with warrants?'

Amina stopped and turned to me, clearly surprised. 'No, not really. All I said to him was I would need access to a couple of systems, one UK bank in particular which I wanted him to get for me, not you. That's what I mean by delegation.'

'Are the HM Revenue and Customs investigating Burgess Data Centre? Under the Proceeds of Crime bill?'

'Yes, but it's different to here,' she said. 'We have access to the Revenue Commissioners through CAB. Chris has no such links with the Inland Revenue. And their forensic financial units are underwater – Brexit has been such an unholy mess they're bogged down with black-market issues in the North and a million other things.'

'Talk about unintended consequences of divorce.'

'I'm just going to say this and don't get mad,' she said, 'but Chris isn't as sound with me as he is with you. Also, I might need some retrospective authorisations for accounts I've accessed.'

'You slipped that in quietly.'

'Well, you were about to go off on a monologue again about what a decent bloke Chris is and I've had enough of that.'

I smiled. 'Sure, what do you need?'

'I've been getting access to various banks accounts under existing court orders –'

'Christ, Amina! Why didn't you tell me? That's illegal.

Get me the names of the financial institutions you need to investigate and I'll get the relevant court orders.'

'OK, Bridge. It wasn't such a big deal in Revenue.' Amina was bright red with embarrassment.

'Sorry, Amina. I forgot how Revenue works. Were you investigating the offshore scandals?'

'Yes.'

'You'd have an open court order on that, given the volume of transactions. How long has the Ansbacher investigation been going on?'

'Twenty years,' said Amina.

'*How long?*'

'It's not a live investigation anymore, but we, I mean the Revenue, can still access accounts and prosecute people under its remit.'

Without realising, we'd exited the park onto Grafton Street.

'Will my accessing accounts without court orders get you into trouble?' she asked.

'No, shouldn't be a problem,' I said, with more bluff than accuracy.

We needed a little treat. 'Want a sticky almond bun and chai latte in Bewleys?'

She beamed sunshine at me.

'Hold off on looking at any accounts until I have the necessary paperwork, will you?' I said. 'It won't take me long.'

Which wasn't entirely true. I'd have to bring back a bun for Joe and Muldoon if I was to get out of this. The current Ombudsman didn't want her gardaí snooping where they'd no right to be.

Chapter 36

My phone danced with an international number I didn't recognise, hissing on my desk for attention despite its silent setting.

'I thought when you muted these things it meant you didn't have to hear them?' I said.

Amina sat across from me. 'Bridge, you don't own that device. It belongs to Google. Sergey and Larry are listening to every word.'

'Christ, that would be funny, if I couldn't hear Siri and Alexa laughing in the background.'

I picked up the call and made my way out onto the second-floor corridor.

'Hello?' I said.

'Hello?' said a rural accent. 'Is this Detective Garda Bridget Harney?'

'Speaking, who's this?'

'Sergeant Brendan O'Driscoll based in the embassy in Madrid. I was Kay's friend when I worked in the Interpol offices in Ireland. We met on a course couple of years back.'

A match struck behind my eyelids, a nebulous memory flared of a jammy posting.

'Yes, I remember, we were looking for a bit of help identifying a victim. Kay mentioned you'd been transferred to the embassy.'

'She was a fine woman.'

There was no arguing with that.

'She was. What can I do for you, Sergeant O'Driscoll?'

'Kay and I discussed Seán Flannery. She said you were hunting him.'

It sounded obsessed and cold put out on a shingle, but accurate.

'Yes.'

'I've sent an update to DCS Muldoon. A flag went off. Flannery was spotted in Barcelona.'

Colourless sentinels of hair rose in one sharp movement, all over my body.

'When? Do you have an exact location? Who's he with?'

'No more,' said O'Driscoll.

I pictured a large countryman with his hand raised in a five-finger splay.

'This was a courtesy for a dead friend. If your DCS wants you on this, you'll get the necessary update. Good day.'

The stairs blurred in front of me as I ran, belting into co-workers and flattening them against the wall. The sixth-floor lobby had the kind of airless quiet I couldn't ignore. It halted my gallop. Barging in on Muldoon wasn't the smart move. The lift *pinged* as I made for the stairwell and better choices.

Choppy male voices heralded the arrival of senior management.

'*Harney!*' It was a bark at my too-slow retreating form. '*To me.*'

DCS Muldoon spoke as though summoning a wilful dog. Joe gave me a raised eyebrow and made space in the copse of men following DCS Muldoon. I slunk in and caught Joe's eye. He mouthed 'Flannery' at me. DCS Muldoon charged ahead and I whiffled in his wake, the aftershave and porcine smell of midday men choking me. I held my breath and waited for Muldoon's entourage to disperse. When they'd moved off, Joe and I followed DCS Muldoon to his office.

Muldoon bristled with energy, his short spiky hair capable of conducting electricity. He stood behind his desk and indicated his visitors' chairs. I sat down, but Joe put his hands on the back of a navy padded chair and used it to support his weight.

'We've had a sighting of Flannery,' said DCS Muldoon. 'One of the lads in the embassy rang me. It'll come through headquarters in the Park soon enough. Flannery's in Barcelona. He was spotted on CCTV in Plaça de Catalunya – feed came in via Mossos Esquadra to the Irish embassy – they bypassed Interpol.'

'Unusual?' I said.

'A little,' said DCS Muldoon, 'but I wouldn't read anything into it. We don't know how the Spanish run their shop and Interpol can take its own sweet time to disseminate information.'

'But it's a confirmed sighting?' I said.

I didn't need to fake excitement to cover my prior knowledge and stood up to contain the plans flashing around my mind with luminous intensity. Joe's eyes were full of misgiving. He looked at DCS Muldoon and a cold finger quenched the wick of my plans.

'Bridge, it's not a certainty you'll go to Barcelona. It may be the Spanish won't want any Irish involvement in the apprehension of Flannery or they might have a sting operation ready to go,' said DCS Muldoon.

'What do we know about it?' I said.

'*We?*' said DCS Muldoon. His intonation wasn't to be missed nor the intent in the hard flint of his eyes. 'Have few details, but those we have are not for sharing. As I said, if you are assigned to this case you will be briefed, but Joe and I have some work to do before any decision is made.'

Joe nodded at me as DCS Muldoon swung away in his chair, as though I needed a further dismissal.

I took my anger out on the steps as I thumped my way down the stairs, texting Liam O'Shea to join me at the Ritzy.

He was already in the doorway of the café by the time I got there and raised a meaty arm, signalling to join him at the top of the queue. Even the smell of toast and sizzling bacon couldn't deflect me.

'You've a face on you like a smacked arse,' said Liam.

'Do you think that's in the spirit of collegiality?'

I was a comic-book harpy, all claws and high-pitched voice. What I wanted to say got caught on my intentions and Liam's laughing face.

He grabbed his toastie and two frothy coffees and we barrelled outside into the soft rain stippling the city.

'They've spotted Flannery in Barcelona,' I said.

'Jesus! When are you off, Bridge?'

'I don't know. I may not be going. Muldoon isn't sure we'll be wanted by the Spanish and Joe is being all . . .' I searched for the word, 'squirrelly.'

'Technical term so.' Liam smiled.

'Please, Liam, I need a bit of support. If Flannery is in

Barcelona it may be a pitstop on his way to Central America. If he gets there we've lost him! There isn't a hope of us finding him outside Europe. This could be my last chance.'

Liam chewed a mouthful of crunchy bacon, food snagging on his even teeth, but it wasn't the time to talk about table manners.

'What do you want from me? To speak to Joe?'

'Yes, if he'll listen to you. Muldoon is discussing it with him and they asked me to leave.'

'Flannery's your pet project,' Liam waved me quiet, 'and you got lucky with Chris Watkiss smoothing the waters for you in the UK, but don't for a second think it's going to happen again. Not in Spain. Costa del Sol is packed with nasty articles that should be extradited, but the Spanish won't budge them.'

An outline of where his frustration lay started to appear.

'Fair enough. Tell me more about Spain?'

He shrugged. A tight movement, more the tensing of shoulders than relaxing throwaway body language.

'Gardaí in Madrid are toothless – they and the Irish embassy staff bring home the bodies or translate. The Spanish won't let us carry guns. We went over two years ago, down to Benalmádena to pick up one of the Dunnes. Guardia Civil wouldn't let us near the place. And their system's shambolic, with infighting between the Ministry of Defence and the Ministry of the Interior. You might get agreement from one and the other will stop you when you're on site. You don't know if their police are coming for you or the criminals.'

His dissatisfaction spun out between us.

'Didn't work out with the Dunnes?' I asked.

Liam shook his head. 'Oul' man Dunne is still out there. Giving us the finger. It's dangerous too, Bridge. Remember that. Place is rotten with officials on the take. It's the gateway to Europe. All the cartels have a presence there. I wouldn't want you or anyone going there on their own.' He looked right into my eyes. 'Don't let O'Connor use your mutual animosity to send you to Barcelona alone. You'll come back in a bag. Do yourself a favour and let Flannery go.'

I leaned up on my tiptoes and was nose to chin with him.

'Can't do that, Liam.'

'So you're going to have Muldoon on your case as well as O'Connor? Not a smart move, Bridge.'

Chapter 37

2007

'It's time for you to meet the chemist,' said Seán.

'Jaysus, not before time,' said Gavin. 'I thought you were keeping her all to yourself.'

'I was, but she needs to know the consequences of non-cooperation. She's finding it "stressful", so it's time she met you. I don't like hitting women, they can't take a beating. Don't touch her head or her hands, mind. She works with the public.'

'Fair enough,' said Gavin.

They walked down Tolka Road past the terraced houses and miniature gardens concreted over to accommodate vehicles. East Wall was Seán's place and a sense of unease dogged him when he was too far away from it, a monster who could find no rest unless on his native soil.

'Where d'you find her? Is she a real chemist, like college and that?' said Gavin.

'Don't be a knob, Gavin.'

'I'm not! The only birds I've seen working in chemists' are the dollies selling perfume.'

'She's a qualified pharmacist and will do what we need. She gets us prescription stuff too – the benzos are going a bomb on the Southside at the minute. There's kit I need to buy for the Farm as well – she can order that for me.'

'Sounds good.' Gavin gave a small grin and pulled at a piece of summer lavender poking its head through a garden fence. He rubbed the seeds in his palms and they let out a sweet, woody oil.

'This is Whack O'Neill's house, lad who grows all the weed out in Rush? Green-fingered fucker all the same.'

'Don't swear, Gavin, you let yourself down.'

'And you let me down – I know the drill, Seán. Was Sister Assumpta so good to you that'd you'd carry her hate of swearing through your whole life?'

Seán shrugged. What he had taken from Sister Assumpta was the idea he was doused in a blackness nothing could wash away and anything he could do, even small things such as never swearing, would be stored in God's bank for the final day of reckoning. A reckoning he didn't believe in, but a younger version of himself struggled to shake off these old superstitions when the darkness inside him massed to a point and pulsed. He had known from the start where the problem lay – in his blood. Not the kind he was born with but the blood he was born into. The nuns and the Vicars of Christ had created this shadow in him.

'No, I don't think she was good to us,' said Seán. 'Looking back, she was a spiteful woman, but hid it well. We weren't old enough to have the words for what she was. If she said it was night in the middle of the day we'd have gone to bed.'

'We had no choice, Seán. They ruled us, looked down on us like we were scum. You know I feel sh–crap about leaving you there. You know that, right, man?'

Seán looked at Gavin and saw truth in his words,

recalling the day Gavin was taken by his grandmother to live in East Wall. Gavin's mother had been useless and left for London after Gavin was born. When she had eventually told her mother she had a grandson and where he was, the old woman had taken off running. Sheila Devereaux had stood in the Home's grand front hall roaring for Sister Assumpta and slapped her across the face when she had declined to let Gavin leave. A picture of Gavin pulling at his grandmother's hand, refusing to face forward or take his eyes off Seán standing at an upstairs window, clicked through his mind like the colour photographs in an ancient red View-Master.

'I know, Gavin.'

They walked in silence, Gavin content to let Seán lead as they walked over the East Link bridge, towards Ringsend and Sandymount.

'What's this chemist's name?' said Gavin, taking out a tin of tobacco.

'Shouldn't smoke, Gavin. Bet you're smoking more than you realise.'

He bobbed his head. 'At least I'm rolling them, so not as convenient as a pack and I never smoke more than ten in a day. Look.' He showed Seán the inside of his tin lid with a list of times written in stiff card. The smell of green wood rose out of the tin, until a sea breeze tore it away.

'That's something,' said Seán.

'Is this chemist expecting us?'

The impatience in Gavin's voice was growing, getting an edge. Seán calmed him with details.

'Her name's not important. She has a pharmacy in Sandymount off the green. We're going there now. I have everything in place. The Farm's rented from an old couple

217

in Kilkenny. They'll stay in the house and have hired out the land to us. Wife is half dead but the oul' fellah's all there.'

'You sure he's OK?'

'Vouched for by the lads in Monaghan. He's a supporter from way back. He spends most of his time looking after his wife, no family apart from a niece in America.'

'You know a lot about him.'

'The boys from Monaghan are thorough,' said Seán.

Gavin supressed a snort and licked his cigarette paper, giving it an expert twirl and putting an unfiltered end into his mouth. The fizz of a struck match and clouds of white smoke left his lungs.

'So what's next?'

'After the chemist?'

'Yeah, Seán, what happens after the chemist? When do we meet the next shipment? You said it would be our biggest yet. Take us off the street corners. You've been promising that for a while.'

'Trawler in Donegal. We've rented it, the lads from Monaghan recommended the fishermen. We go out deep-sea fishing and meet a cargo ship on the way to Rotterdam. It's taking a detour about two hundred nautical miles off the west coast.'

'*What!*' Gavin coughed puffs of smoke, a string of saliva attached to the hand wiping his mouth. 'Two hundred miles out to sea? We'll be killed.'

Seán allowed himself a small shrug. He'd had the same reaction when the fishermen had told him where their trawler would meet the cartel's cargo ship.

'It's nautical miles and the trawler's a deep-sea vessel. Two hundred miles is nothing to them, even in rough weather.'

'Rough weather? In June?'

Seán looked away. He had no desire to concern Gavin further. Weather on land had no bearing on climate so far out to sea, but Gavin sensed something in the quality of Seán's silence.

'Why do we have to go so far out?'

'We can't look suspicious to the coast guard or the navy,' said Seán.

'Won't they see us on a radar or something? They're not as useless as they used to be.'

'Not true, Gavin. They were never useless – ask the fools who dumped bales of cocaine into Dunlough Bay if the coast guards don't know what they're doing. We have to be smart, so we're meeting the cargo ship on the Sunday night of the Round Ireland Yacht race.'

'To unload pallets of drugs, in the middle of the night at sea while a yacht race is on? How is that smart?'

Seán laughed at Gavin's open-mouthed disbelief.

'We'll be out miles further than the yachts can go and even if the coast guard want to have a go, the race will keep them busy. Our coast guard and navy can only handle so much. The *LÉ Eithne* and *Orla* are in port for up to twelve months. The *LÉ Niamh* is the boat we have to worry about according to the fishermen – she has a savage crew and is built for the North Atlantic.'

'So we have Master and Commander Mick coming after us in his boat?'

Seán allowed himself a smile. 'No, they'll be focused on the yacht race in case any of the boats get into trouble. And don't worry about the radar – it will look like two parallel shipping lines. The vessels will pass by one another, not too fast not too slow. The cargo is waterproofed and dropped

into the ocean, the trawler uses its nets to pull the catch in.
The fishermen have done it dozens of times.'

'And we'll be on this trawler?'

'We have to be. Look, Gavin, what are you afraid of?
It's a floating warehouse. We're safe, but we need to make
sure the crew don't mess with anything. These fishermen
aren't playing by any rules. The reason we're being looked
after is because the lads from Monaghan have backed us.'

'Speaking of the lads from Monaghan, how much will
we have to pay them?'

'Half the value of the haul.'

'*Fuck!*'

'Upfront.'

'How are we doing *that*?'

'Guy,' said Seán.

Gavin was quiet, his mind ticking over in the bright
June sun.

They'd walked over the Tom Clarke Bridge and passed
a football stadium, the scrubby sea grass taking hold as
they moved nearer the strand.

'And we have to use Guy and the Monaghan lads?'

'No way out of it, Gavin. We don't have enough
backing or money of our own. Yet. We've an army who
need paying and product to sell. I'm going to brand the
coke with a five-point star, stick the molly in a pillbox and
call them 'Umbrella' after Rhianna. We'll make a killing at
the festivals, especially with the oul' ones at Electric Picnic.'

Gavin smiled and pushed his fringe off his forehead. It
was hot.

'When we have wholesale customers, then we can
expand, stop using the lads from Monaghan, but we'll have
to pay them a tax if we want to supply the North.'

'All right, Seán.'

The words had weight to his ears, because they were laced with the comfort of Gavin's trust. Seán had formed this plan, looked at it from a business angle with financial ratios and strategic planning. This was a new time in Ireland. The property bubble would never burst, people had cheap money, a gaping hunger and not enough orifices to snort it into. Seán was going to help them. When Gavin came out of prison with an army as likely to shoot themselves as the target, the men in Monaghan had taught them how to handle their weapons. They'd seen something in Seán as well and had offered to help with his plans. They were not men he could refuse. However, he knew the biggest problem for drug dealers when business started to flow was cash. Where to put it and what to do with it. Seán wasn't going the way of Larry Dunne, caught on a bridge in Dublin and trying to explain two hundred grand in his mother's garden shed under the cat litter.

Chapter 38

2019

I got off the DART at Sandymount and walked to Harcourt Square, needing some air. The morning train was jammed this time of year, dead-eyed commuters jockeying with school-bagged children. As I walked, I reread the text from Joe telling me DCS Muldoon had given me the go-ahead on Barcelona. The Spanish authorities were allowing one detective to observe and DCS Muldoon had chosen me. Not telling my commanding officer I was pregnant before a challenging assignment broke any amount of Human Resource rules. That didn't bother me but putting the spark inside my womb at risk whipped me as I walked to work.

I'd started to keep a notebook. It helped me fill out the shape of my emotions without guilt, to name what I was feeling and gauge it. Some days I was depressed, others I was driven to the angry end of exhaustion. At no point was I calm and at times I was wretched. It explained why I craved the oblivion of pursuit. The day itself trudged by with little relief, unreturned calls and paperwork awaiting sign-off. There was no information about Flannery or Fuentes. Most of the day was spent justifying travel expenses and making sure Human Resources had my itinerary for Barcelona.

'This is a cost overhead analysis so CAB don't go over budget. We don't need your itinerary to protect you, that's not our job,' said Bluntface, her voice shellacked in spite.

Muldoon and Joe Clarke were curt today, no more information on Barcelona forthcoming. The silence pressed down on me and I found myself outside Paul's floor. It was shut up tight at 7.30pm. The faint shadow of long-gone employees hung in the stale air. I took my phone out, about to face-time Paul. He had the ear of our superiors and might have information I wasn't privy to.

O'Connor burst through the doors of the third-floor stairway.

I stifled a scream.

'There you are.'

'You were looking for me, Detective Superintendent O'Connor?' The mouthful of title gave me a chance to compose myself.

'You're always here, aren't you, Harney? No boyfriend to go home and make dinner for?'

He didn't spit the words or leer at me. O'Connor's sexism wasn't casual, unlike some of the fossils in the force who called the secretaries 'pet'. O'Connor's brand was different, knowingly used and designed to keep women down, but hell hath no fury like a woman on form.

'I'm not sure speculation on my private life is appropriate, Detective Superintendent O'Connor. Is there something I can do for you?'

He gave a wolfish grin, all threat and no charm.

'I hear you're angling to get yourself to Barcelona? Chasing down Seán Flannery at the taxpayer's expense.'

I refused to be drawn or yield to the impulse to take a step back. He would see me flinch.

'What information do you have on him, Harney?'

'It's all in the briefing documents I sent to DCS Muldoon.'

O'Connor was silhouetted against the fading light, a black sun against a backdrop of dusk. The stillness of him was unsettling, no doubt his desired effect.

'It would be a terrible pity if Seán Flannery was ready for you when you turned up. I wouldn't rely on support from the Spanish, they don't like other police forces on their turf. It might not end well for you.'

He gave a sly smile and leaned further forward. I was rocked back onto my heels. He supressed a snort and in the semi-darkness emanated the aggression of a pack hyena when a wounded beast was all but in its jaws. Now, more than ever, I was convinced O'Connor was Flannery's informant.

I cursed the eco-lights and smacked my hand on a sensor. Light flooded the foyer and I made for the stairs.

O'Connor's laughter bounced off the tiled walls behind me.

Chapter 39

Joe's speech pattern was off – he had the intonation of a high-flowing syllable-timed language, where each sentence lolls around. It sounded peculiar in English, which was a stress-timed language. I put it down to worry and talking to Sergeant O'Driscoll too much.

'Look, I'm not sure you should go at all. I spoke to O'Driscoll – he says there's not much by way of support on the ground in Barcelona for us. You'll be on your own – which I'm not happy about – and unarmed.' He rubbed a spot of speckled sun damage at his temple. 'You'll have to stay in whatever station the local police put you. If you do not have permission to accompany them on an operation, you stay in the station. Don't charge off trying to catch Flannery.'

I could hear the capitals in Joe's voice. The neat blue collar of his work-shirt rubbing against sagging skin, a wrinkled man in an ironed shirt.

'Joe, I'll play by the rules and if the Mossos Esquadra tell me I have to sit in an office and watch on a monitor while they apprehend Seán Flannery, I will. You have my word. Now what's the update?'

He pulled a manila folder from his desk and clicked on his monitor, tapping the keys in quick rhythm to log in.

'Flannery was caught,' Joe turned his monitor towards me, 'on CCTV. This is from O'Driscoll. It's in Plaça de Catalunya.'

Plaça de Catalunya was wide and open, a square with lush green areas and a whirling colourful centre. A haven for tourists, it wasn't an obvious choice to conceal a person of interest. Flannery was being shunted across it by two black men. He looked pale and stunned. The video reeled on and Flannery was caught from a side angle by a different camera, then lost into a side street and a CCTV blackspot.

'It's him, but as you can see he's got company,' said Joe.

'How did he look to you?' I said.

'Like he always does, maybe less cocksure.'

'Is he a bit out of it?'

'On drugs?' said Joe.

'Not willingly. The body language is all wrong. He's between those two thugs – they're all bunched up. Doesn't feel right.'

'He may be meeting new buyers or associates. Those lads aren't the trusting type. O'Driscoll said they go into a block of flats off Catalunya Place and we lose sight of them.'

'Could he still be there?'

Joe shoved down his metal window, letting clean air into the cramped office. A spotted magpie landed on the flat roof outside and warned off fellow scavengers with a harsh *yew yew*.

'No idea, Bridge. You'll have to put yourself in the hands of the Spanish police on this one. Human Resources have reserved a hotel room for you and you're on EI 562 leaving Dublin airport at 6.45am tomorrow. According to the Mossos Esquadra you will be met by one of their detectives – O'Driscoll said there's a fifty-fifty chance of that. Be ready to get yourself to Carrer de la Marina, which is the station the Mossos are coming from, if no one meets you.'

'Not the welcome wagon then?'

'Spanish don't want us in their back yard looking for criminals, no matter what the EU directives on organised crime say. You have five days. Don't go missing or looking for trouble. O'Driscoll has all your permits filed with the Madrid and Barcelona authorities. Buy a burner phone and text me the number, I'll get it to O'Driscoll. He and I are the only people who will have that number.'

The subterfuge swayed in the air between us.

'Why?' I said.

'O'Connor. He wants in on this operation. I can keep him out of the loop for five days.'

'Tell him I've gone quiet, Joe.'

He made a smacking sound with his lips. 'And give him a chance to set the Spanish police on you? No, Bridge. Let me handle O'Connor. You'll have more than your fair share going on.'

'We need to call O'Driscoll, make sure you have the latest update,' I said.

He put his phone on speaker and punched in numbers, a run of blips and a single long beep denoting an international ringtone.

'Hello?'

'Brendan?' said Joe. 'You're not a man to give away anything.'

'Well, it's my private line, Joe. If you're ringing it you

should know who you're talking to. Am I on speaker?'

'Yes, Bridget Harney and myself. The room is secure.'

It was a scene from *Dad's Army*. I raised a single eyebrow.

'Hello, Sergeant O'Driscoll.'

'Garda Harney.'

I didn't correct him.

'Take me off speaker, please, Garda Harney,' said O'Driscoll.

'Why? Joe and me are the only people in the office, Sergeant O'Driscoll.'

'Walls have ears, Garda Harney, walls have ears.'

The handset was cold in my ear. 'You can call me Bridge.'

'Fair enough. I take it Joe has told you the gardaí aren't wanted here. It's all politics.'

Sergeant O'Driscoll's voice lowered and thinned. I pictured him crouching under a neat Mediterranean desk with his wide Irish face.

'It's a viper's nest here. There's no other way of putting it. They all inform on one another to their bosses while trying to keep central government in the dark. Bloody embassy's bugged, but we don't know by who. The whole place is crawling with cartel money. Your best hope are the lads in Customs – they have civilian status in Spain and are clean. I'll put you in touch with a fellah there. Ramon Mendes. But remember this, you get into a situation where the Mossos Esquadra are coming to your rescue, you run. Got that, Detective Garda Harney? They're not the cavalry.'

The fast delivery of his information had us both breathing hard.

Joe took the handset and wound the call up.

I turned to face him.

'By the look of you, you're getting the picture,' he said.

I left his office and made my way to Amina's desk. I would use the Garda-approved hotel but book a second place to stay in Barcelona. A bolthole. Amina could book it in her name.

Chapter 40

Arrivals in Barcelona international airport was busy with suited businesspeople looking for drivers with signs. I guessed it was twelve degrees or so, a pleasant change from minus one in wintry Dublin. Barcelona's airport was a bright, efficient place and I'd plenty of time to admire it, as no one was flashing a sign with my name. It gave me the chance to get my bearings and I took the RENFE train to Passeig de Gràcia stopping at a Movistar outlet to get a burner phone. I texted the number to Joe and took the Metro to Liceu, letting Maps recommend a churros and chocolate café on Calle Petritxol. I played the enraptured tourist with ease, Gaudí's flair seducing me. This was a city people had given their lives to and made it vibrant in doing so.

Calle Petritxol was a tiny street with any number of cafés and I was in no hurry to get to a budget hostel Human Resources tried to convince me was a hotel. I ordered at a café window and took a seat at an outside table, relishing the buttercup-yellow sunshine. The chocolate didn't disappoint either – it was thick and rich, the roasted cocoa beans and honey smell had my mouth watering. My burner rang and I swallowed a piece of crunchy soft churro, dusting away confectioners' sugar from the side of my mouth.

'Hello?'

'Bridget Harney?'

'Hi, Brendan, thanks for calling.' My voice was too jolly-hockey-sticks – I needed to take it down a notch. He hadn't called for a chat.

'You came through as a regular tourist? Gave your passport to border control and weren't stopped?'

'Yes, I was waved through.'

'So you think, but there's an alert on your passport – nothing sinister but it will have gone on the national database as soon as I put in for application to travel. Were you met?'

'No, or not by anyone I could see.'

'Fair enough. First time here?'

'Yes.'

'Right so, get to know Barcelona fast, the centre's small enough. You can't trust anyone here. Not when you're investigating the cartels. So you need to know your way around.' He cleared his throat every time he paused, a nervous tic. 'Barcelona's worse than Madrid. The Mossos Esquadra do the policing here, not the Guardia Civil. The Catalan thing is so strong you might as well be in another country. The Ministry of the Interior will try to get involved because it's the Fuentes cartel but the Mossos won't let them. Stay out of that conversation and play dumb.'

This I could do.

'No one met you, officially – it's the Mossos way of telling you this is their turf. You must assume you're being watched. Even if you're any good at losing a tail you'll shake them for a couple of hours, no more. The Mossos own Barcelona and no amount of Guardia Civil boots on the street will make them give it up. The fellah I told you about, Ramon Mendes, will call you on your Irish cell later today. You have one advantage, the Mossos think you're a low-level gobshite over from Dublin who wanted a jolly to Barcelona.'

'I have to thank Joe for that, do I?'

'If it wasn't for Joe Clarke, you'd have been met at the airport, put into a bulletproof vest and thrown into a Comissaria Mossos d'Esquadra station. Where you'd spend your five days. This way at least you can move around. But be careful. The Mossos are known for catching bystanders in crossfire. You're expected at Carrer de la Marina. That'd be my first port of call to show the Mossos you're harmless, although from what Joe says you're anything but.'

With a click he'd gone.

His advice left me shaken despite my bluster on the phone and I darted off across town and into the faceless but clean hostel. Joe had pegged me as a cop who fancied a mini-break and I was going to live up to that. I put my burner in the air vent at the top of my room and lick-stuck a hair across the base. I left my rucksack with everything, bar my badge and money, under the bed. From what O'Driscoll said, the room would be searched. I couldn't look like a complete idiot, so I rolled €150 in a pair of knickers and flung it in the back of a drawer as though it were my emergency money.

A memory floated back to me. I was ten and walking down the avenue with some friends. My mother gave me thirty pence, with strict instructions the ten pence was 'emergency money'. The price of a phone call from the call box on Merrion Avenue if I was in trouble. Of course I had spent all my money in a sweetshop and was half an hour late arriving home, with no prior phone call or emergency money. While my mother hopped off me, I found the ten-pence piece tucked into the lining of a back pocket and produced it in sobbed-out breaths. Horrified at how pointless it was against my mother's wrath.

The same horror held me now as I stuck a smile on my face and left the hotel, making for Carrer de la Marina.

Mossos Esquadra on Carrer de la Marina was a pixelated block, with windows turned a blown-glass green by the late November sun. It was a busy station with an open reception. My visit was no surprise and not an occasion of any interest. The Mosso on the main desk greeted me and asked for my passport. He had a bony face, a snippet of authority in a navy uniform, worn parade-style.

I introduced myself, showed copies of my permits and waited.

He flicked my passport from back to front, and that was when I knew he wouldn't return it.

'Garda identification?' said the Mosso.

'I didn't bring it. I was told I wouldn't be armed and my Garda identification would be useless here.'

No way was I handing over my identification. They knew I had my passport so I couldn't hold it back, but Irish airlines would take Garda ID if I needed to fly.

'*Bienvenida a Barcelona*,' he said in a voice devoid of any welcome. 'We have your phone number if we need to contact you and we know where you're staying. As a courtesy we have arranged accommodation for you at our headquarters in Sabadell, if you find anything . . . *cutre*,' he waved a tanned hand at me, 'not good, with your Garda accommodation.'

'Thank you.'

'What do you plan to do now?'

'I was going to get the hop on/hop off tourist bus and try to get to know the city better.'

'*Vale.*'

He gave me a patronising look – I was an idiot abroad.

Chapter 41

2010

Seán had worked all day in the house. A frenzied quality to his efforts made his blood pump close to the skin, thickening his fingers. Lumps of plasterboard lay in chalky heaps around the hall, together with lumps of old feathery fibreglass. He had dust in his hair, up his nostrils and when he coughed it caught in his chest. The downstairs of his terraced house was covered in a white film. The mess made him redouble his efforts. His girlfriend and her daughter were due back tomorrow evening, and everything had to be back to normal. No one could see him hiding his money. The plasterboard internal wall between the hall and the living room had been pulled off exposing its timber frame and a tic-tac-toe of hollows now emptied of their insulation.

Seán looked at the bundles of money he'd packed into square plastic packets. Six blocks to fit into six hollows, each square of money worth €420,000.

It didn't bother him the cartel took the majority share of profit from their joint enterprise – they were the manufacturer so deserved their cut. Seán was the distributor in this arrangement and entitled to the next largest share. Guy, on the other hand was the money pimp, making nothing, distributing nothing, yet still getting a slice of the pie. Fuentes had a wholesale price which had to be paid, no matter what police seizures or rival gang thefts, and that came out of Seán's end, but it still left plenty of room for profit at the retail level. Guy didn't know how much Seán sold his product for, because Seán never kept to a minimum price. He let market conditions be his guide – he had a nose for desperation, dates of social welfare payments and genteel sham. His army were trained in the subtle art of persuasion, violence alone didn't achieve lasting results. Keen middle-class customers gave their phone numbers to their suited dealers who met them at local car parks, or called to their door as the takeaway guy. A simple phone hack got their contacts and the threat of exposure was all it took to get a price increase. Not everyone was afraid of exposure and in these communities Seán believed in making an example of one individual, something so awful it would travel through the hive mind of junkies. While in Drogheda, he had held down a transgressor and knifed him up the ass, finding that single act was enough to keep all the others in line.

Seán's mind whirred on his strategic plan for the next twelve months. He'd created a niche for his product. The purity levels drew addicts at all levels of society and when people were hooked he would cut supply, sending them like fire ants to other dealers with a fraction of his product purity. Fights would break out in poorer suburbs, local gardaí would be overwhelmed with violent junkies. His dealers would field calls from his middle-class customers, willing to pay whatever he asked to reinstate the flow. His fingers flew over the blocks of money as he duct-taped the ends and stacked them into the timber frame. Over two and a half million would be hidden in the wall between his hall and living room. His 'premium insulation' gave him an ounce of protection and he needed to believe he could protect himself.

Fuentes were vicious, even for a cartel. Seán measured the exact size of the walls and began to score his plasterboard sheets. The mundane task helped him arrange his thoughts. Guy had charged a levy since the early days, called it a 'tithe' like he was some kind of bishop or government department. Seán paid ten percent of what he made every month to Guy. It went straight to his bottom line without Fuentes knowledge and Seán was determined to put an end to the tithe and Guy. The option of trading a kill for a kill with the Dunne gang was tempting, but Fuentes retribution for an unsanctioned hit would be merciless. And Seán had no answer for that. Yet.

Seán hammered nails into the plasterboard, attaching it to the wooden frame. When the time was right, he would shop Guy to Fuentes, offer to kill him and pay this money as a promise of his fidelity.

Time to add the last sheet of plasterboard. Seán's tools lay neat and ready: wire-cutters, Semtex and circuit boards for a booby trap. If someone other than him found this money, a nasty surprise awaited them.

He hammered in the last couple of nails. He had bought rolls of a soft floral wallpaper as a finishing touch, something he hoped would make his girlfriend and her nine-year-old daughter happy.

Lost in his task, he didn't see Sheila Devereux retreating noiselessly out his back door. She'd stolen a key from Gavin. Of course a sentry should have stopped her, but who among them would stop Granny Dev if she was determined to enter? Or own up to flouting Seán's strict instructions to let no one pass?

Chapter 42

2019

The hexagonal shapes on the tour bus pulsed in my eyeline. During winter it ran every twenty-five minutes. This was the blue route and I tried to memorise its times and stops. An angry shiver in my pocket told me my Irish phone was ringing, the screen filled with a jumble of unfamiliar numbers.

'*Hola?* Is that Bridget Harney?' A sun-soaked accent.

'Yes? Who's this, please?'

'Ramon Mendes from Treasury. Where are you now? You sound like you are on a motorboat?'

I laughed over the revving engine. 'Wouldn't that be nice? I'm on a tourist bus.'

'Where is your next stop?'

I checked the map I was given when I bought my ticket. 'Casa Batlló.'

'*Vale!* Get off and look for Bar Nolla. It's near the stop, an old-fashioned Catalan bar. I'll be inside waiting for you.'

'Thank you.'

'*Adiós.*'

Bar Nolla was certainly old-fashioned and authentic. Two squat open wooden doors lay either side of a battered wine cask, now a table. Although ready for business, the place looked empty. The interior was small but bright and the spice of savoury anchovies flavoured the air.

'Bridget?' said the single occupant.

A lanky, dark-haired man with thick-rimmed glasses, he was more town clerk than Treasury detective.

'Ramon Mendes.' He held out his hand and took mine in a warm, dry grip.

'Good to meet you, Ramon, and thank you for contacting me. You're the first real police I've met in Barcelona and I've come from Carrer de la Marina Mossos Esquadra.'

He gave a throaty laugh. 'I hope you didn't give them your passport?'

'I did.'

'You won't be getting it back until you leave.'

He indicated I should join him at a small, neat table. Smoked curled from a cigarette turning to a soft sausage of grey ash. He stubbed it out.

'Your English is pitch-perfect – even, if I might say, Irish-sounding.'

He laughed. 'I went to Ireland on an Erasmus programme. I spent a year studying in UCD. *It was grand.*'

I grinned. He did a good flat Dublin accent, unexpected in these surroundings.

'Ah, good old University College Dublin! I went to Trinity. You should've come to us – we had a better Erasmus programme.'

'You would say that,' said Ramon, an easy smile hanging off his mouth.

We'd found a patch of common ground.

'Juanito! Ponerme un café.'

I couldn't see anyone, but the hissing of a coffee machine from deep in the bar's interior told me something was being prepared.

'Mossos tracked you since your arrival. I'm sure Sergeant O'Driscoll advised you about how things work?'

'He mentioned something about it,' I said.

'They'll rate you as a threat and ramp their surveillance up and down accordingly.' He indicated a brown ramekin containing small white fish steeped in what smelt like vinegar. 'These are *boquerones* – anchovies but with much less salt. Try one.'

I speared a little fish with a small fork and ate it. Dry vinegar exploded on my tongue.

A frothy coffee was put in front of me, wisps of steam rising off it. The server grunted at Ramon, said something and they laughed. My Spanish never passed *'buenos días'* so I was lost.

When the server had gone back into the recesses of the bar Ramon's easy smile slipped away.

'Look like a happy tourist for the benefit of the Mossos and anyone else.' He lit another cigarette. 'When Flannery was spotted, I staked out Plaça de Catalunya. He was moved hours after he was picked up on CCTV.'

'Was he was tipped off?'

'No,' he gave an expressive shrug. 'Well, perhaps, but it is of no account – cartel operatives move freely in this city. I believe Flannery is being held by Fuentes. The two

Africans you see in the CCTV footage are known to us. They took Flannery late in the evening. I tried to follow but lost them around the port. I didn't want to call it in as someone would have alerted Fuentes, but I'm sure Flannery will pop up again on CCTV.'

This didn't fit with Flannery and I shuddered. Something about deep water masquerading as smooth and shallow, with my naked foot at the edge.

'Flannery's a big noise in Ireland,' I said. 'We have a huge problem with controlled prescription drugs and cocaine. He's one of our main drug importers. I thought he was here to do a deal with Fuentes. He lost a couple of tonnes of their product, which would have hurt them a little, but wouldn't he have come here on his own terms? To make amends and pay up for the shipment he lost?'

'I wouldn't be so sure. From the manner in which he's being held, I'd say they're going to kill him.'

'For losing a shipment?' A pulse throbbed in my eyelid, right over my iris – it made my vision flicker as it danced out a syncopated beat. 'That's not right. He can't be taken like this. I have to apprehend him – he has to pay.'

Emotions warred with the words crowding behind my tongue and fought to get out. I made a shucking noise with my teeth.

'You OK?' said Ramon.

I took a breath. 'Yes. I don't understand why Fuentes would kill Flannery. He's one of their men.'

He gave me a long look, measuring me. I wasn't alone in taking risks.

'Couple of things. Flannery isn't a kingpin in Spain. Maybe in Ireland he's *El Jeffe,* but not here – there are too many cartels, each with their own generals. I'm guessing from his docile behaviour that he is drugged. It is a standard way of operating for Fuentes. What is not standard is how they're going after Flannery. You lose a shipment belonging to Fuentes and your options are limited to pay or die. But Fuentes will shoot you where you live – Flannery was brought here to be interrogated and disposed of. I would say Fuentes are trying to protect an informer. Someone who's of value to them and hard to replace. Do you have informers in your police or government?'

The café closed in on me. A buzzing heat in my chest climbed to my face, scorching my throat along the way. DS O'Connor's face flashed in my mind.

'Anything's possible. How do you know this?'

Again the shrug. 'I've seen it before. Fuentes have any amount of rising stars wanting to fill the boots of the men like Flannery. But officials, people who can clear a path for their shipments or keep operatives out of prison, are gold. Fuentes will protect them at any cost. Which means this is dangerous. If your Flannery is being sacrificed to keep an asset in place, the Mossos in the Fuentes pay will want to keep any investigation into Flannery at a minimum. Do you have a second place you can stay?'

'I can get one.'

Ramon smiled and flicked his cigarette into the crenelated ashtray. 'You're right. Don't tell me if you have a place. Take a circuitous route when you go there and check for a tail. A little information . . .' Ramon took a pull from his expresso. 'I've been told the Mossos are focusing on three locations Fuentes have used in the past.

They're narrowing it down and should have something solid in the next twelve to twenty-four hours. Flannery may be captured within the day.'

I had condensed a lifetime of pursuit into Flannery and here he was, to be plated and served to me. Something so easy was not to be trusted.

'You don't look satisfied,' said Ramon.

'I want Flannery apprehended, for sure, but it's difficult to be so removed from the intelligence-gathering. I've no idea how solid your information is.'

Ramon tore at the left corner of a ridged napkin.

'I understand. I'm not in on the intel either,' the outer corners of his eyes creased as he scrutinised me, 'and I get why you are suspicious. You are right to be. The Mossos can't be trusted – it may be a small bunch of them, but we've no idea how far up the chain the corruption goes. We are being "presented" with this information. If you were back in Carrer de la Marina you'd be given this same information by whatever Caporal would talk to you.'

I ate another *boquerone*.

'You believe a cohort in the Mossos know where Flannery is and are drip-feeding this information to their superiors?' I asked.

Ramon's mouth turned down on one side. 'Yes. They've known where Flannery is from the moment he was brought here. Fuentes traffic more cocaine into Spain than any other cartel. Do you have any idea how much money they control? We estimate Fuentes have the GNP of a small country. They're pulling everyone's strings on this.'

His face didn't change expression so I kept mine neutral too.

'Do you still think you can arrest Flannery? Take him home to Ireland?' he asked.

'If I find him first, I believe I have a chance.'

'Will you be able to prosecute him? Dismantle his organisation?'

The body in the Dublin Mountains would be hard to explain away. The difficulty the drugs seizure had caused Flannery's OCG and his lieutenant being bugged were bound to unlock something for me.

'We're closer than we've ever been and the drugs seizure is causing cracks in his gang.'

'My gut is we'll find Flannery dead in an alley, but who knows? You might get lucky and force the Mossos to apprehend him. Trick is to do it in the glare of the press or another agency. The Mossos are wary of Treasury, but we can't carry guns. Check in with me a couple of times a day, text or something. You don't want to get embroiled in a Mossos shootout. You won't survive it.'

His face split in a grin at the comic-book terror he must have seen in my face.

'You afraid?' he said.

'I'd be an idiot if I wasn't.'

'Good, it will keep you alert.' He stood to pay and put some crumpled bills on a silver change plate I hadn't noticed was there. 'Hey, Juanito! The service in this place is terrible!'

He added something in Spanish and a shout came from the back of the bar. Juanito appeared and raised a fleshy fist in mock outrage.

'Let's go. I'll take you to Plaça de Catalunya. It's what they would expect.' He nodded over his shoulder at two navy uniformed Mossos slouching outside the bar, their distinctive red-and-navy berets at a fashionable angle.

'Not subtle, is it?'

'No,' said Ramon, 'but I'd say you played it well in Carrer de la Marina. They don't rate you so they're not bothering to disguise themselves.'

I laughed. It sounded nervous and tinny.

Chapter 43

There was a powdery tickle at the back of my throat, the last thing I needed was a cold from the flight over. Ramon's briefing stayed with me as I walked around the city. I spread out my obsession with Flannery and viewed it from different vantage points without much luck. My quarry was too near. I had white line fever. My route back to the hotel was lengthy – I wanted to orientate myself in this city. The air was crisp and a uniformed Mossos saluted me as if I were a visiting dignitary riding around in an open-top car.

In my room I checked the hiding spot – nothing had been moved. A longing to hear Paul Doherty's voice came over me and I dialled him on my Irish cell. He picked up on the second ring.

'Hi.'

He had a voice like a pair of leather cowboy boots.

'Hey, I'm glad you picked up,' I said.

'Why wouldn't I?'

'I'm not disturbing you, am I?'

'No more than usual, Bridge.'

We both laughed.

'It's good to hear you,' I said.

'Is everything OK? This Flannery thing doesn't sound safe. I was talking to Joe about it today and he's worried.'

The idea of him talking about me when I wasn't in front of him brought rare comfort.

'It's strange. Spain has this reputation of being the girl next door, easy-going and sunny. But not so. I'm being stonewalled and our own authorities are telling me to keep my head down. The Mossos are closing in on Flannery so I should have a location soon.'

Silence.

'It doesn't sound safe,' he said then. 'Will you be part of the squad that arrests him?'

'No. I might get a vantage point at the outskirts of the operation but from what I've been told I'll be at the station away from everything.'

'That doesn't sound like you.'

'You're smiling,' I said.

'I am.'

'So what will you do, Bridge?'

Everything so straight at the beginning of our conversation twisted and tangled at the sound of his voice. The pregnancy and his impending fatherhood was a splinter in my mind that skin had grown over and was now so deep I'd have to get a hot needle at it. So I said nothing.

'I'll stay in the station like a good little Blueshirt.'

'I find that hard to believe. Do you know where Flannery is right now?'

'No.'

'That's something.'

'Why? What do you think I'd do, Paul?'

'That's a loaded question. Do you want me to answer?'

A picture of how others saw me swirled in the peppery

smoke of my brain.

'Go on, tell me.'

'Are you armed?' he said.

'No.'

'You're not thinking of approaching him on your own, are you?'

The question dulled the digital line or sharpened it to a fine point. I couldn't decide which and my breath came hard.

'Of course not.'

He gave a growl of agreement. 'Please stay safe, Bridge. Don't do anything rash.'

'Sure.'

'When do you get back?'

'I'd say the end of the week.'

'OK, see you then. And Bridge?'

'Yes?'

'Come back in one piece.'

We hung up, but I'd no sensation of a trouble shared.

I was alone with my thoughts, yet I wasn't on my own and would never be again. Fears for a clutch of cells rippling inside me piled on. I had lost something in the pursuit of Seán Flannery, learning everything about his existence and watching him every opportunity I got, all but swapping my life for his. With so much violence in my world, who was I to bring a defenceless child into it? My true nature was being revealed to me. I was the violence. My mother once told me decent people had the same urges as everyone else – it was how they acted on them that made the difference.

The day dragged on as I played the happy-calamari-eating-plod, ignoring a staring face in the queue for

Sagrada Familia and again reflected in a shop window on Avinguda Diagonal.

It was late when I got back to my hotel room, but sleep wouldn't come so I stopped trying to entice it and I washed my face in the tiny bathroom. The neon backlit mirror did me no favours and the face looking back was a death mask with holes for eyes. The night lengthened and still I couldn't find any rest. I got out of bed, sinking to the floor to change the shape of my environment. I could kill Seán Flannery in combat, but what if he was drugged and a captive? Could I stop myself murdering him in cold blood?

I left the hotel in the dark hours, nearer to dawn than midnight and made for my second location.

Chapter 44

Gavin rang back with an address. It was long. Seán got the first words of the address inked out on his hand, using the dregs of a biro he found near the phone boxes, *Numancia 30*. He stopped writing, his heart raced and the words swam in front of his eyes. He must have said something before he sank to the ground as Gavin had shouted at him.

'Hold on, Seán! I've a driver coming to get you!'

He was exhausted, dehydrated and dizzy as a newborn foal. Gavin sent a pre-paid taxi for him. The driver was well compensated and dragged the half-conscious hobo into the back of his Skoda.

Seán sat in the back seat and asked for a phone. He punched in Gavin's number.

'Hey, man?' said Gavin. 'How you holdin' up?'

'OK.' Seán sounded rusty as though he'd borrowed someone else's vocal cords and they didn't quite fit. 'Thanks, Gavin. You still got Guy with you?'

'Right here beside me, Seán. Glock 19 to his head, ready to squeeze the trigger the second you say.'

'You tell him, if he's sending me to Fuentes contacts he'll be dead before I've walked in the door.'

'He knows, Seán.'

'Tell him, Gavin. I want to hear his voice.'

'Guy,' said Gavin, an upbeat menace in his voice, 'is Seán going to a safe house? Will Fuentes grab him when he walks in the door?'

'No . . . no.' Guy sounded as frightened as Seán wanted him to be. He heard the connecting crunch of bone on bone and a splatter.

'Just giving my man here a reminder of what will happen if you're jumped, Seán,' said Gavin.

Seán heard a low moan in the background.

'And, Guy?' said Gavin. 'Don't think your razzer friends can help you – no one knows where you are. If anything happens to Seán I'll take my time with you, so think on. Kept a man alive for four days once. I reckon that's a record.'

Guy was weeping and with each sob Seán felt drops of cold relief.

'Who am I going to see?' said Seán.

'Bloke called *Pablo Gar-ce-ah* – that how you say it, Guy?'

Seán heard another low whimper from Guy and hoped Gavin hadn't lost the head too soon – he had a bloodlust when activated that he struggled to switch off. Seán wanted nothing more than Guy dead – Guy's fingerprints were all over his current predicament – but Guy would die at his hands.

'Pablo Garcia,' said Guy. 'He's a pawnbroker, high end. Gold and diamonds, I've used him before for personal stuff. He'll make sure you have money and can get out of the country. You should know Interpol have an international warrant out for your arrest.'

'Mr Helpful now, are we, Guy?' said Gavin.

'I've arrived,' said Seán. 'I'm giving the phone back to the driver. If you don't hear from me in ten minutes start cutting his fingers off.'

'Sound,' said Gavin.

The pawn shop was at the base of a huge block of flats – to Seán everything in this city sat under blocks of flats. He walked past the smoked-glass frontage, a filthy loon in ridiculous shiny shoes. An older man with a head of pomaded hair pranced out of the shop. He was a black sparrow in a three-piece suit with his moustache manicured to the last hair.

'*Señor* Seán?' he said. 'I am Pablo Garcia, and *Señor* Guy said to expect you. This way, please.'

He indicated to a doorway next to the shop, opened the door and waved Seán in. It was a modern foyer that smelled of regular cleanings and green plants. Pablo called the lift and kept his eyes ahead, one hand playing with the side of his moustache. He opened an apartment door, clean and clutterless, lived in by a person with precise habits. Seán assumed it was Pablo.

'Please take this phone and ring your friend Gavin,' said Pablo. 'After your call I will show you where the bathroom is and make something to eat for you.'

'No,' said Seán. Not because he wasn't famished – he might faint from lack of food and water – but because he couldn't change his nature. His need was for control at all times. In all things. He rang Gavin.

'Seán, man?' said Gavin. 'How's it looking? Good?'

'Yeah, so far. I'm going to eat and cleaned up. If I don't call you back in three hours kill Guy.'

'No worries, man,' said Gavin. 'Did you hear that, Guy,

I'm to kill you if Seán doesn't ring back in three hours.'

Seán hung up.

'Please tell your friend to calm down,' said Pablo. 'I don't work for the cartel and Guy does, but if they try to contact him, because you've escaped and he is compromised, the cartel will kill him and there will be no one to pay me. Also, do you want the cartel to come looking for you, *en serio*? In earnest? They'll start by killing everyone in your organisation in Dublin. Your friend Gavin will be first on the list.'

He indicated to a soft forest-green chair to Seán's right.

'Please sit. I will be well paid for my services, so rest, eat. Then I will take you in the boot of my car to the port, where a yacht is waiting and you can sail back to Ireland. Or anywhere you care to. Guy said you are a master yachtsman.'

Seán's mind was unable to package his thoughts in any rational way.

'OK, I'll eat first and you eat what I eat.'

'Of course, *Señor* Seán, come into the kitchen and watch me prepare.'

'Can you make ham and cheese sandwiches?' They reminded him of Sunday tea in the convent, where the sandwiches were more cheese than ham, but he'd liked them. You had to like something.

'Of course. In Spain we call them bikinis, because they are triangles, you see?'

Deftly he made a sandwich and held up a half, cut on the diagonal. Pablo was quick, with compact movements in his tiny kitchen, nothing a full arm's length away. He made tea to go with the sandwiches.

'Please come and sit in the salon to eat,' he said and

smiled at Seán. 'Can you call your friend Gavin and ask him to get back to normal. I will buy a burner phone for you when we leave the apartment as that is my work phone and I will need it back.'

He was wearing a '*Kiss the Cook*' apron so ridiculous it was comforting, but weariness threatened to lay Seán out.

'You are not well and, were my intentions bad, it would take nothing to overpower you. Sit. Eat.'

The man had a point and Seán sat in the armchair and let it swallow him. He watched the man nibble at the sandwiches and sip his tea. It was like dining with a hamster. Seán wolfed into the food, drinking two pots of tea and losing count of how many bikinis he ate.

'Why not call Gavin?' said Pablo.

Seán punched in Gavin's mobile number. 'Gavin?'

'Yeah, man – everything still on the up and up?'

'I'm good, going to rest for a bit now, then I'll get a burner and sail for home. Let Guy go – you can't keep him there anymore – someone's bound to notice. Fuentes might call him and we can't let them know I'm safe. Make sure Guy knows you'll slice his face off if he tries to alert Fuentes. Cut him now to give him a taste.'

'Will do, Seán, but you'll call me in a couple of hours?' said Gavin.

'Yes, maybe five hours, have your phone on.'

'Cool. If anything happens I'll come back and kill Guy.'

'I know you will, Gavin.'

Seán hung up and Pablo regarded him.

'You know, Guy isn't a bad man. He does want to help you, *Señor* Seán.'

Seán sat back and crossed his legs, a feeling of warmth

stealing over him. He listened to Pablo patter on about when he first met Guy, how he helped him buy gold pieces and good diamonds to be kept safe for a rainy day.

Seán looked out the apartment window and saw it was dusk. He jumped up.

'How long have I been here?' He swayed.

'Only an hour and a half,' said Pablo.

Seán's head pounded and he flopped back down into the chair. His eyelids had a mind of their own and started closing like theatre curtains at the end of a show. He shook himself.

'There's no point in fighting it,' said Pablo, 'and you've had much more than me. It was in the tea. Rohypnol. You'll be unconscious in minutes. I'm going to call Fuentes now.'

Seán couldn't see anything and his system was shutting down. His mind thrashed like a bird caught in a net, but his listless body didn't stir.

He heard Pablo Garcia's phone call but couldn't say anything.

'I think Guy is compromised – you may want to retire him. This happened because Seán's associate found him. I'm going to go now as I'm close to collapse. Send the men in the service entrance, you have the keys.'

Chapter 45

Bobbles of gold hung off the departing night's curtain. I was in 20 Carrer d'En Roca, an alleyway of eight-storey buildings lying between Las Ramblas and Placa del Pi. An Airbnb Amina had reserved in her name. My apartment was the size of a foldaway bed and Ramon's words unspooled in my head as I breathed in ribbons of muggy air. If I opened my window, I could reach across to touch the balcony of the building opposite. The fifth floor of a sandstone building with a barrel-tiled roof. The barrio had a ferrous smell, as though rusting from all the angry graffiti on its architecture.

Fully dressed I lay on the bed, too early to get up, too late for sleep. My phone was face down on the jaded pine locker. Light leaked from the sides and it made the same sound as a faulty desk fan.

The number was withheld.

'Yes?'

'Bridge?'

'Amina? Is everything OK?'

'No.'

It was a tiny sob.

'I'm sorry, Bridge. I was told it was confidential.'

She was keening now, a hopeless sound.

'I don't want to do this to you because you're so far away, but if I don't tell you I'm no friend. Your dad's being brought into the station later, to be questioned about money laundering.'

The room melted and slid down its own walls.

'Bridge? Bridge?'

'I'm here, Amina. It's OK.'

The frontal lobe of my brain looped with civilities while the rest screamed. I made for the double windows and flung them open. The tang of a port city rushed into the vacuum of the apartment.

'It's my fault, Bridge – I followed the trail – and it was so convoluted – there's so much not filed –'

She was chuffing, a small toy train doing endless figures of eight.

'Slow down, Amina. Start from the beginning.'

'Joe told me. He knew I'd tell you. Muldoon called him up to the office yesterday – he said your dad would be called in to discuss money laundering. He's not being arrested. He's helping with enquiries.'

It was a blow to the side of my head. A fuzzy pain fogged my vision.

'Not being arrested,' I repeated.

'Bridge, it's to do with two companies Chris and I have been investigating. They're involved with a massive money-laundering service. They're using a Finnish cryptocurrency company operating on the dark web using tumblers –'

'Stop!' I couldn't process details.

In a few short hours my dad would be in his dressing gown and pyjamas. Turkey-skin neck with white bristles, sitting at the breakfast table feeding the dog scraps.

Amina snuffled on the phone.

'My father has trouble logging onto his laptop – how in God's name is he supposed to have access to the dark web?' I said.

'He wouldn't have to. Money was dumped from a clean wallet – as a legimate currency – into the Isle of Man branch of Munster Banks plc in the name of Nasda Holdings.'

The edges of my mind curled up. Nasda Holdings bank statements winked up at me from the floor of my mother's study.

'Remember the Ansbacher accounts? The tax evasion scheme set up by Des Traynor? Politicians, builders, judges – oh sorry, Bridge!'

Heat pulsed down the phone.

'It's fine, Dad knew them, but it was from the cocktail circuit. He wasn't in their camp.'

Amina's embarrassment continued to radiate until my ear was hot.

'The Ansbacher accounts weren't concealed, just the Revenue weren't wise to how devious those bastards were. Can I just point out these accounts were set up when the weekly wage was less –'

'Amina! Please stay on track. This is my dad!'

'Sorry, sorry. Nasda Holdings is a different animal. It was set up in the seventies in the Caymans, same as the Ansbacher accounts, and had a bank account that was managed out of an office in Fitzwilliam Square, but the company never traded. Nasda Holdings was set up to look banjaxed.'

'Never traded? Then it's defunct.'

'That's what I said and it's a sign of criminality.'

A gnarly stone rolled around the pit of my stomach.

'It's forward planning on an epic scale, Bridge. The company never traded and is lost in time, you'd never know to look for it. But Nasda Holdings bank account receives crypto-currency, bitcoin and Ethereum. Both are a red flag for –'

'Money laundering,' I said.

Amina was silent.

'But doesn't crypto currency leave traces?' I said. 'The bitcoin blockchain is a public ledger?'

'Yes, in theory, but it's an unregulated market with new blocks being added every ten minutes. It's not as simple as typing into a search bar.'

'So what are Nasda Holdings doing?' I said.

'When the crypto-currency is clean it's traded for pounds and transferred to Munster Bank Isle of Man. Nasda Holdings shouldn't have a bank account so there's some crooked employee helping in the bank. It's the only way this account could receive money.'

'So that bank branch is colluding in this fraud. So what's my father got to do with this?'

Amina gave a hard swallow. 'Your mother's one of the named directors of Nasda Holdings, the other is a company which we know –'

'*Jesus!* There's no way my parents are involved in this! How can my mother be a director of anything?'

'I don't know, but there's something else of interest.'

'What?'

'The guy who set up the whole Ansbacher Scheme – guess who was his articled clerk in the fifties?'

I had nothing. My mind was pinballing around the facts Amina had given me.

'Richie Corrigan. You know him, right, Bridge?'

Chapter 46

I didn't suffer from prescience. Richie Corrigan inveigling my mother into some financial misdeed shouldn't have surprised me – after all, I had read their letters. It was too early to call my father and today he would need all the rest he could get. He needed a plan for his upcoming interview and my feet took me to the local bakery, while I tried to understand my parent's involvement in Nasda Holdings. I wasn't having much luck.

Panaderia del Nuestra Señora was no more than a window with a half door for serving. The buying of bread in the small panaderia had a timeless quality to it, a challenge and response going on for hundreds of years unchanged. I walked back to my apartment with a couple of croissants, needing the morning chill and the thought of coffee bubbling on my stove to keep me upright.

My burner phone rang.

'Ramon?' I was walking up the stairs and the phone reception bounced with metallic-sounding holes. 'I can't hear you, wait until I'm in the apartment.'

I ran to my floor, unlocked the apartment door and rushed inside.

'I have Flannery's location, Bridge.'

A moment of eerie stillness.

'Where is he?'

'*Tranquila* – let's take a beat on this.'

'Where are the Mossos? Have they taken Flannery?'

Ramon sighed. 'Fuentes want Flannery dead, but they don't want some cock-up killing disturbing their business. The Mossos in the Fuentes pay have to earn their keep, but the Intendents – you call them inspectors – want to manage the capture of Flannery and the dirty cops. You're up against many agendas.'

'Will the corrupt Mossos get caught?'

He gave a bark of dry laughter. 'Unlikely – and it's another reason you'll be kept in the dark. The Intendents don't want another national police force to see how we're struggling with corruption. I'm going to give you some information, what you do with it is your business. According to my informant Flannery's in Carrer del Marquis de Barbera. It's in the old town, but it's full of rat runs, alleys backing onto laneways barely the width of a person and everything enclosed by high-density buildings. It's where the *chicas* and the illegals live.'

'*Chicas*? Girls?'

'Few of them are girls now. It's home to the black economy. The cleaners, childminders, everyone middle-class Barceloneses use to make their lives easier. My point being, people will turn a blind eye.'

'What else have you got?'

'He's in Building 38 and from what I understand he's in the Fuentes' custody.'

A cold finger pulled an invisible thread, puckering my insides.

'Custody? So you were right – he was abducted from Dublin.'

'My source says he's handcuffed with some other men the Fuentes have scores to settle with.'

'Are you sure of your source?'

'Yes, she's a chica, cleaning the building Flannery's in. There's a pop-up brothel above him, run by one of the low-level gangs Fuentes use to ship product.'

'Why is she telling you this?'

'Her son's in the gang, she wants to keep him safe, says the bosses are like rabid dogs.'

I stood in the mouth of the apartment's balcony and looked at the early stages of activity in the square. People scurried back and forth, a harried look to them. I kept my eyes peeled for Mossos.

'Tell me about Building 38,' I said.

'All those buildings are ancient, they lean over and nearly connect at the top, but if you're thinking of breaking and entering someone's apartment for a vantage point I wouldn't advise it, Bridge. Lots of those occupants are illegally armed.'

I changed tack. 'Tell me, if the cartel blame Flannery for the drugs seizure in Kilkenny, why didn't they kill him when he got here?'

'It's not Venezuela, Detective Garda Harney. We have some semblance of government.'

I'd offended him, my world-class talent.

'Sorry, Ramon.'

'Believe it or not, we have a dedicated anti-corruption task force for *el funcion publica,* but the cartels have too much money.' He sounded beaten. 'Something else you should know – we're working on the Fuentes schedule.'

'What do you mean?'

'I'd say Fuentes paraded Flannery around waiting for Interpol to flag it. Contact is instigated with the Garda through the embassies, a slow process with information going back and forth. Ending with a single member of the Garda – you – coming over unarmed to observe the operation in Barcelona. Fuentes, through the Mossos, know what's happening.'

'But doesn't it complicate everything if the Mossos kill Flannery?'

'Last year a Fuentes hitman killed one of their Dutch associates near Sagrada Familia outside his hotel, in front of tourists. The Spanish authorities won't let anything disrupt the tourism industry and the Mosso's investigation was overseen by the Guardia Civil, who were brought in from Madrid. The interruption to Fuentes business cost them millions, lost them operatives and closed shipping lines for months. Fuentes won't let that happen again, so if the Mossos kill Flannery, it's clean. No federal government involvement.'

'But there'll be an investigation?' I hated thinking of Seán Flannery in the past tense – it was too good for him. 'I want to arrest Seán Flannery and take him home to face the courts. My Detective Chief Super wants it too.'

'Won't happen. While all the talking is going on in the diplomatic channels, the Mossos will take Flannery to a prearranged area and kill him – with the necessary narrative for the authorities, shot while escaping custody or something – if things get complicated they'll kill him in Carrer Marquis del Berbera, but that would be a secondary option.'

'So Dublin isn't in the loop on this?'

'In this equation the Mossos control everything, the only unknown is you. They'll have eyes on you. Remember in this situation you're the goalie and the Mossos are the penalty shoot-out strikers. The Irish are not known for their goalies.'

'You've never met Shay Given.'

'I've heard of him.'

He gave a harsh laugh that died on the doorstep of his next subject.

'Does O'Driscoll know where you are?'

'No, but he has this number. I rang him last night to check in.'

'Don't mention where you are at any point – to anyone – even over the phone.'

'Right. The Mosso I met first day here told me they'd arranged accommodation for me as a courtesy – in Sabadell.'

'Sabadell. Mossos headquarters. It figures. Listen, the Mossos don't expect you to show up. Inviting you to Complex Central is *el ardid*, a trick. They've done their duty and if you show up near Flannery and get shot they, the Mossos, have plausible deniability. Be careful, Bridge, you're alone in this. It's your decision to pursue Flannery.'

His tone frightened me. It was a glowing cigarette being held to my skin, the hairs scorching.

An engine backfired outside and I jumped. '*Oh!*'

'Bridge!'

'It's fine. A Vespa or something.'

We were jittery.

'Let me make it easy on you.' Mendes seemed to be puffing an early-morning cigarette.

I pictured the smoke coming down his nose and out of

his mouth as he formed his next words.

'Go to Mossos HQ and wait until Flannery has been dealt with. Is this guy worth being shot for, Bridge? Fuentes don't leave witnesses.'

Chapter 47

Ramon's comments about Fuentes and the way they did business had a chilling reality to it. If I wanted to arrest Seán Flannery it would be tantamount to a rescue operation. My skin tingled and my clothes chaffed. I was rescuing a man who'd hurt a young girl, killed the woman he lived with and killed my partner. Who could suffer such a man to live? I could let Fuentes and the Mossos kill Flannery, pretend I didn't know what was happening, but if I left any human being to state-assisted murder, what did that make me?

I had to phone my father, to warn him what was coming, but mostly for selfish reasons, to hear his voice before I left the apartment.

'Hello? Who's this?'

In my haste I'd used my burner phone.

'It's me, Dad. Bridget. You OK?'

'Yes, Bridget, of course I am. Are you all right? Has anything happened?'

The fear in his voice was my fault.

'I'm good, Dad.'

He let out a breath. 'Thank God.'

There was no easy way in.

'Dad, someone from the DOCB is coming to take you in for questioning. It's about Nasda Holdings and laundered money.'

A pause.

'You shouldn't be telling me this, Bridget. It's illegal.'

'Dad, what kind of a daughter would I be if I didn't?'

'You're a good daughter, Bridget. Don't worry about me, I can handle myself. You stay focused on your job in Barcelona.'

'*Dad!*' My voice was grainy with panic. 'Don't hang up! In Mum's study there are statements from Nasda Holdings. Richie Corrigan was involved and –'

'Bridget, you can't tell me any of this. And if what you say is correct, they'll subpoena my phone records and this call will show up. From an unregistered number.'

I was an idiot. 'Sorry, Dad.'

'It's all right, *alanna*. Listen to me, your mother and I haven't done anything and I'll prove it. You're the one I'm worried about. For God's sake, stay safe.'

He sounded strong.

'Dad, I love you.'

'Are you all right, Bridget?'

'I'm fine, Dad. Honestly.'

'Stay that way.'

Chapter 48

A tenuous plan spun in my mind with a single tenet, get Flannery away from Fuentes and the Mossos. My best idea was to find him, intervene and trust some of the Mossos were real police and would back me up.

It was no plan.

The burner rang again and Joe's number flashed on the boxy screen. I didn't answer, knew I wouldn't be able to tell him I'd no design other than to forge ahead.

Grabbing my black windcheater, I took the stairs instead of the creaking lift. The base of the courtyard was busy and I was going for the lone holidaymaker on a guided tour look, complete with padded windcheater, hop-on-hop-off bus map and fanny pack, but I had my running shoes on. Ramon said I was being watched – problem was I didn't know who was tracking me. I prayed the Mossos were as broke as An Garda Síochána and overtime was an issue.

I took the metro to Jaume, wandering in and around the wider avenues of Via Laietena, and had a *café con leche* in Heaven, a tourist haven with hundreds of reviews on TripAdvisor. It was bustling with self-importance and confusing coffee recipes, a place to be seen, and many of the customers were queuing for selfies with the baristas as much as the matcha coffee. The noise level was similar to a jabbering aviary. No one noticed me heading for the toilets. I ditched my jeans and windcheater and took my running gear out of the fanny pack, leaving with the help of a bathroom window onto the street behind the café.

I jogged away, heading for Carrer del Marquis de Barbera.

A stiletto knife of grey street.

I waited behind a corner and watched for someone to come out of the building where Seán Flannery was captive. Excitement had mixed with fear, coiled itself too tight around my gut and snapped. I had no way back to Matthew and the children other than to tell them I had apprehended Kay's killer. I owed Lorraine Quigley, whose life Seán Flannery had horribly snuffed out, and countless others. All those innocent lives stacked against mine – it wasn't such a sacrifice. I put my father's face from my mind. He would survive. It's what he did. The main door of the building opposite where Flannery was being held opened and disgorged a young family with their mother. I held the door for her as she backed out with a buggy, shouting '*No te separes!*' at her children and pulling them close.

'*Gracias.*'

'*De nada.*' I'd learned something from the Duolingo app I'd downloaded.

Inside, the foyer smelled of garlic and bike oil. I took the stairs to the second floor. While the stairwell was dark, the landing was bright from a frosted window that faced the street. It was open and the building needed air if the

271

foyer was anything to go by. From the shadows I chanced a look out to Flannery's building. Two men were smoking handrolled cigarettes on a second-floor balcony, the ember ends glowing and their cruel faces thrown into sharp relief by each drag. The smell of burnt rubber swayed in the tepid morning air.

A man I recognised from the CCTV footage exited the main door of Flannery's building. He had a machete strapped to his leg. Despite his swagger, he looked furtive and walked towards the other end of the alley with quick, backward glances.

I ran to the third floor and skittered to the ground. The landing window had been jammed fully open with a bar. It was nine thirty. According to Ramon, this area housed most of the low-paid workers in Barcelona, which might account for the stillness of the building. I crawled over to the open landing window and lifted my head slightly up, not wanting to catch the eyes of the men on the balcony below. One was slouching on the railing. The other turned towards him in a fluid movement, the deep notes of their laughter reverberating in the close space, a church choir. My eye was drawn into the interior of the apartment and three men bunched on the floor in a kneeling tripod.

Seán Flannery's outline was so familiar it didn't matter his face was turned away. The men were bare-chested and Flannery's network of white weal scars grizzled against the pale of his skin.

It happened fast.

Chapter 49

Machete Man came shouting down the alleyway. He pumped his legs and roared. I couldn't understand his words, but the guttural urgency of his tone was plain. The men standing on the balcony laughed, one gave a gaseous snort. It was an unusual reaction, unless they were stoned.

A minute later Machete Man barged in the apartment door where Flannery was being held, shouting, and kicked out at the group of kneeling men. Flannery was hauled up, his eyes shiny and hard, a shark's face. He gave nothing away, fear or calm. Machete Man brandished his blade and swung it at Flannery, close enough so he'd feel the air split in front of him.

The captors shouted and shoved one another. Flannery stood, immobile, while the other two prisoners cowered. The bar holding the window open was rough against my palm as I pulled it out and took it with me as I raced down the stairs. No one was visible but doors clicked shut behind me. Of course I had been followed, one against many, in spite of my paltry subterfuge. I had no element of surprise, but I could be unpredictable. Psychotic.

They hauled Flannery and the others through the

building's front door and six pairs of eyes greeted me as I lunged towards them. Flannery didn't need an invitation to any fight. He took Machete Man. High Boy pulled a gun gangsta-style, on its side with his forefinger flat against the barrel. His movements were theatrical and gave me time. I fell to the ground and took his legs out from under him. Then popped up jack-in-the-box style and hit him with the window bar, kicked him in the face on his way down, his doped eyes never registering what happened. Commotion on the balcony above us as the other men ran at the remaining guard. Flannery bent over a slumped Machete Man, searched his pockets and pulled out the handcuff keys. Sirens split the air behind us.

'*Seán Flannery, don't take those handcuffs off! I'm arresting you on suspicion of the murder of Kay Shanahan and Lorraine Quigley –*'

'Now?'

'Yes, now.' I pulled the chain between the handcuffs. He was barefoot and his feet were in shreds. We made for the end of alleyway in an awkward pantomime-horse formation.

'*You are not obliged to say anything – unless you wish to do so – but whatever you say will be taken down in writing – and may be given in evidence!*' My words came out in gasping heaps and fell between our fleeing feet.

'*There's no time, Bridge. They're coming for us! Can't you hear them? The Mossos!*' Panic made him shout, but he was fast and kept pace with my long strides.

We were making good ground.

'*Tell me you have a plan or they'll shoot both of us!*' he said.

I didn't have a plan.

'We need to get out onto Via Laietana,' I said. 'It's a

main thoroughfare. The Mossos can't corner us there. There'll be too many people. Tourist bus will be passing by in five minutes.'

'That's it?'

'It's all I've got, Seán Flannery!'

We ran, puffing, up the alleyway.

'Up there,' he said. He jutted his chin towards an open first-floor balcony window. 'That balcony. We have to go through a building – the Fuentes Mossos will be at either end of this lane.'

Much as it galled me, he had a point. He made a stirrup of his hands.

Cars screeched in the distance, blue-and-red lights blistered the alleyway.

Yet I paused.

'*Come on! They'll start coming down the lane!*' he said.

Against all my instincts I put my foot in Seán Flannery's hands and he boosted me up. I got onto the balcony and pulled him up after me. We raced through an apartment full of circular-shaped mouths and out their front door. From one building into a basement café of another. Up through their back stairs and out through a family apartment. To a soundtrack of shock and what I took for expletives. People reaching for phones to dial 112. This time we went from one balcony to the next door one, jumping the meagre distance in a panicky scrabble.

The plaster crumbled under my sweaty hands. Flannery kicked in the balcony window. The frame was swollen and burst with his first kick. We flung ourselves inside. The place was furry with decay, and empty. We were on the fifth floor and my lungs burned with hot holes. My body shook with adrenaline overload, but no one was following us.

'This isn't good,' I said. 'It's too quiet. They're clearing the area –'

A clean *crack* tore the air around me. Plaster puffed in a cloud inches to my left. A deep hole, big as a five-cent piece in the wall.

'Snipers,' said Flannery. 'They'll be looking for a clean kill and no witnesses.'

We shrank further into the darkness of the apartment.

'If we can get out the back of this apartment, it should bring us onto Nou de la Rambla, it's close enough to Palau Guell. The Mossos can't shoot us there, it will bring too much attention,' I said.

An acrid, vinegar smell found us. Flannery looked at me.

'Tear gas. They want to get rid of bystanders with their camera phones. The Mossos will say they're trying to get us out of the building.'

We were on the run again.

Down through the building, into the basement and out the caretaker's back door, but it wasn't onto Nou de la Rambla. The street was too small. We were lost.

The Mossos had made a perimeter and were banging out tear-gas canisters the way a vending machine pops out Sprite cans. Gas rose in a laneway near us.

'The buildings will give us some protection and it takes the tear gas a couple of minutes to get hold of you,' I said.

I held my badge out and blocked Flannery's body, preparing to make a run for it.

He pulled me back.

'You can't get shot for me – let me go in front, Bridge.'

An odd shiver went down my back at the way he said my name.

The Mossos had stopped shooting tear gas and turned off their sirens. Coming in for the kill.

'I'm not saving you, Flannery, I'm making sure you come home to face murder charges for Kay, Lorraine and fuck knows who else you've killed.'

'Don't swear, Bridge, you let yourself down and you let me down.'

His words echoed around me. They were sacred to him, a catechism taken from childhood and in the eerie quiet they triggered a shadowy memory.

'I never killed Kay, Bridge.'

The shape of the words left his mouth and hung over his head in silty speech bubbles.

'They will shoot me, no matter what, if they have to shoot through you to get to me, they will. You need to go.'

He stepped away from me.

'*No!*' It was a hissed shriek. 'They don't know we're here yet – we have about a minute to get to the end of this laneway. There has to be a main street near here. More people somewhere!'

'Look around you, Bridge. There's no one here. They've scarpered or are indoors. *Go!*'

He turned as if to run back to the Mossos. I grabbed the chain.

'You're handcuffed and I'm a police officer. *You will not be shot!*' I pulled him around. 'Follow me! You're not going to be gunned down in an alleyway. It's too good for you, Seán Flannery.'

'But it's not good enough for my sister.'

Chapter 50

I pivoted towards him.

There was a kind of relief on his face.

'There are two kinds of blood, Bridge. The kind you're born with and the kind you're born into. I was born into your blood. Your mother is my mother. I'm the child she left at the Mother and Baby Home.'

A burning rag scorched through my mind, charring everything I knew about my family.

Did I jerk? Did I deliberately move?

Crack!

Flannery fell, the lower part of his left leg all but torn off. They were using hollow-point bullets that expanded on impact. I dragged Flannery back into the building. A mop trail of blood followed us.

'Bridge . . . leave me . . . they'll kill you . . . if you're here with me.'

'*No!*' I screamed, trying to staunch the blood flow. It was impossible. My hands were red to the wrist.

'Go out the front of the building! Leave me here. They don't want you.'

I was sobbing. Yet the rational part of my brain was still

working. He was a monster, but not even a monster deserved to die this way. I tried to marshal the reserves of hate I had nurtured for Seán Flannery since the moment I had met him. Nothing, other than a cold fatigue.

'This isn't right. You have to be brought home – if we get medical help we can save you.'

We sank down into the emergency exit of the building, holed up in the shadows. I put my head out and saw one of the Mossos d'Esquadra, his tags obscured and face unidentifiable with his red-and-navy beret pulled low and sunglasses covering his eyes. His gait casual, a man on a coffee break. He'd kill us both.

'I never learned to swim, why was that?' said Seán.

His leg was the texture of a soggy woollen blanket.

'I don't know, Seán. I don't know why you never learned to swim.'

'And me a sailor.'

Pain had locked his eyes away – he looked at me through frosted glass.

'Can we call O'Connor? Or do you have a tout in the Mossos?' I wrestled with my burner phone, my chest on fire from the gas.

Flannery wheezed out a laugh. 'Here? I never had an informer in the police except Joe –'

His body leaped in my arms as a bullet fired from a long-range weapon hit him in the stomach.

'*Noo!*'

There was no spurting or dramatic exit wounds.

Specks of blood sparked when he drew breath, the sound of a fire trying to catch. His body lying across me, with life seeping away.

'Guy is Richie,' said Seán.

Logic was leaving him, pathogens and toxins had breached his blood-brain barrier. He was raving.

Seán Flannery searched my face, looking for some understanding or traces of his mother. I never knew which.

Chapter 51

The stillness surprised him.

A webbed brightness in the foamy grey clouds,

Pinpricked with blue and red fairy lights.

His sister to one side, her beautiful face contorted into lines and circles, but even that softened.

Sister Assumpta, her country girl's laugh, loud and firm.

The days on Bullock Harbour.

A flaked white tender, a skillet for cooking fish after landing a catch.

Joe.

Waving from the granite harbour, the hopeful cries of seagulls overhead and endless sky racing the dark sea.

Seán sat in the boat and spent he didn't know how many hours looking at the horizon.

Chapter 52

Three hundred short yards separated me and the first Mossos shooter. Not enough. I eased myself out from under Seán Flannery's dead body. My badge had fallen as we dived for cover. I grabbed it and made the conscious decision to look right into the guy's face. Then I ran. Let him and his sniper pal on the balcony explain to An Garda Síochána why I was shot in the back fleeing brother officers.

A downpour had drenched the city and left it bad-tempered. People ran for shop doorways and back into their offices.

I ran too.

Doubling back on myself, using random zigzag patterns until I was lost. All the while looking for people making eye contact in the rain, or a hat where there was none before, a pair of glasses trying to mislead me. Anyone with a gun needed seconds, no more, to snuff out a life.

I took an FC Barcelona peaked cap from a shop display. Small black birds twittered on balconies, tattle-tattling my location to an unseen foe. My mind folded and knotted over the last minutes, longing to blot out what it had seen. I hummed a song about morning breaking from my childhood in an effort to keep everything live and in place. My burner phone rang.

'*Ramon?*'

'Bridge! Are you OK?'

'*No!*' My voice was charged and the word stung as it came out.

'It's all over the news. TVE and Sky have reporters at the cordons around Carrer Marquis del Berbera. They're are saying the body of a male has been recovered. Is it Flannery?'

'Yes, it's him.'

A fog of numbness had descended. It wouldn't help me stay alive.

'Did you see who did it?'

'No.'

'OK, any witnesses?'

'None I could see.'

'*Val-eh.*'

The word drawled out of his mouth, but he didn't sound OK with it and I had a sinking sensation Ramon was of no use to me now.

'Do you want to meet me? Do you need me to contact your people?'

I needed time and some space. 'No and no. Mossos were outside the plaza, they chased us into an alley and shooters came at us from an upstairs balcony. I'm done.'

'*Suerte,*' he said.

I would need some of the luck he was wishing me. I hung up on Ramon, appalled at my own rudeness but wanting to be gone. I'd let the embassy make arrangements for getting Flannery home.

I made my way back to Plaza del Pi.

I landed on the bed in the apartment and took off the hat, turning my head to the side. My eyes stung from the gas and tears leaked down my face, pooling on the polyester bedspread. I made no sound, didn't know who I was crying for and had no idea what to do next.

'Liam?' My voice sounded faint, travelling miles through the dead air in the apartment to get down the phone.

'*Jesus! Fuck!* I had no idea where you were – are you all right? What the hell happened with Flannery? It's all over the bloody news! Joe's shitting himself with worry over you! We all are – thank God you're OK!'

Liam's words were running into one another and his tone was harsh, but it sounded soothing as a waterfall.

'I'm OK. I'm OK.'

'Bridge, what happened? Have you have checked in with anyone? O'Driscoll in the embassy doesn't know what's going on, the Spanish police said you never reported into their Headquarters. We're relying on Sky News. Said a shooting between police and a known Irish criminal happened today at Carrer Marquis del Berbera. Like where the fuck is that?'

The expletives were pouring out of him as his mind fell into a ravine.

'Calm, Liam. I'm OK. I need to get out of here.'

'Can I help?'

'Yes, please.' Lumps of gratitude, big as hailstones, hit me. 'Can you book me a flight on Ryanair out of Girona, please? I'm not flying out of Barcelona on Aer Lingus. Could you book it in your sister's name and I'll show my badge to the Ryanair officials. They'll let me on. I don't want any record of my name on flight databases.'

'Jesus, what's going on?'

'The Mossos are the ones who chased Flannery and me. More of them went into buildings and set up sniper positions. If Flannery hadn't forced me up onto the balcony of one of the buildings, I'd be dead.'

There was a black silence on the end of the phone.

'The Spanish police are after you?'

It sounded absurd coming from such a stolid person.

'No, corrupt cartel cops, they're the ones who shot Flannery.'

Deep breath.

'They're not chasing me in earnest, but if they happened on me who knows? I'm not going to walk into Mossos Central with all the tourists on Nou de la Rambla and ask for a police escort to the airport. I'd be expected to take a direct flight from Barcelona – it's a small subterfuge but I'll take it.'

'Do they have your passport?'

'Yes. Will you start enquiries our end to get it back?'

'Of course.'

The bones in my ankles cracked as I rotated them, trying to free the tension binding my body.

'Seán Flannery thought he was my brother.'

I was weightless in the silence – untethered – stretching until I tore at the edges then came together again.

'Is that possible?' said Liam at last.

'My mother had a child before she married my father. It could've been him.'

'Jesus, I'm sorry, Bridge.'

I sat up and looked in the mirror.

My hand moved up to my hairline and scratched at some dry skin near the centre of my forehead. My fingers were rust-red with Flannery's blood, white lines on my knuckles. My running shirt stiff with the last of his life.

'Bridge?'

I wanted to tell Liam that Joe was Flannery's informer, but those words wouldn't form yet.

'Flannery told me he didn't kill Kay.'

Liam grunted. 'You believe him?'

'Yes. I have no evidence other than he was dying and didn't want to leave the world with deception on his lips.'

How to say Flannery had wanted something from me, wanted some of the love I had always received, had the awful human instinct to matter.

'He told me to go, leave him, that they'd shoot through me to get to him. The Mossos were using tear gas.'

'What for! Was there a riot?'

'They wanted to clear the area, stop bystanders filming.'

'Ah, Bridge . . .' His voice was shot through with worry.

My eyes were red-rimmed and bloodshot. 'He should've faced trial for his crimes at home. There's no justice in this. It's a dirty cover-up and no closure for anyone.'

'Bridge, this isn't on you. Anyone else would have left him.'

'How's my dad?' I needed to change the subject.

'He's fine, bearing up. O'Connor's doing the questioning. He's no match for your oul' lad. He has some high-price solicitor in with him – that dude will have your father out by 6pm. You'll be home by then. Yeah?'

'I don't want anyone treating my father like a criminal when I'm not around – he's to be treated with decorum.'

'Muldoon said to treat him like a sitting judge and call him Mr Justice Harney when referring to him.'

The idea of my father sitting in a musty interview room was an iron weight.

'You need anything else, Bridge?

'No, I'm good.'

I wasn't.

I wanted to tell Liam everything was churned up. The life inside me was no more than a conscience, fighting for its existence against my own sense of inadequacy. Flannery's cold-blooded murder, Joe being an informer and my father sitting in Harcourt Square, all revolving around and picking up speed.

I hung up and vomited down the side of the bed.

Chapter 53

Café Sol was horseshoed into the basement of a Georgian redbrick coach house near Harcourt Square. The sun was making a rare appearance and Joe Clarke waited for me on the flickering granite steps of the old house, holding two roast-bean Americanos. He stood up and handed me a coffee, black with an ice cube floating in it, the way I preferred. His sell-out was a filleting knife gutting me.

Flannery was dead, his involvement with the Fuentes cartel clear. I was to be lauded by my own force in exchange for silence on Flannery's police killers, a bartering of sorts that sat like orange coals.

'You got back OK?' said Joe.

'Yes,' I said.

'It wasn't your fault, Bridge, the way Flannery died,' he said.

He must have misinterpreted the look on my face.

We parked our backsides on the cold steps and the sun did a vanishing act.

I said nothing.

'Wicklow granite, from the 1850s,' he said, 'those steps. They hewed it by hand, the workers on Lord Wicklow's estate in Enniskerry. Read about it when I went to visit the gardens one year. These steps have seen more trouble and blood than you or I ever will.'

'Stop trying to make me feel better.'

My words slapped his down, recent events bundled up inside me, knotted sheets in a dryer. I was wrung out, my interest pinned on why Joe would have passed information to Flannery.

Joe gave a hacking cough that spoke of bronchitis.

'How's your dad faring?'

'Good.' I moved around on the hard bones of my backside, unsure of Joe's change of subject but deciding to match him. 'How're things at home with your family?'

'Wife is still in Spain costing me a bloody fortune and the girls are in Trinity.' He nodded towards the Green and my alma mater. 'Living it large in Dublin, pretending to study and putting their hands in my pockets every chance they get.'

From the mouth of babes.

'Please, not money.' It was a whisper, unheard by Joe as he lounged on the steps.

A formless pain rose inside me and I wanted to tear my clothes from my body screaming but gagged it all down. Instead street noises filled the silence, passers-by, traffic, grey street-water sluicing into a gutter.

Joe gave my knee a rough squeeze. 'You blame yourself for Flannery dying. From what O'Driscoll said you were lucky to get out. You might've stayed too long with Flannery.'

'He told me to go. Told me they'd shoot him through me.'

Joe took a swig of coffee and turned his face up to the sky.

'Then it was the best thing he ever did in his life. I'm

289

glad he had that in him, after all the damage he's done.'

Tears were lodged in my nose and leaked out. I took cold breaths into my stuffed head.

Joe fumbled in his pocket, pulling out a clean cotton square and I put it to my face.

'You know if you were ever in trouble you could tell me,' I said.

'Me?' said Joe. 'God, Bridge, you're the one we're all worried about! Did Flannery say anything to you when he was dying?'

His eyes were full of sympathy but a horrible eagerness lurked around his face. It helped me get some distance.

'He thought he was my brother.' The taste of rot from those tainted words.

'*What!*' Joe's eyes darted around my face looking for something. 'Why would he think that? Was he deranged? Did the fellahs who caught him have him on drugs?'

'Flannery said it to me when we were holed up in the alleyway. A gunman shot him from one of the balconies.'

Soft rain started to fall.

'Christ, what a situation to be in. Are you going to get it checked out?'

'Yes, I've asked a friend in Forensic Science Ireland to compare our DNA.'

'Hope it's someone you can trust? You don't want the world and his wife to know the last thing Flannery did was play you.'

I said nothing, but his responses puzzled me.

'Wait and see, Bridge – he was lying.'

'He believed it.'

Joe dipped his head as if deep in thought. 'What else did he say?'

His hands had navy veins twisted under spotted skin, and I still expected him to ask the obvious question.

'Not much else.'

'Nothing?' said Joe.

'Just about my mother being his mother. I think . . . I feel it must be the truth.'

'Now you're not making sense.'

Joe's patronising tone took me by surprise, although I don't know why – even a canary will peck when its cornered.

He put the coffee down and brushed droplets off his shoulders. 'You're feeling sorry for yourself and believing the words of a man who couldn't tell the truth if his life depended on it.'

'*You weren't fucking there!*'

'Bridget, don't swear. You let yourself down and you let others around you down.'

The street, the noises of traffic, even the rain stopped.

'Say that again, please?'

'What?' Joe cocked an eyebrow at me, a small smile on his face. 'You've heard me say that before – my old mam used to say to us. Me and the sister.'

'Joe, did you know Seán Flannery when he was a child?'

The desire for Joe to confess cleaved at my insides, my fingers interlaced of their own accord.

He gave me a quizzical look. 'What? Like socially?' He snorted at the absurdity of my question.

'Did you?'

'Are you serious, Bridge? Dear God in Heaven, of course I didn't know Seán Flannery! Wouldn't I have declared a conflict years ago when he first came to our notice?'

I was in a fairground hall of mirrors. Joe's lies were reflections distorted and expanding, laughing at me.

'Are you alright, Bridge? You're as white as a sheet.'

'I'm fine, Joe.' I stood up as though basking in the sun. My left leg shook, jiggered with adrenaline. 'Leg's gone to sleep,' I said, over-explaining.

'Come on, we'll go back inside. Do you want your coffee?'

'No, I'm fine thanks, Joe.'

I forced myself to walk back to the Square beside the man who'd been Seán Flannery's informer, who'd hobbled me at every turn.

At the entrance he turned to me.

'You know, I don't feel so well. I might head home. Take the rest of the day off,' he said.

Chapter 54

I darted forward, with feet falling over one another, my body a fraction behind my will and stumbling to keep up. If I stopped I wouldn't go into Muldoon's office. I'd run home and hide under my bed sobbing.

'Bridge?' It was Liam O'Shea, his face bent out of shape with concern for me.

I handed him off. To explain, to stop, to do anything other than get to the sixth floor would be fatal, for whom I was unsure.

Detective Chief Superintendent Graham Muldoon's door was shut. Glimpses of him flashed through the sidelights of his door.

His secretary stood, observed my rocking and said nothing. She walked over to the closed door, giving three sharp raps. *Tat-tat-tat.*

'Detective Garda Harney for you, Graham.'

Not a man for small talk, he took his seat and told me to stay standing. It suited, my body was receiving too many electrical pulses. His window was open and my mind fixated on the frustrated drivers grinding gears up and down in the looping traffic.

'Bridget?'

I heard but didn't respond.

'Detective Garda Harney?'

'Yes, Chief Super. Sorry, I lost my way there a bit.'

'You have something to say to me?'

My head swung around to check the door. It was locked. I crossed over to the brown metal window frame and brought it down with a screech.

DCS Muldoon was visibly losing patience with my odd behaviour.

I walked back to face him.

'I have reason to believe Sergeant Joe Clarke was Seán Flannery's informer.'

Muldoon's stillness was stark. A compression on one side of his mouth the single clue to his inner thoughts. A rhythm rose off him in waves, matched in some way by a tone inside me. A diving bell filled with a bubble of air waiting for the hammer knock.

'What do you have?' he said.

'Flannery told me. Just before he was shot in the chest. Said the only informer he ever had was Joe.'

Muldoon's face was a mask, but there was an echo behind his eyes, so I plumbed its depths.

'Flannery was always in front. We never surprised him, back as far as 2018 when we picked up Lorraine Quigley and baby Marie, he knew we were coming. Had the Gardens cleared and was standing awaiting our pleasure.' I searched Muldoon's face. 'The drugs seizure in Kilkenny was a joke, he knew we were coming and ditched the stuff in a service station. The shipment was tracked by MAOC, which means Flannery had an informer at senior level with access.'

Muldoon's silence was wrapped in restrained fury.

I ploughed on. 'Lorraine Quigley, at one of our last meetings, told me Seán had an informer.'

Muldoon stood up from behind his desk, walked to his window, the fingers of his right hand splayed and clenched.

'You can't trust someone who's bargaining for her child's life,' he said.

'I agree, but her information isn't taken in isolation.' I took a punt. 'You have doubts about Joe, too.'

He turned to face me. An eternity of moments rolled through his office as neither of us spoke.

Muldoon's eyes strayed off to some inner place. 'Yes.'

I was biting the inside of my cheek, the blood on my breath a tell-tale.

'I believe he has money troubles,' I said.

Again the pulse from Muldoon.

'His wife is in Spain most of the year and his daughters are in college. He sold the family home a few years back and not by choice.'

DCS Muldoon rubbed a hand through his hair and the bristles bounced back. 'There'll be no way to keep Joe off the NBCI radar.'

The National Bureau of Criminal Investigation's brief covered anything from anti-racketeering to murder to postal theft and wedged in a subsection of a subsection, was 'review of all major crimes'. They were internal affairs and called their reporting structure fluid, which meant they could tell any ranking officer outside their own department to jog on. They weren't a popular bunch and no one outside their department knew how their accountability worked. The Commissioner had taken a real interest in what they did – it stood to reason with the amount of money the criminal gangs threw about– and was in the process of upgrading them to Anti-Corruption. This didn't bode well for Joe.

'Flannery was a monster,' I said. A flip book of Seán Flannery's broken body and pale fingers attempting to stem his own blood played for me.

'He had no human feeling as an adult, but children don't start out that way,' said DCS Muldoon. His eyes moved to the picture on his desk of two boys, his mirror-image sons. 'If Joe profited from Flannery's empire he'll answer for it.'

His voice was hard as oak and as knotted. His thumb flicked against his bent index finger, ticking off options.

'You'll take O'Connor.'

A loaded gun to a stick fight. My skin stretched and tightened in response to the danger. 'Please, DCS Muldoon, O'Connor isn't the man for this.'

'He *is* the man for this. Don't think for a second that you got away with planting evidence. You were so desperate to convict Seán Flannery of Emer Davidson's murder you framed him, then Joe convinced Chris Watkiss to destroy that evidence for you. When Joe came back to Dublin, I asked him if he'd any skeletons that could haunt me. I know what you owe Joe and what you'd do to protect him.'

There was steel in DCS Muldoon, but I hadn't known how well he'd use it.

'Sir.'

Muldoon eyed me. 'I'll brief O'Connor.'

He turned his back to me in dismissal and I slunk out.

Chapter 55

D16 E991

Joe's Eircode. It wasn't what I had expected, a block of bleak rendered apartments with chunky rough redbrick balconies.

I swung around a small car park, with nowhere near enough car spaces. I drove, of course, and Detective Superintendent Niall O'Connor sat in the back lest there was any confusion in our demarcation.

'Put it anywhere, Harney. We won't be here long.'

DS O'Connor wasn't wasting any pleasantries on me. Wearing a boxy overcoat cloaking his rank, he should have looked ridiculous, trussed up in the back of an unmarked Avensis with his perma-tan and comb-over – but he looked vigorous. A dog who had tasted blood and knew more was coming. It made me queasy. DS O'Connor knew how to shape a person's fear – his high conviction rates spoke of how successful he was at breaking a person. DCS Muldoon knew this, yet here we were.

Joe buzzed us in. The foyer had a transient air, painted in bright colours with an empty bike rack and the smell of new carpet, complete with scuff marks on the steps. It was more hostel than home, full of people at the start of their lives, not wanting much privacy, enjoying long hours of purpose and fun, bursting with smugness. Joe was invisible here.

Students came down the stairs as we made our way up to the fifth floor and Apartment 14. Detective Superintendent O'Connor had said little or nothing to me on our drive over.

'Get up the stairs, Harney.'

There was no 'Detective Garda' from him.

'Yes, sir.' I resisted the suicidal urge to call him 'Ma'am'.

'Don't use your upper-crust voice with me, Harney. And it's Detective Superintendent to you and don't bother to shorten it to Super – we're not on good terms. And you'll stand outside.'

'With respect, Detective Superintendent O'Connor, it would be advisable to have another garda present, to corroborate statements and assure witness safety.'

To my relief I sounded relaxed, even strong. Self-doubt, my abrasive friend, lurked around me but was undetectable by DS O'Connor. Any of that flammable anger I lit off two stones in my twenties was gone. Joe had stymied our operations, but it didn't help ignite any fire. I was bringing an executioner to a friend's home, not repaying the exit he once marked for me. My thoughts must have played out on my face and DS O'Connor granted me a rare smile, or a rattlesnake bite.

'You're worried about the witness? You've an idea about what went on when up the North, do you? Of course your old man was perched up in the Special Criminal Court, hiding behind layers of protection and worried about the human rights of terrorists. The rest of us didn't have that luxury.'

Bolstered by the silence, he frogmarched me on.

'Mind you, things have changed.' He had the temerity to laugh. 'Your oul' fellah was so high and mighty on his wooden bench with his stiff neck, but he turned out to be bent. We'll see how he gets on with the lads in NBCI. They'll have the measure of him in no time. You know, if it'd been me, I'd have you suspended, but Muldoon is soft on a pretty face.'

If I didn't give it to him over my father, I wasn't going to be baited by crude chauvinism. I held my tongue – and had a moment of disassociated pride, or the ghost of a smile from Kay. I needed O'Connor to be in as good a mood as possible – one word and I could be denied access to his interview with Joe.

We reached Joe's landing. He stood in the doorway of Apartment 14. He wore an open-neck shirt and slippers moved his weight from foot to foot as he stood in the doorway.

'To what do I owe this pleasure?' said Joe.

'Get inside, Clarke,' said O'Connor, abandoning all pretence of fairness before he was even through Joe's door.

We went inside.

Joe was grey and smelled of mucus – the whole apartment was a shrine to eucalyptus and the flu. It invaded my nostrils and glanced off the back of my throat. O'Connor coughed, looking overpowered by the menthol.

There was a brief pause.

'I am arresting you under the Criminal Justice –' said O'Connor.

'*No! Sir!*' I said.

'Corrupt Offences Act 2018 –'

'*Detective Super –*'

'Section 7 Subsection 2 –'

'*We need to discuss –*'

'You are not obliged to say anything unless you wish to do so, but whatever you say will be taken down in writing and may be given in evidence. Is that clear, Joe?'

Hit by a bomb, Joe was dazed.

'Interrupt me again, Harney,' said DS O'Connor.

For an instant I misunderstood, opening my mouth to ask a questions, but he leaned in and Newton's-cradle-shunted me away.

He looked at Joe. 'I don't want to cuff you. Insult to both of us, so put on your shoes there's a good man and we'll go back to the station.'

Joe said nothing as I got his coat and he changed into a pair of slip-ons straight out of an eighties music video, with built-up heels and distressed leather. He squeezed my hand as O'Connor led him out of his house. His bowed shoulders beside an upright, exultant O'Connor was painful to witness.

PART 3

Wash yourself of yourself
-Rumi

Chapter 56

Amina stood in an airless Terminal 1 in Dublin Airport.

Something had gone wrong and potential passengers milled around somewhere in the middle ground between frustration and clear rage. Airport staff tried to look nonchalant, with limited success.

Amina's headscarf was neat and pinned to the side of her face, stiff and formal. A meet-and-greet committee of one. Falling into step beside me, she rattled off our itinerary as we walked towards Departures.

'I heard about Joe – are you OK, Bridge?' said Amina.

'No.'

I had a low buzz of anxiety from a bad night's sleep.

'Is he OK? Are you OK, Bridge? Can we talk about it or not?'

'Sorry, Amina. I don't have any information about Joe, I'm not in Muldoon's confidence. Sorry.'

She gave my arm a light squeeze. 'Why don't we walk by Butlers and get a coffee? Our gate is 107, our flight to Birmingham is at 6.35. I have our boarding passes all printed out, both ways because it's a one-day trip. I brought a salad box each as the food on the flight is either too cold or plastic-tasting. We can go straight through security – I rang ahead and told them we were coming, so we'll be treated as airport staff. We land in Birmingham at 7.35 and Chris will meet us outside the Departures hall.'

She rattled off this brisk information and we took a side gate, bypassing security and screening. I showed my badge to the airport policeman and we nodded at one another, nothing more.

Amina's fussy generosity was soothing and, as per her itinerary, we were making our way out from Arrivals in Birmingham International Airport to the Departure set-down car parking by 7.45.

Chris stood waiting beside his Alfa Romeo 156 like they were on a date.

'Hullo, ladies! Let's get you in and we can start the niceties,' he said.

His whole body was smiling. He rubbed chapped hands together against the early December cold and opened the door for Amina when she couldn't work out where the handle was.

We got onto the Ring Road to Holloway Circus quickly. The city centre wasn't as tidy as I'd expected. Hotels had been finished and much of the hoarding was gone, but a confusing collection of diversions meant I didn't know where we were. The city shone with Christmas decorations, reminding me of the presents I had stashed for Matthew's children in a spare room.

'Curry leaves?' said Amina. We inhaled the spicy green smell living in Chris's car.

'Gamthi curry leaves, lemony. Wife uses them in everything, including me. Makes the best butter chicken this side of the River Rea – reckon it's why I've a bit wood on me unfortunately.'

'Not at all!' said Amina. 'A little weight looks good on a man –' She stopped, two pink spots on her cheeks.

'On a man my age!' said Chris. He chuckled, a deep rumbling bass. 'Reckon you're right – wife seems to think so.'

There was comfort in Chris's stolid presence. His accusations of me not doing enough on the Burgess Data Centre case and Amina doing too much unauthorised had lost much of its heat after my trip to Barcelona and subsequent events. Chris and I would have to have words, but I'd had about as much discord as I could take.

Chris palmed the steering wheel with his right hand and squeezed my arm with his left.

'Sorry to hear about your dad, little 'un.'

'He was questioned and has no case to answer. Nothing to back up their claims. If there was any doubt I'd have been suspended.'

My voice was tight with emotion.

'Aye, you've had a time of it since we last met. I'm sorry you had to go through it on your own, Bridge.'

The kindness in his voice undid me and easy tears swam up. I couldn't blame it on pregnancy, but my bladder had moved to my eyes.

Chris kept the chat flowing.

'Ruddy Queens Parkway, digging the crap out the city again – honestly the council are experimenting on us. It's Crystal Maze around here.'

'The decorations are lovely though,' said Amina. Her voice was wistful.

The decorations were festive, but Christmas with my

mother in a nursing home tasted like burnt feathers.

Amina was already searching through her carry-on case, a sturdy affair propped up on the car seat beside her, laden with sheets of printouts, ancient yellow forms and the brilliant white of paper taken off a fresh ream.

'I have all the documentation we discussed here, Chris,' said Amina.

'We'll hold it, Amina, till we're at Circus if you don't mind. You've done an amazing job. Be handy to take me through it same as Bridge, from the top.'

'Thank you,' said Amina. She shone new-penny-style at Chris's praise.

My phone gave a piqued bleep, irritated it was in my back pocket being sat on. The message on the lock screen threw my head back for a deep inhalation.

I've tested yours and Seán Flannery's DNA. No match. No familial connection.

Chapter 57

'You've perked up no end,' said Chris.

I put the phone back in my pocket. 'Some good news. More than good.'

'Right, we're here!' said Chris.

The Circus was as I remembered, an edifice of grey concrete made less dusty for a recent shower of rain.

We ran inside, over the greasy-looking tarmac, and Chris signed everyone in. We followed him up the stairs.

'I've a meeting room on fourth floor – it's quiet enough and we'll not be disturbed.'

We grabbed mugs of black, prison-grade tea with bobbing sugar cubes from a self-service drinks station inside the door.

'You could trot a mouse across it, but it's wet and warm,' said Chris.

We sat down to work in a meeting room, the size of a walk-in wardrobe and redolent of armpits.

'First off, I owe you both an apology,' said Chris.

His face was brick-red.

'Couple of weeks ago I threw you rightly under the bus.'

Steam from our polystyrene cups curled into the silent air.

'I'm not proud of it. Maitland's been sat on me about Burgess and the Data Centre. Our Deputy Chief Constable was on Maitland's back. She were giving him heat about missing a narcotics ring supplying the Midlands and beyond. So Maitland were passing it all down to me. And not giving me the resources to investigate it. I believed it were constructive dismissal and reported him to our Deputy Chief, told her Maitland were using DS O'Connor to put pressure on you about the Emer Davidson case. Maitland has form for this kind of thing, so there'll be wigs on the green for those boys.'

He smacked the desk in triumph, thinking he was giving me O'Connor on a plate.

I gave him a frayed smile, unable to go into Joe's treachery and unwilling to relive his arrest.

'Right, we'll move on,' said Chris, perplexed. 'Amina, there's no overhead so you'll have to use your laptop.'

She was organised and handed each of us a pack in a blue folder. Much of this work was a result of the court orders Joe had fast-tracked for me. The irony wasn't lost. I undid the elastic toggle with an awkward fumbling of fingers and it snapped.

'No matter, Bridge,' said Amina.

Her laptop was on, the first slide chock-a-block with black lines and boxes bisecting the harsh neon. A complex topology of banking transactions. We were going straight in.

'The documents in your packs are to back up my claims about Seán Flannery's drug business,' Amina said. 'There are gaps and I'll need your help. Do you want the abridged version or line by line?'

'Oh, abridged please,' said Chris.

Amina's downcast face was comical.

'This was decades in the making. Richie Corrigan incorporated two companies in the Cayman Islands during the 1970s, Nasda Holdings and Slowell Ltd. He moved undeclared money from the Ansbacher Cayman Bank to Dublin in 1997. Corrigan got it over to Munster Bank Isle of Man branch and away from the Irish Revenue Commissioners. Seán Flannery lodged it for him – it's his name on the docket – so I'm assuming Corrigan gave Flannery money for his trouble. And Flannery used it to start his drugs business.'

'How did Corrigan find Flannery in '97?' I said.

'Corrigan's involved with Slowell?' Chris said.

We were speaking over one another and too loud for the small room. A half thing stirred in my memory.

'You wanted the short version. You both have bits of the story – let me continue with the top-line summary. Then we'll try and piece together the detail,' said Amina. 'We'll take Slowell Ltd. first.'

Chris half stood then sat again, unable to stay quiet. 'Slowell Ltd. is only the logistics company Burgess Data Centre uses.'

'Mike Burgess is involved with Richie Corrigan?' I said. My neurons were firing, trying to remember if I'd ever seen Richie Corrigan and Mike Burgess in the same room. I was coming up short.

'We've been working on it for a bit now,' he said. 'I told you the financial controller in BDC contacted me back in October. Saying there were anomalies, costs out of sync and such. We matched the revenue to BDC's customers. It took some time, but Amina's great at figures.'

He took off his suit jacket and placed it on the back of his seat.

Amina's head bobbed in time with the words pouring out of her. 'None of the BDC records fit. They're overstating their revenue. Customers with domain names, which should cost thirty pounds or less are being invoiced for massive server configurations for tens of thousands of pounds, but these invoices are embedded among genuine invoices and held back. In fact, the sample customers I contacted were delighted with Burgess Data Centre sales and service. I can see how they got by the Inland Revenue – whoever advised BDC was an expert. All the Inland Revenue found was Declan Swan's embezzlement. Slowell Ltd. are at the centre of Burgess Data Centre's operation. They put in a water-based cooling system for BDC last year. Slowell Ltd. drive BDC's profits down by 70% or more every year. It's a legitimate business practice, many tech companies have European services centres generating administrative costs to reduce profits.'

'We know Burgess wasn't a dealer on a big scale,' said Chris, 'and this product is from Fuentes – found some of those markings you told me to look for, Bridge. Could be Burgess Data Centre were a holding depot for Fuentes? There's upwards of a hundred million pound going through BDC annually.'

'Cartel-size lolly,' I said.

'Aye. We reckon Richie's using BDC to launder Fuentes money,' said Chris.

'It's a perfect cover,' I said. 'It has a field crew for deliveries, a logistics company it can drain cash through and warehouses of space for drugs.'

'And whatever else the Fuentes cartel fancy bringing in,' said Chris.

My face darkened.

'Moving to Nasda Holdings,' said Amina. 'Given Flannery went from nought to sixty when he started his drugs business, it's fair to assume he had a backer. An angel investor.' Her cup was split down the middle, her fingers working piles of polystyrene snow in front of her.

'Why would he have needed to be bankrolled – lad like him, wouldn't he have stolen the money, Bridge?' said Chris.

I shook my head. 'He didn't have the skills in '97. He was eighteen. Gavin Devereux ended up in prison for having the guts of ten ounces of high-quality cocaine in his possession and trying to sell it near a Dublin bridge. I bet Flannery was there too but escaped.'

The scene built itself in my mind – Seán Flannery hiding by one of the granite walls lining the Liffey, making its way to the sea.

'I know how Flannery got the money to the Isle of Man for Corrigan,' I said.

'How? It was a cash deposit, so a rucksack of money,' said Amina.

'He sailed there. Flannery sailed from Dalkey to Newnham on Severn last year to get rid of Emer Davidson's body – that can't have been easy. The Isle of Man would be no challenge to him.'

Chris scrunched his eyes. 'When he were eighteen?'

'There's nothing on file as to when Flannery learned to sail, but I checked last year with the yacht club he crewed at. They said he was gifted and must have started sailing young. He was brought up in a State home run by the church, so maybe sailing was a way of escaping.'

The pen in Amina's hand froze mid-note-taking. The reality of Flannery's childhood hung between us, oppressive and colourless until it had burnt off all the oxygen in the room.

Chris pushed open the meeting-room door and outside air billowed in.

'So Richie gets Seán to sail over to the Isle of Man with a bag of money, to kick things off,' he said. 'Then they hit their stride, so Fuentes supply the drugs, Flannery sells 'em and Corrigan launders the money with the help of Burgess and BDC. How does Nasda Holdings fit in?'

Amina moved to her next slide and I closed the door – we needed privacy.

'Nasda Holdings were set up in 1971 with two directors, Richie Corrigan and Slowell Ltd. In 1982 Richie resigned as a director and was replaced by Mrs Elizabeth Harney,' said Amina.

'Your old mum is a director of Nasda Holdings, Bridge?' said Chris. He put his arms behind his head, revealing two damp circles.

I twiddled the aircon buttons and got a background fan going.

'Yes, Mum has bank statements for Nasda Holdings at home. Richie Corrigan worked for the banker who set up the original Ansbacher scheme. Corrigan and Mum corresponded.'

I tilted my head back to give a moment's respite before what came next, an airing of linen rotten from decades in the dark.

'Mum had a child before she met my father. She was seventeen and had a baby boy in Clarendon House, a Mother and Baby home. Richie Corrigan, although not the father, was her friend at the time. It goes a lot deeper on his side. He was twenty-one years older than her.'

'He were thirty-eight and hanging around a girl of seventeen? Man of that age came sniffing around my girls

I'd box his teeth in,' said Chris.

'I wish my mum had a dad like you, Chris, but she didn't. Her closest friend was a cousin in Canada.' My eyes found the compacted fibres of the carpet.

'Corrigan told you he'd been having an affair with your mum for decades. Told you in Harcourt Square when we was interviewing Seán Flannery about Emer Davidson's murder. I remember your face! You looked like you'd been run over by a getaway car.'

I smiled at Chris's apt description.

'Yes, I did. But it's not true. Corrigan was blackmailing my mother. I read her correspondence. She believed Richie had access to the child she gave up for adoption and the child's safety was dependent on her compliance with his wishes. Flannery said Richie's name when he was dying. His exact words were 'Guy is Richie'. I thought he was raving, but he was trying to tell me Corrigan was more to him than a solicitor. I believe Corrigan manipulated Flannery as well, told him my mum was his mother. Flannery told me he was my brother. However, there's no genetic material linking us.'

I shook my head and tried to push away the memory of what he'd said. His blood-filled breaths and belief in another kind of life.

Chris's mouth was agape.

'I'll find out what happened to your mother's baby, Bridge. If you want?' said Amina.

She was looking at me with eyes the size of dinner plates.

'How?' I said.

'I have high level Revenue clearance, access to any Irish state system I want – for example, I can get into Dublin corporations live traffic feed and search for cars if I have the registration number. TULSA – that's the children's agency, Chris – will be easy.'

'Sweet Jesus!' I said.

I couldn't tell what amazed me more, the thought of Amina tracking people down, or the utter lack of regulation on the Revenue's access into Irish citizen's lives. 'Have you been accessing systems without authority again, Amina?'

'No,' big grin, 'this is Ansbacher and I've lodged it under the investigation.'

At least it was legal.

'If you could try, Amina, I'd appreciate it.' My voice caught on the words. 'My mother's maiden name was Flannery. Elizabeth Flannery born July 2nd, 1962.'

There was a naked silence.

'It's a common name,' said Amina. She gave a brisk nod of her head. 'If there's any information on the system I'll find it.'

'You're a ghost!' said Chris. 'Wish I'd someone helping me with Her Majesty's Revenue. I can get f– little or no information out of them.'

'They don't have our history,' said Amina. She gave a weak smile. 'We've had so many corrupt politicians and bankers that Revenue get access to what we ask for. It's why Corrigan moved his money in such a rush. In 1997 the McCracken Tribunal found out about money hidden from the Revenue in the Ansbacher Bank in the Caymans. Munster Bank were up to their eyes in it as well – they gave me the information about Nasda Holding's account in Munster Bank Isle of Man. They're the biggest retail bank in Ireland and the state's a majority shareholder – the management in Munster Bank would prefer a bill from Revenue rather than a criminal conviction.'

'By heck,' said Chris.

'It's not our finest quality,' I said.

Chris moved around in his seat surreptitiously, scratching his back. He spoke again, his eyes full of questions.

'So Richie Corrigan had leverage over your mother and Seán Flannery? What did he get for it?'

'Money. I'd say with Mum it's more complicated.'

'Bridge, you'll need to stay calm for this.' Amina gave a series of taps on her scroll-down button. 'Your mother withdraws money from Nasda Holdings account every quarter. €200,000.'

I reached a hand out to my seat-back, unaware I was standing. My knees concertinaed of their own accord, a broken toy.

'Easy, lass,' said Chris.

'It's a bank draft, so I assume it's going to Richie Corrigan,' said Amina.

Chris was puce-faced. 'And it's a good assumption, but what if Bridge's mam and dad have numbered accounts somewhere we don't know about?'

Chapter 58

I admired Chris's drive for the truth, even though it was costing both of us.

'I've checked all available and not so available financial records on Bridge and her old pair,' said Amina.

'Excuse me?' I said.

Her hands were hummingbirds either side of her head.

'I had to.'

'It's OK, Amina.' She needed reassurance from me.

'There's nothing, Bridge – I mean your folks have a lot of money by ordinary standards, but your tax returns all check out, everything matches. You've no offshore accounts and nothing like the money a drug business generates. But your mam's signature is on all the withdrawal slips for Nasda Holdings. I think Muldoon got wind of this and that's why your dad was brought in for questioning. The last withdrawal slip was Friday 28th June 2019, but no withdrawal from the account for quarter end in September.'

Electricity streaked through the grey coils in my brain.

'Mum's getting worse and we moved her to a nursing home this year. In July. Richie doesn't have access to her, we

316

supervise the visits. And,' hard breath, 'I doubt Mum can write her own name now.'

'Wouldn't Richie Corrigan forge it?' said Chris.

Amina's small hands buzzed through a stack of paper. 'Up to the last transaction he was bringing Mrs Harney into the bank with him,' she said.

Rage burned a hole in me. I was unaware I was moving until I had the cold steel handle of the door in my grasp. I needed to get on a plane back to Dublin to beat the living tar out of Richie Corrigan.

'Bridge!'

It was Chris. He was barring my way.

'This won't help, lass.'

He looked around.

Amina scrabbled in her bag and handed me a bottle of water. When she spoke her voice was small.

'I wanted Chris to be here when I told you. I thought this might happen.'

Her small face chastened me. 'I'd never hurt you.'

'I know,' said Amina. The soft material of her hijab rustled as she shook her head. 'But you might see the omission as a lie, and I didn't want you to think I'd lied to you.'

I reached out and touched her shoulder. 'You haven't lied. None of this is your fault, we've got this far because of you.' Anxiety pecked at me. 'Did my dad know about this?'

'I wouldn't say so,' said Amina. 'He's never with your mum. It's a heavyset woman in the car outside. It's all on CCTV. I'm guessing Richie Corrigan goes to your house when you're not there and takes your mum. I can't track the car from the departing destination, there's not enough

CCTV where you live. I find it at Munster Bank on College Green then going into Trinity Street carpark after it drops your mum and Richie off.' She paged down on her screen. 'It's an ancient BMW. Here's a photograph of the woman driving.'

Nata.

Solid, kind Nata. With a fur coat and a burnished platinum ring.

'I'm an idiot.' It was a withered whisper and I gulped at my water.

'Pardon, Bridge?' said Chris.

'Later.' I batted him away. 'Keep going, Amina.'

'Nasda Holdings only ever took one cash deposit, in 1997, now the account takes laundered Bitcoin or Ethereum. The crypto currency is converted to cash and waits for Mrs Harney's quarterly withdrawals, but there's a problem due to your mam's illness. So Slowell Ltd. is now a payee on the Nasda Holdings account and a recent electronic transaction moved €600,000 out of the account. I reckon it's a test run. To see if any red lights start flashing. Remember Nasda Holdings is banjaxed.'

'Banjaxed?' said Chris.

'Defunct,' I said. 'It shouldn't have a live bank account.'

'Correct,' said Amina. 'Munster Bank believe an employee in the Isle of Man branch is helping.'

'No shit,' said Chris.

That got a laugh from both of us.

'Is the employee still in play?' I said.

'Yes,' said Amina. 'I told them to do nothing and you'd be in touch with a "recommendation".' She made air quotes.

I was reeling. My mother, Richie Corrigan, Seán Flannery

and Mike Burgess connected in some dense web.

'Why would Corrigan risk taking your old mum to the bank, Bridge?' said Chris.

Two puzzled faces turned towards me.

'It's his nature. He's spent the last forty years inserting himself into my mother's life, resorting to deceit and blackmail to keep their connection. She's his obsession.'

'I'm sorry, lass,' said Chris.

My mother had borne Richie Corrigan's obsession alone – her courage stopped the words in my throat.

'Drink some water, Bridge,' said Amina.

I took another gulp and looked at the slides, trying to get some distance and start again.

'You say Mum withdrew money in '98?' I said.

'First withdrawal from Munster Bank in College Green, Dublin March 1998. £20,000. The withdrawal amounts increased over time,' said Amina.

She turned her laptop screen to face me. Lists of line items in headache size font.

'Mum's been taking money for over twenty years from the Munster Bank's head office, so they know her. They know the routine of Richie and Mum coming in and she signs the withdrawal slip. They've been watching for years and have seen her deterioration. Banks aren't slapdash about withdrawals, so if Richie wants to change up the way money is withdrawn, with Mum in her current condition he'd have to get Power of Attorney over her and he can't. So Richie was forced to show his hand and use Slowell Ltd. to withdraw money.'

Amina took some bottles of water from her bag and handed one to Chris. He twisted off the cap and bubbles clambered to get to the top.

'I like a bit of fizzy, me,' said Chris, as much to give our minds a rest as make us laugh.

The cupboard we were in had taken on war-room status and the air had a thick, unventilated quality despite the fan.

Chris circled his neck and a small bone clicked.

'So Richie Corrigan uses Slowell Ltd to drain money out of Burgess Data Centre, converts it to crypto-currency, washes it around then puts it in Nasda Holdings,' he said.

'Wait,' said Amina, holding up a small white hand. 'Don't get ahead of yourself. Slowell Ltd. puts *some* money in Nasda Holdings – remember how much money's coming out of BDC – well over €80m a year. I would imagine most of that's going to the cartels.'

'Right so, it's fair to say the money Richie's putting into Nasda Holdings and getting Bridge's mum to withdraw is his fee from Fuentes?' said Chris.

'Or he's skimming,' I said.

Amina brought up the transactions she'd found for Nasda Holdings. 'Both are reasonable assumptions. The deposits and withdrawals have been constant over the years. We're looking at €13 million and change taken from Nasda Holdings.'

'How much?' I said.

Chris made a popping sound of disbelief. 'Right, let's try putting this together,' he said. 'We know Mike Burgess and Seán Flannery are acquainted from the Emer Davidson murder, but Flannery was a liar so might have met Mike years ago. Let's say Mike starts buying drugs off Seán Flannery. When did Flannery move into wholesaling?'

'A tout I have said he had a chemist as far back as 2005, a woman by the name of Avril Boyle. She had a small pharmacy and helped him process his cocaine, gave him the 'recipe' users wanted. She committed suicide and according to her family she was an addict, met Seán Flannery at Narcotics Anonymous. She thought he was her boyfriend.'

Chris cocked an eye in my direction. 'He were an evil bugger, Flannery.'

I couldn't disagree.

'Reckon we've gone as far as we can on our own,' said Chris. 'Why don't we go and visit our old friend Mr Burgess? See if he can corroborate any of this?' He rubbed his hands together.

'In Winson Green?' I said.

'No.' Chris shook his head. 'Strangeways.'

Even the name was terrifying.

Chapter 59

Strangeways was a fitting name. A maximum-security prison with layers and levels of security behind imposing Victorian architecture. A purpose-built prison. The architect dreamed of six prisoner wings converging on a centre tower, in imitation of a snowflake. The centre was a tower known as the Rotunda. There's nothing like a self-deluded Victorian for building cages of public misery and calling them art.

Amina stayed in Holloway Circus. There was no need for law-abiding civilians to be exposed to maximum-security male prisons. Few prisons bothered me, truth be known, but Strangeways was different. Unhappiness and discontent boiled through those wings and belched out of the seventy-one-metre-high ventilation tower. The November sky was bruised from its fumes.

Chris had organised for Mike Burgess to be brought up from the cells and we waited in a room embedded in the Governor's wing.

'Why is Burgess here?' I said.

'Keep him safe, they've got some of the best segregation units in Britain.'

I raised an eyebrow.

'You'll see.'

The door rattled and Mike Burgess came in. He wasn't cuffed as he presented no threat.

The prison officer nodded at Chris and they exchanged pleasantries about their families. 'Back in twenty minutes, Chris,' he said and closed the door.

If I was surprised at the shortness of the interview it dissolved at the sight of Mike Burgess. I was shocked.

The big, blustering fool I'd pegged Burgess for was gone, in its place was a scared man living inside his former husk. Mike Burgess looked as scraped out in the inside as he was scarred on the outside. He sat down and folded in on himself.

I indicated to the side of his face – the skin was raw and smeared.

'One of the prisoners in Winson Green threw a kettle of boiling water on him,' said Chris. 'Bastard put sugar in it. Makes it stick and burn deeper. You all right, Mike, lad?'

Chris's tone was kind and the way an emasculated Mike Burgess put his face up as though feeling sunshine, was pitiful.

'Thanks for putting me here, Chris.'

'You're all right, lad. Not long to go, last two years of your sentence is suspended so you'll be out in no time.'

Chris looked at me, signalling questions should be brief and to the point.

'Why's she here?' said Mike. An old badger, who'd known too many teeth in its hide.

'Just over visiting Chris, Mike, nothing to alarm you.'

'I'll not talk to anyone but you, Chris.'

There was no comfort Mike Burgess could get from my words, so I kept quiet.

'Mike's had a rough old road. Managed to get through those first couple of attacks, but this last one were the end, weren't it? You tried to top yourself, didn't you? Got a bit of washing line from an obliging prisoner. Might've been the end if one of the prison officers hadn't found you, right, Mike?'

He nodded, his once raven hair the colour of city snow.

'Took you here, I did. Kept you out of harm's way, pulled in a favour or two to do it, but you're all right now? Aren't you, Mike?'

Chris tried to get Burgess to engage. Which he did, by lifting his eyes for a fraction of a second each time Chris ended with a question. A frightened smile on his mouth.

'But you never told me the truth, did you, Mike? Why you were attacked so many times? You said it was money, they were looking for cash off you, for their friends on the outside. And it were a credible enough story. But it's not true.'

Mike's eyes flickered.

'Oh, I'm sure money's at the root of it, but it's not local lads giving the orders, is it?'

Mike's muscle memory kicked in and he shook, a trembling of old pleated skin dangling on a coat hanger.

'Come on, lad, don't have me change this situation.' Chris circled a hairy finger at his surroundings. 'It's not what either of us want and I've shown I can keep you safe, eh?'

Mike Burgess sucked on a nicotine-stained finger – somewhere in his memory he was puffing one of the Havana cigars he was so fond of and trying to conjure the sweet cherry tobacco smell.

'You've kept me safe, Chris. And I'm grateful, but you can't keep Lydia safe.'

'We can, but from who?'

Mike's milky eyes sharpened. 'Fuentes cartel. I'm not testifying against them. They'll kill her, they've said as much.'

'OK, lad, but fill in a few gaps for me. This is off the record.' Chris looked around and put both his hands out. 'We need to know what we're up against.'

Mike gave a morbid laugh, wheezy from prison cigarettes.

'You've no clue what you're up against. They've said the same to Anne, told her to stay put and do her time or Lydia will pay the price.'

'You correspond?' I said. Surprise had the words out of my mouth before my brain could shut it down – the bitterness between Anne and Mike Burgess at their sentencing was acidic.

'What's it to do with you? The Judge never said we couldn't and I know why you're here.' He poked a bent finger at me. 'You've found out Fuentes were Flannery's supplier and he were my supplier. Thought you were so smart, didn't you, lady? Thought you saw through us all with what happened to Emer, but you knew nothing. I'd have given anything to get the case closed. Fuentes lurking around watching everything. Flannery informing on me every step of the way. He's an ambitious bastard, always wanted me out of the way so he could take over the Data Centre operation. Suits him I'm banged up.'

Mike wasn't in the loop. I chanced a side glance at Chris and he read it.

'Flannery's dead,' said Chris. 'Fuentes had him shot in Barcelona.'

Mike's dog-eared body crumpled in on itself. 'Can you keep me here, Chris?'

'Course I will, lad, but you have to help me. How did this start?'

'It was never me who started this. Fuentes found Richie Corrigan in the seventies. He worked for some dodgy banker and they set up money-laundering on a big scale. The cartels were always looking for ways to clean their money. Richie was in this business a long time before me. It was his idea to buy the Data Centre. Don't let them get me, Chris.'

Fear dissolved holes in Mike Burgess, and he babbled his daughter's name over and over.

It pelted rain as we drove out of Strangeways. The urgent rhythm of the drops matched my desire to put as much distance as possible between myself and the prison. Chris fixed his front mirror and toggled the wing mirror on my side a fraction. It was a sign of nerves.

'Well? What now?' he said.

Chris was good at reading body language and putting people at their ease – it was his nature. So I was sure he knew what was coming.

'We've a lot of intel. Much of it unactionable in isolation,' I said.

'Meaning we've not got the firepower to go after Fuentes.'

'No, but we can work with Interpol, try and get on their task force in-country or at least put a case together for our evidence and claims.'

'Christ! It could take years! No chance you'd leave it?' Chris looked at me with searing eye contact.

'Can't do that, Chris.'

'What about your pal, Richie Corrigan?'

'With the stuff Amina's got we can take every penny off him and I believe money's his motivator. Do you remember his wife? She took off to the South of France?'

'Sort of, something about her wanting your dad to join her.'

I snorted. 'In her dreams. But you should see the place, size of a hotel and renovated top to bottom. It's stunning, yet I never twigged how Richie paid for it. I believed his business covered it. Still I'll be letting CAB know all about Mrs Corrigan's chateau. They can add it to the pile of confiscated assets.'

'Who'll head up the investigation? Will you get a chance to be on it?'

'No, I'll be a witness, as will my father – we'll be helping with enquiries – due to Mum's unwitting involvement, but I trust DCS Graham Muldoon. Our problem is time. We may not have enough of it. Corrigan's a flight risk. At least we've found Fuentes' informant in the DOCB, so that channel's closed off.'

'You had an informer?' said Chris.

Chapter 60

The sky was full of grey wool treaded together and drenched in rain, you could smell it straining at the edges. I had asked to meet Paul at his house, not having any desire to bring my personal business into the Square before I was forced to. Paul's home was a sandy coloured brick mews at the back of Waterloo Road. It was near the centre of town, but an expensive leafy hamlet with huge beech trees, now denuded of leaves. My sense of smell had been in overdrive the last couple of weeks – I had read somewhere it was to do with pregnancy and could be the reason I was so sick in the mornings.

When Paul opened the door the musky male scent that was his alone greeted me, weakening my resolve.

'Come in,' he said. His mouth was open in a grin reaching his eyes. 'How was Birmingham?'

'Good, we got back late last night. I won't stay long.'

'OK, but at least come in. Have a coffee?'

He walked down his hall, the soft carpet stealing his steps. He was barefoot and the house was warm so I shut the door against the stinging cold outside. I could smell fresh coffee and warm bread, and my stomach churned. I'd had a couple of gingernut biscuits and although nothing would have suited my taste buds more than toast with marmalade, my stomach wasn't going to allow anything else for a couple of hours.

'You said it was important?' said Paul.

I stood in his neat kitchen – wooden floors and stone sink – it didn't strike me as a family kitchen. I checked out his notice board.

'You're still diving?'

Something passed over his face I couldn't name – it might have been surprise at my blatant nosy-parkering.

'Not so much, those pictures are old. Can I get you coffee?' He was smiling and tamping down a shot of ground coffee from Darboven. 'You got me hooked on this stuff.'

I gave a small smile. 'I won't have coffee today.'

His look of surprise would have been comical if I weren't so keyed up.

'Bridge, you're pacing around and it's a pretty tight space,' he said.

Small talk was never my forte and the more I tried to slide something into a conversation the less it succeeded.

'I'm pregnant.'

He stopped mid-tamp.

'I wanted you to know, but it's important you understand I don't want anything from you. In fact, if you have any role in my baby's life, it will be at my behest.'

There was an imprecise, broken piece of time where neither of us knew which end we were holding, so let it roll away.

His body language was unreadable.

'Is it . . . ? You're sure you're pregnant?'

What he wanted to say was too gauche and he'd tapered it off into another question.

'I'm just over twenty weeks.'

'Jesus!' His eyes flicked back and forth trying to calculate, but we hadn't slept together often. 'The time in the stationery cupboard?'

'Yes, end of June. We were halfway finished with those stupid evaluations O'Connor had me doing after the Emer Davidson case. We were a bit reckless.'

There was no point in continuing, he got the picture.

His face softened at the edges and he pressed his hand to his chest. 'Are you OK? Do you feel tired? How come you're not showing?' His eyes scanned my body. 'I can't see anything, apart from being a bit pale you're no different. Maybe around the eyes?'

'What? Wrinkled and wrecked-looking?'

We laughed and it was a wrench releasing a compacted bolt.

'Why didn't you say something before now? Why didn't you let me come to the scans? I would've helped. I want to help.' Realisation light-switched across his face. 'What were you doing chasing that mongrel Flannery? You could have been killed . . .'

'This is why I didn't tell anyone. And you should know I haven't been to see any obstetrician yet.'

'Then how do you know you're pregnant? Might it be the menopause?'

I looked at him. 'No, apart from the obvious of my period being months late I did a couple of chemist tests. I'm pregnant, Paul. There's no doubt. You're the only person I'm involved with. But this is a courtesy call. I'll be doing this on my own.'

A fear, from a much younger, frightened version of myself came to contradict me.

He crossed over and held me close. His body radiated heat. 'It's OK, Bridge, we can do this together. You're not on your own.'

I took his arms away from me. The comfort came too easy and I distrusted a thing not fought or worked for.

'I'm fine, Paul. I had a bit of a challenge to accept the pregnancy.'

How much to tell of my feelings of inadequacy?

'If I have what's needed to be a mother. I'm not sure I have, but I love and want this baby. All we've had is a series of one-night stands.'

'Ah Bridge! When you say it like that it sounds awful! This changes everything. I want to be in a relationship with you. I care about you.'

This was costing him. He leaned on the countertop, white bones pressed out from the flesh of his knuckles.

'I haven't been so hot on the whole relationship thing. My divorce was a mess and I didn't want a relationship with someone at work in case I messed it up.' He gave a self-effacing laugh. 'So now that I have messed it up, please don't shut me out. Not if we're having a child.'

My emotions were a dizzy mess and letting me down. I had expected a terse nod and to be sent on my way, not a do-over because of our baby.

'Paul, I have no expectations of you. We haven't had the best of starts and a baby's not going to suddenly make it better.'

'Yes, but what will your colleagues think! That bog bastard O'Shea will beat me to a pulp.'

He was laughing, but underneath the humour a nub of panic.

331

'You think the lads will have a pop at you if you don't stand by me? What year is it? 1980?'

'No! No, that's not it, but I'm older than you, Bridge. I've been married before. People will blame me and we're at an age now where we need to do things right.'

'Christ, you sound like Richie Corrigan!'

'What?'

I swiped his question away. 'Paul, you need to respect my wishes. And you can take that worried look off your face. Do I strike you as the type of woman who invites questions on her private life?'

He gave a tight laugh.

'Well then, I'll leave you to your breakfast and we'll carry on as usual,' I said.

'What about scans and the safety of the baby, where are you –'

He got the flat of my palm. 'I'll let you know my plans in due course.'

I left in a hurry. I didn't have a whole lot of plans and needed to research how to give my baby the best start. The first twenty weeks were hardly textbook. My phone rang and Amina's number flashed on my dial.

'Hi, Amina.'

'Hey, Bridge. You on your way in? Muldoon's looking for you.'

'Yes, I'm on my way in.'

I paused, unsure of my next line.

'Amina, I'm pregnant.'

'Oh!'

Her thoughts braided down the phone as squad-room sounds filled the silence on her end.

'Are you OK? Is Paul the father? Can I help?'

'I'm fine, Amina.' Her buzzing excitement was infectious. 'Paul is the father but he's not in the picture. I'll be doing this by myself.'

The rightness of my words was a comfort.

'Listen, I don't pretend to understand your choices, don't understand some of my own, and it's your decision to have your baby by yourself. But that decision shouldn't mean you're alone.'

I laughed, hearing the echo of my own words from weeks ago.

Her laughter came back at me. 'I want to be there when you tell Liam you're pregnant.'

'He might be able to help – his sister's had four children. He'll know her obstetrician.'

'Careful, Bridge, Liam will want to be your birthing partner.' She was enjoying herself. 'Well, this is probably as good a time as any. I found your mam's baby.'

A silence so thick it could envelop my hand, if I reached out to it.

'Will I go on, Bridge?'

'Yes.' A gulping sound. 'Please, Amina.'

'His name is Ben Williams. He was adopted by a couple in Ohio – Meredith and John Williams. I don't have much more, but he got out of that Mother and Baby Home.'

I had pulled the car over, tears spilling down my face. 'Thanks, Amina.'

'Want me to check some more?'

'Not at the moment.'

For now it was enough that Ben Williams existed, out of the range of Richie Corrigan and his ilk.

Chapter 61

Muldoon had his head in his hands. It was no more than a glimpse as the door closed and his secretary barred my way, but his head was bowed.

'He's expecting me,' I said.

Ms Goddard eyed me as if I had *access denied* stamped on my forehead.

'Wait here,' she said.

I noted she didn't rap on the Muldoon's door, instead walking in and half closing it behind her. Their voices were too low to catch any conversation. Muldoon walked out wearing a navy fleece, giving no indication of his rank, followed by his harried-looking secretary. She trailed him to the lifts, worry furrowing her forehead.

'You're sure you need nothing else, DCS Muldoon?' she said.

'I'm fine. You hold the fort. Is Joe ready?'

'Downstairs and waiting,' she said. Each word a nod.

I wasn't part of this conversation and had no death wish, so kept to the side and looked at our little tableau in the gleaming lift doors. They opened and disgorged a creosote-coloured DS O'Connor. He spotted Muldoon and opened his mouth without thinking.

'What's Clarke doing sitting in reception like he's off on an outing?' he said.

It wasn't how I'd have started a conversation with DCS Muldoon and I smothered a smile of satisfaction.

DCS Muldoon's face didn't register DS O'Connor's presence or his remark. The oaf was unseen.

'After you, Detective Garda Harney,' said DCS Muldoon.

O'Connor's trapdoor mouth hung open.

'You'll be briefed in due course, Detective Superintendent O'Connor,' said the redoubtable Ms Goddard.

The doors closed on O'Connor's face.

I won't lie, it was a sweet moment and would have been enough, if not for the curiosity tickling me about what I was doing with DCS Muldoon going to the ground floor to meet Joe Clarke, who by all accounts, was waiting in the foyer when he should have been in the cells.

We arrived at a convent in Glasnevin and DCS Muldoon parked by the gate lodge. I hadn't spoken throughout the journey – other than to salute Joe – by his grin my astonished silence was amusing him.

The builders had gone home for the day and we were out of sight of the main building. A russet Virginia creeper grew up the side of the cottage and into the eaves, a selection of roof tiles in its fiery teeth.

'Joe, why are we here?' said DCS Muldoon.

Joe sighed. 'It's not going to change much. I'll be investigated for owing money to a loan shark and no doubt will be charged.' He raised his eyes to skyward, but got no further than the car headliner fabric. 'I wanted you pair to know the truth. I've no way to prove it, but will you listen?'

He had our attention.

'Bridge, you've been a great officer and I don't know what Flannery told you, but I lied to you and that was unforgiveable.'

Words wanted to tumble out, but it wasn't about me comforting Joe. My heart knocked in my chest at the sound of his voice. He was broken.

'Never heard you so quiet,' he said.

'I missed the briefing so for once in my life I'll hold fire,' I said.

Joe put his left hand up to his head and pressed until his fingernails were white.

'Will you keep questions until the end, please?' he said.

'Of course,' said DCS Muldoon.

'Up there,' he indicated to the convent's main building with a steady hand, 'is where my sister lives. Ellen Clarke her given name, but Sister Assumpta when she took her vows.'

The car blurred around me as cogs slotted into place. It was all I could do to keep my promise.

'Ellen's ten years older than me. She was born in 1959.' Joe's shoulders hunched up to his neck. 'It was a different world back then, no internet, no mobile phones, people lived and worked in their own parishes. The State of Emergency had ended thirteen years before. We weren't well off,' he gave a snort, 'in fact we were dirt poor. Small holding and never enough of anything. My parents wanted a vocation in the family and it fell to Ellen. I believe they thought they were giving her a better life. When I was eight she went off to Clarendon House, the Mother and Baby home. I don't know if Ellen wanted to be a nun. She was a great woman for . . .' He grappled with something. 'These short-lived bursts of affection, hugging and making a pet out of me, but it was play-acting, there was nothing behind it. She and my parents had so many rows growing up, but it didn't knock a whit out of her. She could have a blazing row one minute, Mammy in tears, then ask you if you wanted to go out and pick berries off the hedge or bring in the cows. Things didn't stick to Ellen, but Jesus she was fearless. Run into a field and ride a horse bareback, while all the local kids watched.'

Joe was quiet for a moment, lost in a reel he had exclusive access to.

'Either way, Ellen and I weren't close and she didn't see Mam and Dad that often. Dad died when I was about twelve, so Ellen visited us more. But she'd changed. Hard and hot with self-righteousness, a poker stuck in the fire too long. Mam wanted us to be closer. When I finished up in Templemore and got stationed in Drumcondra I'd go up to her on a Thursday evening in the convent for a bit of tea. Ellen could be charming when she wanted. It got to be a habit and I'd tell her about my day, what I was doing. At first to have something to say, but Ellen was a good listener and a nun. She wouldn't tell anyone anything.'

I chanced a squint over at DCS Muldoon to see what he was making of Joe's story. He was fascinated. It was a glimpse into an Ireland I never knew, of rosaries at tea time and *Ireland's Own* magazine setting your world view.

'So it went on. I found myself unburdening to Ellen. I couldn't talk to my wife about my work and she was focused on our girls. When Ellen asked me to look out for a little lad I couldn't deny her.'

Joe's face was flushed.

'It was Seán Flannery. He was a small, even by standards

back then. That fucking pervert priest – God forgive me for swearing, I'm letting myself down – was taking an unhealthy interest in him, I swear.'

He made the Sign of the Cross.

'If I'd known what Father O'Mahony was like I'd have killed him myself. But no one had any idea what went on in those homes. We're not even getting the full story now, despite all the investigations.'

The hurt in his voice was raw.

'Seán was a good little fellah. Full of chat when you'd take him anywhere. Me and Ellen used take him out by Bullock Harbour – he was mad for the boats. Even at that age. It's fair to say I was fond of him.'

Joe waved a hand in the air at his sentimentality.

'Either way I kept an eye on him, but when he went to St Augustine's he didn't want to meet me anymore, thought the other lads would give him a hard time for knowing a *shade*. St Augustine's was a one-way ticket to Mountjoy for many of the residents. But not Seán, he was clever – in truth I never knew how clever until he was older – and times were changing. The system of Mother and Baby Homes was unravelling with the likes of the Single Parent family allowance. Clarendon House closed and Ellen was moved back here. Seán didn't keep in touch with her, but he kept in touch with Richie Corrigan.'

I couldn't stay silent. 'How did he meet Corrigan?'

'Ellen. Richie Corrigan came to Ellen in the seventies – she wasn't long in Clarendon House then. He wanted to sponsor a boy. Not adopt but help him out in life.'

'She gave him access to a child like he was a rescue dog?' I said.

Muldoon, who had been silent through all this, made a

rasping sound as his hand connected with the bristles of his five o'clock shadow.

'Not in the way you think,' said Joe. His mouth was a harsh knot.

'It was a different time,' said DCS Muldoon. 'Many of the more prominent families in Irish society would have given donations to the nuns and priests for orphans.'

Joe was nodding. 'And nothing untoward ever happened with Corrigan – I'll stake my life on that – he financed the boating trips, gave the convent money for clothes, schoolbooks for the children and the like. Richie had access to Seán all his life. He always asked me to say nothing about my association with the boy, I wasn't sure why but I accepted it. God help me, I thought Richie was a benign influence, in particular when Seán turned to criminality.'

Joe's hope hung in the air, so much stale smoke after a cigarette has been extinguished.

'I never covered up anything for Seán. That time Gavin Devereux was pinched for drugs Seán wasn't with him.'

I wasn't sure if I believed that, but let it slide.

'I-I told Ellen what the gardaí knew about him in our weekly chats. I never thought for a second that she'd pass on any information, but she might have.' He looked sheepish. 'Ellen's a bitter woman, but it's twisted in on itself now. You'll see when you meet her.'

Chapter 62

The convent smelled of Holy Thursday, altar candles and obligation, a lonely ritual for its own sake.

Sister Assumpta, or Ellen Clarke hadn't changed.

'You're looking a bit dishevelled, Joe. Got yourself in trouble? I'll wager it's that wife of yours and the fine style she likes to be kept in,' she said.

She gave a curt laugh, not insensitive but unafraid to show what she thought of her sister-in-law.

'Come in.' She walked at a brisk trot across the shiny parquet flooring into the formal parlour at the front of the convent.

We followed.

Sister Assumpta sat facing us, with quiet composure, her workman-like hands folded.

'I can't say your visit is unexpected – what has Joe done?' she said.

'Detective Garda Harney,' said DCS Muldoon. A clear indication to start.

'Sister Assumpta, you worked in the Mother and Baby Home where Seán Flannery was born. How well did you know him?'

'Detective Garda Harney? You're back at detective now, are you? Joe told me you had a little problem with planted evidence he sorted out for you.'

Her statement was heated by Joe's discomfiture. If she was waiting for DCS Muldoon to react she'd have better luck with a lottery ticket, but the raising of her eyebrow showed she enjoyed humiliating me.

'Answer the question please, Sister Assumpta,' I said.

'Yes, I knew Seán Flannery when he was a youth.'

'I'd say you knew him for most of his life, Sister Assumpta. You lost contact with him during his time at St Augustine's but he found you again. How?'

Emotions flitted across her face, an inner debate we weren't privy to.

'He wanted to find his mother. He came looking for me when he was eighteen. I didn't know who his mother was. The records are a bit sketchy, but I told him it was a woman who'd married a rising barrister.'

'Is that true?' I said.

She gave a cruel little snort. 'Not at all, but he wanted to believe it.'

'Why?'

'No doubt,' here she looked at Joe, 'my squealing little brother has told you of our association with Seán Flannery. Richie Corrigan met me when I was in Clarendon House and asked for a baby boy. Richie wanted him to use the surname Flannery.'

'So you changed a child's name?' The enormity of their actions was chaos-sized.

'Detective Harney, you imagine these children had surnames? Most of the girls ran out of the convent and didn't want their names on birth certificates or

341

documentation. Look at how difficult it is to trace these women even now – do you think that's because of the nuns?'

The facts in her words were serrated rocks on the shoreline when a wave pulls out.

DCS Muldoon spoke into the silence.

'Did Richie Corrigan specify anything else?'

'He wanted the boy told his mother had married a rising barrister and showed me a picture of a woman the boy had to resemble.'

I fumbled around in my phone, trying to bring up some of the old photos of my mother.

'This woman?' I said.

'Yes.' Sister Assumpta gave a bob of her head. 'That could be her, but the photo Richie had was of a younger woman, an old-fashioned studio portrait.'

'Why did he want a boy that looked like this woman?' I wasn't telling her about my mother, she didn't deserve that level of transparency.

She tilted her head to one side, the way a predatory bird moves to get a single view of its quarry.

'That's your mother, isn't it? You're the image of her. How amusing, Detective Harney. I remember when I first met you, when you were trying to find out if I knew Seán Flannery. I knew there was something familiar about you.'

I wouldn't let her distract me. Muldoon eyeballed me with the same message.

'Richie Corrigan. Why would you help him?' I said.

'The church needed funds, always needs funds, to build convents, places of worship, send missionaries out to the world. Richie donated thousands to Clarendon House – we built grottos all over the country, helped build the

Church of the Assumption in Walkinstown –'

'That's what you spent the money on? Statues and buildings! What about the children?' My voice was loud, but the room absorbed it. Not the first voice to express discontent here.

Sister Assumpta shrugged. 'We did what was right. Those children were born of original sin. It was a stain they could never wash off, even though we baptised them.'

'Did you care about any of them?' I said.

A momentary chink, then she got back inside her religion, sitting in the fortress her church had built. 'They were our burden, begotten of sin.'

Despite evidence to the contrary I had always believed I was safe with nuns, the women who had educated me. They were kind and good, as though God had given them a store of grace and their job was to share it with the children they educated. Sister Assumpta's seasoned cruelty to the children put into her trust shocked me to the point of speechlessness.

DCS Muldoon intervened.

'Let's not get side-tracked,' he said. 'Sister Assumpta, Richie Corrigan paid the convent for access to Seán Flannery, correct?'

She shook her head. 'Not correct. Richie Corrigan gave a donation to the convent – as was proper – he sponsored Seán.'

'Was Richie in touch with Seán when he was in St Augustine's?' said DCS Muldoon.

'Yes, he never lost touch with Seán.'

'So Seán got in contact with you when he was eighteen and that contact continued for the rest of his life, correct?'

'On and off,' said Sister Assumpta, her mouth hard as a mechanic's vice.

'Here's the crux of the matter – did you pass information

on to Seán of a sensitive nature? Information you gleaned from Sergeant Clarke?'

'Loose lips, eh, Joe?' said Sister Assumpta. She was diverted.

Joe perched on the edge of his seat as though the couch were made of cactus prickles.

'You should know Joe was compromised the moment he married a woman he couldn't afford.' Sister Assumpta turned on him. 'You knew she'd want more than you could give. God forgive me, the hours you sat in here moaning about how you'd make ends meet and the amount of overtime you had to do to keep her in Spain. If I hadn't switched off from your mindless patter I would've gone mad. The boredom was excruciating.'

Joe looked awful, a beaten dog. My heart went out to him, but I had to press her.

'Did you tell Seán Flannery about a shipment of cocaine being tracked from overseas in November?' I said.

'Who's to say?'

'Christ, you're in full disclosure mode now, aren't you, Ellen?' said Joe.

'Did you contact Seán Flannery and tell him we were tracking that shipment?' said DCS Muldoon.

She made a hacking noise, turned out it was laughter. Discordant and ugly.

'You're idiots! I never told Seán Flannery anything. If he was to meet his end down the barrel of a gun it's what God intended. Joe's information was never any good. It was all nod-and-wink rubbish. The fool thought he was spilling his guts, but it was never clear who was doing what.'

'But you said you did! Why did you lie to me?' said Joe.

'To fuck with you,' said Sister Assumpta.

A swearing nun was rare and despite my ideas of how cosmopolitan I was, it shocked me.

Sister Assumpta laughed. 'Joe thought we 'owed' Seán. He was' – she paused – 'abused by a priest. But you must remember these children were tainted with original sin. Born out of wedlock from women who were unchaste.'

She had a skein of normality, but below the dermis bitterness had honed itself into madness.

'I kept my vows,' said Sister Assumpta, 'unlike those girls.' She pointed a long finger at me. *'They will be judged by God and I will sit at His Right Hand!'*

Her voice rang around the cavernous room. A sheen of sweat on her face, delusion shining out of her eyes and caked into the spittle on her lips.

'Why now?' I said. 'Why are you telling us this now?'

Joe looked at her and leaned forward, tapping her knee.

'Are you ill?' he said.

'Well, aren't you the quick one, Joe?'

'Colon cancer? Same as Daddy?'

'Give him a sweet from the jar,' said Sister Assumpta. 'You would've made a great detective, Joe.'

'How long have you got?'

'Six months, maybe less.'

Chapter 63

Sister Assumpta had shaken me – to see such a lack of empathy in someone who had children in her care pared me to the bone.

My father texted me saying my dinner was cold and being eyed up by the dog. The smart move was to call it a night, go home and eat, chat to the Judge – but I was no good at taking advice, especially my own.

I sat in Harcourt Square's car park and rang the bug in Gavin Devereux's car. He was on the move and not alone.

'*Why did you contact me now? We've never met before.*'

'*I'd no choice.*'

A woman's voice, somewhat familiar, but coated in anger.

'*Does Richie know you're meeting me?*'

'*No, Gavin, you'll inform him when we've finished. I'm not meeting Richie again. Go out the back roads to Delgany.*'

'*Where the fuck's that?*'

'*I'll thank you not to swear at me, Gavin Devereaux.*'

'*Go right up here onto the N11, I'll tell you what exit to take.*'

'OK. Why are we meeting?'

'They've gone out to meet someone. I believe they'll find out about Richie and the extent of his involvement. Which means they'll find out about me. I won't be going back to the office. She came back from Barcelona with information about an informant.'

'Yeah, but she got it wrong. Joe Clarke was never an informant.'

'Don't interrupt me! Take the next left for Enniskerry. I believe Seán Flannery told her about Richie. She and that oaf Watkiss have put two and two together and uncovered what Richie's doing. I told him Mike Burgess was a buffoon. That Emer Davidson case last year nearly blew it wide open.'

'Are you sure about this?'

'Gavin, you're not the brains of the operation. You're an enforcer. Stick to what you know. Circle the roundabout and take the exit back towards Dublin.'

'OK, but are you sure the razzers know about Richie?'

'I've worked for Graham Muldoon for over twenty years. He's wise to something and isn't telling anyone.'

The phone fell from my hands. It was Ms Goddard. That sanctimonious bitch. Josie Goddard. Not *Joe. Josie.* I threw myself out of the pound car. Roaring for Liam O'Shea and Muldoon in jagged breaths. In my haste I hit the emergency button on my Tetra radio. Gardaí came from every direction in Harcourt Square, pouring out of doors, tracking my signal.

'We need to go now!' I shouted at Liam O'Shea.

'Jesus, Bridge, what in God's name?'

There was a pile-up in the car park.

'It's all right! I'm sorry. Everything's fine.'

I was shouting at ten gardaí who did not think everything was fine, judging by their faces. I snatched at Liam O'Shea who was standing in the middle of them and put a hot mouth to his ear.

'Josie Goddard was Flannery's informer! Muldoon's secretary! She's in Devereux's car. They're on their way back from Wicklow. We can track the bug's GPS signal.'

'Go up and get Muldoon,' said Liam. 'I'll get armed support and we'll go after them full strength.'

'Right.'

DCS Muldoon must have heard the commotion as he was on the stairs. The time for discretion had passed.

'It's Ms Goddard, she's Flannery's tout. She's in a car with Gavin Devereux right now and wants to warn Richie Corrigan we're on to him.'

To Muldoon's credit he didn't flinch at the rat in his woodpile.

'You have their location?' he said.

'Yes, I'm tracking it now.' In my haste to get to Muldoon I'd hung up on the bug. 'We can listen on the way?'

'Fine, where's the ASU?'

'Liam O'Shea's getting them – they'll be waiting in reception.'

As I fell into step beside Muldoon, an urge to speak overwhelmed me. 'DCS Muldoon, my dad told me you had copies of my mother's signatures on Nasda Holdings withdrawal slips – may I ask where you got them?'

'Josie gave me a dossier. It was handed in for me anonymously with photocopies of the slips. We believed it came from a whistleblower in the bank.'

'Maybe not.'

'So it would seem,' said DCS Muldoon.

He opened the door to reception and, true to his word, Liam had an Armed Support Unit waiting for us in the foyer.

'I need a second unit,' said DCS Muldoon, 'covert please. I want Richie Corrigan under surveillance while I wait on a warrant. Liam, travel with the ASU, assume Devereux is armed. Bridge, with me in the undercover car.' A hissed whisper. 'I want every part of Josie's life investigated. With extreme prejudice, Detective Garda Harney.'

I was the right woman for that.

He walked down the stairs, his shoulders set and heels clicking. No rest tonight.

Chapter 64

Described by one of my former commanders as a match player, unpredictable and always in for the long haul, I stood outside DCS Muldoon's office, folders and back-up documentation in hand and waited to be seen. With Josie Goddard in custody and the National Bureau of Crime Investigation preparing a file on Joe Clarke's financial issues, DCS Muldoon wasn't in a good mood.

'Detective Garda Harney!'

His bark took me out of my reverie.

It was 8.30am, Muldoon bristled in full uniform and his office had a woody clean smell.

'Good morning, Detective Chief Superintendent Muldoon.'

He rubbed a hand over his bristling head and I half expected a blue spark of electricity.

'Sit down, Bridge.' He sat behind his desk and flicked the elastics off an A4 folder. 'Seán Flannery's body is being transported back from Spain, we will perform a full post-mortem, but the Spanish have examined him.' He held up a hand to cut off my open mouth. 'As is their right in their country. They've promised an internal investigation of the police who attended the crime scene but have stated

Flannery was not shot with a Mosso Esquadra weapon.'

I snorted. 'So they got the guns from Fuentes. Big difference.'

'There's nothing else we can do, Bridge.'

'It'll be a whitewash. They'll say it was person or persons unknown.'

'The Mossos have lodged a complaint about you through diplomatic channels, said you were suspected of assisting Flannery in his escape. They've no proof to back up this allegation, but it's caused problems for the Commissioner and the Minister for Justice.'

'That's ridiculous!'

'I agree, but if you had some proof to back up your allegations about Fuentes involvement, it would be nice. The Commissioner will go to bat for you, as he's aware of the corruption in the Mossos and that Spain is a portal for the cartels – don't get me wrong – if we had any kind of proof we'd go to the EU Commission. O'Driscoll in Madrid has your back on this.'

'I've Joe to thank for that.'

Muldoon paused at the mention of Joe's name.

'Is there anything we can do for him?' I said.

Muldoon shook his shovel-shaped head. 'No, but there are positives. He didn't do anything for financial gain, he's up to his eyes in debt and he has questions to answer about his relationship with Flannery – but Joe didn't pass on information to his sister. And by her own admission she didn't pass anything onto Flannery. Joe's retiring, that's about the height of it.'

'And Josie Goddard?'

The wrinkles on Muldoon forehead raised up into a V.

'DPP are preparing a file for prosecution.'

'And Corrigan's murder?'

'We have the man who pulled the trigger but he's nothing. An enforcer.'

'Did you talk to Josie about it?'

The ground might have shook at my temerity, but Muldoon didn't.

'I listened to one of her interviews. She's not dancing, maintains she and Corrigan were friends and never passed on any information to anyone about anything.'

'We'll find something on her, DCS Muldoon.'

'The DPP will struggle as we can't admit any of the recordings in the car into evidence, but the Criminal Asset Bureau will leave her without a farthing. Josie maintains she met Corrigan when she was a girl, staying in a hostel in Dublin. He helped her get a job in some accounting firm in the seventies. She said Corrigan was obsessed with your mother.'

Muldoon's face narrowed at my sharp intake of breath.

'Corrigan also 'helped' my mother get a hostel and a job. He lied when he said they'd had an affair. I remember her looking at Richie Corrigan, wherever he went – as a child I thought it was admiration, but now I believe she was watching him.'

Muldoon shook his head. 'Hard to see him as the brains behind Flannery's OCG. He was such an old duffer.'

'On the outside,' I said.

'Indeed. Were Fuentes his backers?'

'I believe so – he was their asset, laundered their money but with Josie in custody they moved against him. Or who knows? The decision to kill Corrigan might have been made at the same time they decided to kill Flannery. Maybe Fuentes are waiting for the dust to settle and see who rises up to replace Flannery.'

DCS Muldoon gave a wintry smile.

'What's happening with Nasda Holdings and Slowell?' he said.

'Everything Richie Corrigan touched is coming under investigation. We have a Munster Bank Isle of Man employee co-operating with us and we're preparing charges against said employee. Amina is working on warrants for assets held in the country and in France, those we can fast-track based on testimony, your belief and audit trails. The Inland Revenue and West Midlands are working on Slowell Holdings and Burgess Data Centre, but it's going to take time.'

'We've disrupted Fuentes cash flow and supply chain in here, the UK and possibly Europe. To what extent I don't know,' said DCS Muldoon.

'There's something else,' I said.

I debated with myself as to whether I wanted to discuss this with anyone, but if I had learned anything it was that I couldn't do it alone.

'I have a tout.'

'Is your informant on CHIS?' said DCS Muldoon.

My face screwed itself up. 'Not so much. I knew there was a leak, but thought it was O'Connor so I kept information on the tout to myself and Joe. I've been running Sheila Devereaux.'

'What? Gavin Devereux's grandmother has been informing on him and Flannery? All the while this has been going on?'

'Yes, she told us about the drug shipment coming in and the Farm in Kilkenny where Flannery processed his cocaine. She told us about his chemist. It was all her. That's why the intelligence was so strong. Flannery had no idea.

Now he's dead Gavin Devereux will step up. I'm pretty sure that's what Sheila Devereux wanted, but the material point is we've a way into the Fuentes cartel. Gavin doesn't know his grandmother is our informant.'

Calculations floated across Muldoon's eyes.

'You know the guy heading up MAOC – we can deliver real intelligence to him,' I said. 'We may never be in a position to do anything significant to Fuentes, other than keep our own patch clean, but MAOC have power. They work with the DEA. If Sheila Devereux can give us intelligence, who knows where it will lead. I'll need your help in running her.'

'You will,' said DCS Muldoon. 'And she'll have to know we'll offer her up to Gavin if she doesn't do as we say.'

I'd picked the right man to work with.

Chapter 65

A coiled sensation built in my throat until it became a full dry retch. I put my feet on the cold floor of my bedroom and sat in the inky darkness, a darkness made for slumber, not scrabbling for gingernut biscuits. I kept them on my locker for morning time nausea which had formed its own routine over the last week. My body looked the same but the person living inside me was making him or herself known. I stumbled downstairs, surprised to see a light on in the kitchen. The house was warm with our central heating rattling through the pipes. My father had the radio on and Shay Byrne was wishing everyone a good morning and introducing James Taylor's 'Fire and Rain'. It was about all I could put up with at 6.15am.

Nata had been taken in for questioning by the Gardaí and was facing possible charges of elder abuse, but she'd get a warning, nothing more. My father had wanted a custodial sentence but what had she done? Other than given 'a family friend' as she described Richie Corrigan, access to my mother and brought her on a couple of outings. It was a stout defence, still her brush with the Gardaí meant she'd lose her working visa.

'Morning, Dad.'

'Good morning, Bridget. Too early for scrambled eggs?'

The lumpy liquid texture had me running for the kitchen sink and bringing up any gingernut I'd managed to swallow.

'Are you all right, Bridget? Do you have a stomach bug?'

My father's face was creased with concern. It was time.

'No, Dad, it's morning sickness. I'm pregnant.'

I didn't know where to laugh or cry as my father stood there with a frying pan in one hand, in his full-length silk dressing gown and white hair standing up in tufts.

'Oh.'

'Yes, indeed, Judge – oh.'

'No, I don't mean that – are you all right about it? Are you happy?'

'Yes, I am, Dad.'

He put his cooking equipment down and went to the cupboard. 'Your mother used to take a liquorice-bark tea when she was carrying you. Couldn't stomach anything else in the morning.' He turned and smiled at me with some loose-leaf tea in his hand. 'I got some in, just in case.'

'You knew I was pregnant?'

He raised his thin bony shoulders up to ears rushing down to meet them. 'One of the mornings a couple of weeks ago you got sick. You looked so like your mother. Leaning over the sink and running the tap.'

'Oh, Dad, why didn't you say!'

'I'm not sure. You always have everything under control and I didn't want to interfere.'

I let out a weak laugh. 'Dad, I haven't a clue what do with children. I always expect them to behave like characters from a parenting manual. Even my own pregnancy, I treated it as if it was happening to someone else, but I can't anymore. I'm never going to be prepared for a child, but is anyone on their first? I have to give control over to the baby now. Let him or her set the pace.'

'I'm glad to hear you say that, Bridge. We haven't been open over the years. It's my fault. I didn't come from a family where anyone talked about emotions or their troubles. It was seen as shameful and I brought that silence to my own family. If I'd been more open with you and your mother I'd have known what a scoundrel Corrigan was. And saved her decades of pain.'

My throat closed with unshed tears. The years had marked my father and not in a good way.

'Why don't we try to be a bit more open? You and me? Help each other. It'll be nice being a grandad.'

Now I did cry, fat tears down my face.

'Don't worry, *alanna*, we can do it.'

'Thanks, Dad.'

'Right, let's get you the best obstetrician we can. The chap who did your mother is long retired but I'll have a chat with him, see who's top of their game at the moment. Your mother went to the Rotunda. Good hospital.'

I gave him an encouraging smile. He was at his finest when helping. He was full of light and it lessened some of the sorrowful lines my mother's illness had soldered onto his face.

'I'll call you later when I've a couple of names.'

'Thanks, Dad.'

I got dressed and drove into Harcourt Square.

Liam was hanging around the corridors, a stupid smile on his face.

'So you've heard?'

'What? I've heard nothing, Bridge.'

'Don't ever go into politics, Liam. You can't lie for toffee. Seeing as you're here, want to go out to the Gardens? See how they're marking Il Duce's death?'

'Flannery would've loved to hear you call him that. All right so, I'm driving. And if you want any advice about babies, my sister's had a few and I – '

'Liam, if I want your advice I'll ask for it.'

He was a grinning idiot.

'But thanks, O'Shea.'

'Right, the Gardens it is.'

He drove and we turned onto St Martin's Garden's cul-de-sac and entered a war zone. Gavin Devereux's sentries blocked the avenue, the fire brigade and an ambulance sat outside Flannery's house. Trails of harsh-smelling black smoke sat in the air as though they'd made a funeral pyre of his East Wall home.

'What happened?' I said.

A young sentry eyed me.

Sheila Devereux was in Flannery's front garden. Her face singed and bloodied, skin hanging off her neck in gluey blobs. She was keening, a hollow sound full of pain, as the paramedics helped her into the ambulance. Gavin stood beside her, no kindness on the hard planes of his face. He moved closer and said something to her. Of course I leaned in – as if I could hear from this distance – but I saw the animosity. It was stark.

'Stand back, Bridge. Leave the emergency services to their job,' said Liam.

I never listen.

'Is Mrs Devereux all right?' I said.

'Takes more than a booby trap to kill her,' said the

young sentry. 'It went off in Seán's house, but she made it out. Youse probably never copped it but Fuentes cartel kidnapped Seán a couple of weeks back. Sheila must have known something as she told everyone to stay inside, said it was a big meeting with the bosses and everyone had to be out of sight. Even Gavin, lied to his face –'

'Sheila Devereux has a back channel to Fuentes?' I said. An acute pain behind my eyes.

'I never said that!' He was high-pitched with panic. 'You fuc– you razzers are putting words in me mouth!'

His voice had drawn the eyes of Flannery's people to us. Liam and I made for the car. A more senior member of Flannery's gang was deliberately making his way towards us. He had the face of a hornet and I didn't want to provoke him or the wasp's nest Flannery had left behind.

Liam reversed the car out of St Martin's cul-de-sac just the right side of unseemly haste.

'You could feel the anger radiating off the lot of them. What's going to happen now?' he said.

'Don't know, Liam, but I'll tell you this – Gavin's in charge. Interesting times ahead. You still looking at that posting down the country?'

He looked at me. 'No, think I'll stick around. You'd never know when I'd be needed.'

'We need to find out who killed Kay,' I said, grimacing.

'Knew that would come up at some point.

My stomach rumbled. 'Can't think when I'm hungry. Fancy a toastie in the Ritzy?'

'You're buying,' said Liam.

THE END

ALSO BY POOLBEG.COM

47 SECONDS

JANE RYAN

I HEREBY SOLEMNLY AND SINCERELY DECLARE BEFORE GOD THAT I WILL FAITHFULLY DISCHARGE THE DUTIES OF A MEMBER OF THE GARDA SÍOCHÁNA . . .

Detective Garda Bridget Harney's obsession with Seán Flannery began when he claimed his assault on an underage victim was 'consensual'.

WITH FAIRNESS, INTEGRITY, REGARD FOR HUMAN RIGHTS, DILIGENCE AND IMPARTIALITY . . .

But the case against him fell apart. Bridget realises no rules hinder Flannery, so why should they hinder her?

UPHOLDING THE CONSTITUTION AND THE LAW AND ACCORDING EQUAL RESPECT TO ALL PEOPLE . . .

When a severed arm is found in a pig carcass in Dublin docks, her instincts tell her Flannery is involved. Her colleagues say there is no evidence. But Bridget refuses to let Flannery slip further into the darkness.

ISBN 978-178199-7758

CPSIA information can be obtained
at www.ICGtesting.com
Printed in the USA
LVHW021814280222
712230LV00016B/2067